In My Heart
The Sweetbriar Mountain Series

Nora Everly

Editing: Rebecca Kimmel

Editing: Nicole McCurdy, Emerald Edits

Proofread: Marla Esposito, Proofing with Style

Cover: Yummy Book Covers

To Jenna
For always encouraging me.

Chapter 1
Luke

One more swing and the tree fell. The scent of dirt blasting into the air filled my lungs while the sunlight filtering through the pines cast the forest floor in spiky patterns of shadow and light. I let my senses fill, grounding myself against the regrets threatening to derail the progress I had made since returning home from Afghanistan.

I was a father.

I had a son. If I got a handle on myself, I might be able to meet him and see his mother again. My Lily was also back in Sweetbriar, our small Oregon hometown. The thought of seeing her again after everything I had done and how I had ended it all—

I cut Lily out of my life. I had thought she deserved so much more than what I could offer. After a certain point, the things I'd seen and done in the Army had blended together into a black cloud of hurt and pain and I could no longer process what was happening to me. My grandfather tried to help but you can't help someone who feels worthless, so I cut him out too and stayed away from Sweetbriar.

Frustrated, I wiped the back of my hand across my sweaty brow, then took swing after swing at the fallen tree, splitting it into manageable pieces. Some of it I would use for firewood; the rest I would carve into animals, or chess pieces, or paperweights, or whatever else crossed through my thoughts the next time I needed to disconnect from the world.

My muscles burned and my still-injured back ached as I straightened but pain wasn't enough to make me forget what I had done. Nothing ever was. I could never disconnect from Lily. She was branded on my soul. No matter how far apart we were or how many years went by, she was always there. Memories played on a loop in my mind like an old black and white movie—sometimes skipping, sometimes blurry, but never gone. Those memories pulled me through some of the worst moments of my life, even when I had wanted so badly to let go of everything and fade away.

When I found out she was coming home my life burst back into color. Everywhere I went in this town held a moment we shared. She was on my mind constantly and it was driving me to distraction. It hurt. The desperate yearning in my chest grew bigger every day, overwhelming all other facets of my world until all I could think of was how to convince her to let me back into her life again.

I wondered how she was now. My heart broke for her when I found out her husband died. Then I was sick at myself for being happy I might have a shot to get her back. And my son? I wanted him too. I wanted my life to be the way it should have been before I fucked it all up.

All these years, I had told myself I'd done the right thing. But now that I was home and finally healing, I knew letting her go was the worst mistake of my life.

After my medical discharge from the Army, I was a disaster. My grandfather Jed, or Pops as I had always called him, a Vietnam vet, convinced me to get help. I was diagnosed with PTSD, which should have been obvious to me, but it hadn't been. Denial is a powerful tool when your only goal is to forget. Pops took me to his therapist, talked me through panic attacks, comforted me when I realized all that I had thrown away, then gave me Rocky, my sort-of emotional support dog. Rocky had failed out of Jed's ESD program, but I fell in love with the brown and white boxer when he refused to leave my side. He woke me from nightmares, nudged me whenever I got down on myself, and provided me with the kind of love only the best, most loyal dogs could. Rocky was currently dozing off under a tree.

Pops and his employees trained service dogs of all kinds on his ranch right outside of Sweetbriar. I stayed with him for about a month before moving back to the house where I grew up. And it must be said, there is something about being surrounded by puppies and wide-open spaces that could put anyone at ease. It was the perfect way to begin settling back into a normal life.

I inherited my childhood home after my father passed. He'd made quite a few changes to the house while I was in the Army, to the point it almost felt like a different place. But the land was the same—fifty acres that backed into the Cascade Mountains in Oregon. I had since readjusted to the quiet sounds that had been so familiar in my childhood: animals rustling through the brush, the rush of the river, wind blowing through the trees. After being surrounded by people and near constant activity it was difficult at first, but I finally realized getting acclimated to peace and solitude was a blessing.

"Yo, McCabe!" My former sergeant, Liam, called to me from the trees. He was my brother, bonded irrevocably not by the blood that flowed through our veins but by the blood we had lost together over the last few years.

Rocky's ears pricked up, but he didn't budge; by now he knew Liam almost as well as he knew me.

"Hey." I took another swing and left the axe in the wood. "How was work?"

"Typical. Boring. Quiet." He grinned at me. "Small town life is exactly what I needed."

"I grew up here. It's not always boring and quiet, you know." Like any small town, Sweetbriar had its fair share of gossip and low-key intrigue.

His lips tipped up in a grin. "Duly noted. How was therapy?" I was glad to see him smile. I wasn't the only one who was a mess when we got here.

"The physical stuff is always easier. Talking about myself was never my thing." Liam and I served together, we were both medically discharged due to the same IED attack. I convinced him to come with me to Sweetbriar and help me run my late father's construction company.

"Swinging that axe can't be good for your back," he remarked.

I shrugged. "As long as I do it right, I'm fine."

He smirked. "You're full of shit."

"I needed to—" I ran a hand down my face, unsure of what I was trying to say. But Liam knew.

"You needed to get it out. The way you feel about her being here . . . it's real now. No more *if* or *when*. They're both in town and it's just a matter of time before you see them."

"I'm nervous as fuck," I admitted.

"I can't blame you for that. You've been building this up in your mind for a long time."

"It's everything, man. If I screw this up, what do I have?"

"Hey, look. For one, that's not going to happen. And two, both of us know by now it's not healthy to think that way. We have each other, and Jed, and my grandmother. Neither one of us is alone."

"Is that your therapist or mine talking?" I joked. The mood out here had gotten too serious for my liking.

"Hard to tell lately, but that doesn't make it not true." He passed me a bottled water before sitting by Rocky beneath the tree and scratching him behind his ears.

"You're right." I sighed.

"Let's go get coffee. That's what I came out here for." He chuckled.

"Good idea." Lily's sister, Violet, owned the only coffee shop worth going to in town. If I got lucky, maybe I'd run into Lily there. Last time I spoke to Violet, she had mentioned hiring Lily for the summer.

"Call Jed, have him meet us."

"The old man texts now. I taught him how to use his smart phone. The memes are endless."

He huffed a laugh. "Let's go."

I shot Pops a text, Liam woke Rocky, then we took off. Liam drove, just like he always had when we were deployed.

"Pops is busy. Just you and me this time."

He nodded his answer as he took us out of the mountains and down into town. I lowered the window in back for Rocky and cranked the air conditioner up high for me and Liam. It was an unusually hot summer day in Sweetbriar and, since returning from Afghanistan, we were all about creature comforts. Air conditioning, warm blankets, endless hot show-ers, and sleeping in. Don't get me started on hot coffee and good food. Violet got my business more than once a day, and I'll leave it at that.

We also set our own hours at my father's—well, now *my* company, McCabe Construction. Dad had built it to unbeliev-able levels while I was gone. I'd inherited enough money that I never had to work again if I chose not to. But I couldn't sell the business and leave his employees jobless. Plus, I needed some-thing to do, so I stayed and gave them all raises, just to spite my father's cheap ass ghost in case it was lurking around some-where, still disapproving of my choices.

He pulled into Violet's parking lot and cut the engine.

"There's my guys!" Violet greeted us from her perch behind the counter. She was older than me by a few years and I'd known her my whole life. She'd always been like an older sister to me. "The usual?"

"Please," Liam affirmed with a huge smile while I hung back and nodded. It was after lunchtime, and her shop was always slower this time of day. We practically had the place to ourselves. She turned her back to prepare our orders and I contemplated how to get her to start talking about Lily without having to ask.

She slid our coffees and a plate of scones across the counter. "Lily won't be in town until tomorrow. She was up all night with Calla. The poor little thing is cutting a tooth." Calla was Lily's baby, about six months old.

"Thanks, Violet." Liam paid for our orders and headed to the sofa in the back corner of the shop. I let Rocky follow him.

I took my drink with a sheepish smile. "Uh, I was going—"

She reached out and patted my arm with a knowing grin on her face. "And now you don't have to ask me about her. You're welcome."

"Thank you, Vi. You've made this easy on me, and I appreciate it."

"Well, I'm glad you're finally home. You and Lily belong together. You always have."

"I didn't realize how much I missed her in my life until I got back and got my head on straight. She's essential—I can't be myself without her."

Her eyes melted as she gave me a smile. "I love the way you talk about her."

I pressed my lips together and studied my shoes, embarrassed. What if Lily wouldn't talk to me? I'd end up a lovesick idiot with his unrequited feelings on display for an entire town to ridicule.

"Hey, it's okay." Her smile grew sympathetic. "Your face shows your love, Luke. It's in your body language and the words you choose when you talk about her. You have always loved her, ever since you were little kids. Once she sees you and hears you out, that simple fact will sink in."

"I hope you're right. But I'm not going to rush anything.

We started off as friends, and I have to be okay with it if that's all she wants."

"I know. But if ever any two people belonged together, it's the two of you."

"Well, I can't imagine not having her back in my life. She's been in my heart forever, Violet. I never let her go."

"None of us let you go either. You're part of the family, Luke."

Violet gave me a nod and turned around to tidy behind the counter. I joined Liam and kept trying to come up with a way to get close to Lily again.

Chapter 2
Lily

Each time I drove this road it felt like I was driving straight back to him. Years had stacked up between us. Miles too, I assumed. I didn't come home very often, trying to avoid the memories this place stirred up. There was a hole in my heart that nothing could ever fill. My husband hadn't filled it; my children can't even fill it. Will had done his best to help me put the pieces of my life back together, and I had been content with the life we'd made. But Will was dead. And I was headed home to start over.

Then, I couldn't stand to be here.

But now, there was nowhere else for me to be.

I never thought I would lose him, but I did. I never thought I could be with anyone after him, but I had been. Being a thirty-year-old widow running back to her family was never in my life plan. Yet here I sat, watching the same roads I'd traveled as a kid pass by as I drove back to the beginning. Back to the past I had fought so hard to leave behind.

Funny how what should have been a three-hour trip could turn into five. Time had no meaning for first-graders and babies. We'd already had three pee breaks and a Happy Meal break, I was sick of changing diapers in the car, and if I had to take a walk around another rest stop, I would scream.

"Are we there yet?" echoed in my ears and I couldn't wait to stop driving. Dylan, my six-year-old, stirred awake in the back seat as the speed limit dropped and I slowed to a crawl as the highway led into town. Sweetbriar, Oregon. The gateway to Mount Hood, population 5249. When I was growing up here, the population had been 5197. This meant there were about fifty-two people who didn't yet know my business. Memories sprouted up in my head as I passed familiar sights. Some were pleasant, but most I wanted to bury again. Some things never changed, and this town was one of them. I felt like a stranger even though this used to be my home.

"Mommy, look! There is Aunt Violet's coffee shop. Can we go in and have a smoothie and some cookies? Please, please, *please*. We've been driving forever and my butt is so tired," Dylan complained from the back seat.

"You know what? My butt is tired too. It's smoothie time, bud." I laughed as he let out a whoop.

A break was necessary before facing the rest of my family. My big sister Violet was the least intrusive of the whole lot of them. Or maybe she was more subtle about it. When you grow up as one of eight siblings, you learn that privacy is a luxury you will never have. Plus, my mother was the queen of all pushy, in-your-face mothers throughout the land. Luckily, my dad was mellow enough to balance us all out and keep the peace. I turned my SUV into the parking lot and pulled into a spot right in front of Vi's shop.

Violet spotted me from the window and rushed out, arms waving crazily in the air with her brunette waves flying out behind her.

"Lily, yay! You're finally here! Where are my babies?" She ran right past me to the back, opened the door before Dylan had even had a chance to unbuckle, and peppered his cheeks with kisses as he giggled. "Dylan! I've missed you, little bug."

She pulled him from the car and wrapped him up in a huge hug. "Today is snickerdoodle day, and I have a big one with your name on it. Go on inside. Grandpa is sitting on the big couch, and Finn and Nick are working at the counter."

Dylan had a major sweet tooth; she didn't have to tell him twice. He took off like a shot into the store with a huge smile plastered on his face.

"Hey, Vi," I said as I lifted Calla from her car seat.

"Ooh, Lily! Give me that baby," she demanded, rushing around the car to snatch her from my arms. Violet had two kids of her own—sixteen-year-old twins, the aforementioned Finn and Nick.

"Aunt Violet has presents for you, you sweet little thing," she crooned, laughing as Calla wrapped Vi's hair into her drooly little fist and pulled. "Look how much she's grown already. It seems like only yesterday we were in the hospital. She has her daddy's green eyes and your red hair. I bet she'll get your freckles too. She's so cute I can't stand it!" Her face turned wistful. "God, Lily, before you know it, instead of pulling hair and drooling, she'll be driving around in your car, asking for money and sneaking in after curfew."

"I missed you, Violet," I said, pulling her in for a side hug. Nostalgia kicked me in the gut as she wrapped an arm around my shoulder. Hopefully coming home would turn out to be a good thing.

She leaned into me and kissed my cheek with a loud smack. "You're going to get sick of this face. I want you to work with me here in my shop until summer vacation is over and you start your job at the school. I already asked and Mom will babysit." She took in my dubious expression. "Don't bother arguing. You need to get out of the house and get your life back. You need to be social, Lily. It will just be for a few hours in the mornings. Say yes, please?"

Violet's coffee shop—simply called *Violet's*—was the nexus of this town. Mornings were always chaotic because everyone in Sweetbriar came here for their coffee. In the ten years since she'd bought the place, she'd turned it from an average, nondescript coffee shop into a hotbed of gossip and social activity unparalleled anywhere else in town. Working here would be like diving right back into being "social" on the first morning. Nope. No thanks.

I had a whole lot of brooding and being alone with my thoughts planned for this summer, and I wanted to stick to that. When school started this fall, I would take over as the librarian at Sweetbriar Grade School, the same school I attended as a child. My identical twin sister Rose taught kindergarten there, which was great, but I could already see the privacy I'd enjoyed while living out of town start to disappear.

"What? I can't work here. I have a baby. I'm nursing." My argument was halfhearted because I knew it would end up being fruitless . . . and I also sort of wanted to do it.

Her lips twisted to the side as she scoffed at my attempt at an excuse. "I know you pump too. If Calla needs you, Mom will drive her over. You need to get out of the house. You were cooped up on bed rest for months, then you were all alone living the hermit life up in Tacoma. Calla is six months old. She'll be fine with Mom. All babies love her, you know that." She pointed at my face with a cajoling grin. Calla grabbed her finger and giggled. "Plus, it will give us time to chat and catch up. I missed you."

"Oh, all right." I caved like I almost always did when it came to my family. Plus, Violet was beautiful and funny and being around her always cheered me up and I needed huge amounts of cheer. I was sick of being sad.

"I'm glad you stopped here first. There's something we need to tell you, and it will be easier to hear it from just me and Dad first, rather than the whole family." She chuckled nervously.

Why did that sound so ominous?

I followed her inside to find Dylan perched at one of the high tables near the counter, his face covered in chocolate frosting. I cringed as he dunked a snickerdoodle into a huge glass of chocolate milk with his entire hand. "Finn gave me a brownie and a snickerdoodle. I couldn't decide, so he gave me both! I love it here!"

I shook my head. "Dylan, your chocolate face matches your chocolate-covered eyeballs." I always teased him about his big, brown eyes—eyes that look just like his father's.

"I think he got more frosting on his face than in his mouth, Aunt Lily." Nick laughed as I hugged him.

"Hey, Finn, come over here and give me hugs too."

With a grin, he came out from behind the counter. Violet's sons were both tall, just over six feet, with brown hair and beautiful hazel eyes exactly like hers.

"Are you getting shorter?" he teased as he patted my head.

"Nope, I'm still a statuesque five feet and two inches. You must be getting taller. Stop growing," I ordered. "Rose and I will be the shortest members of this family once all the little kids turn into teens," I called over my shoulder as I passed through the tables to the fluffy, pillow-covered purple sofa at the rear of the store to sit next to my dad.

He stood and gave me a hug, then sat back into the corner of the couch to prop his feet on the dark wooden coffee table. Violet sat in the brown leather chair perpendicular to the couch. After exchanging a look, they both stared at me.

What the heck was going on? My eyes darted between their suspicious looking faces.

"She's gonna be pissed," Violet said to my dad. They started to look nervous, and I started to get worried.

"Just tell me." I sighed as I flopped back against the cushions.

After inhaling a huge breath, Violet finally started talking. "Lily, none of us told you this before you moved back because we were worried. The bed rest, the hard pregnancy, Will's death. We didn't want to cause you any more stress."

My husband, Will, had been a police officer. After pulling over to help a stranded motorist, a hit-and-run driver ran Will down, killing him instantly. To date, the driver still hadn't been caught. A week later I had discovered I was pregnant with Calla. To say I've been "stressed" was an understatement. I had spent the last almost year and a half in a state of perpetual confusion laced with grief, just putting one foot in front of the other and trying not to think too hard about anything.

It was my father who decided to drop the bomb rather than Violet. "Honey, Luke is back in town and he's here to stay."

"What?" I breathed. "Here in Sweetbriar? Luke? Are you sure?" I gasped as my head turned to the door, then to the windows, stupidly looking around for a sign of him.

Lucas Michael McCabe.

I had tried hard over the years to banish that name from my thoughts, and I always failed. Our mothers had been best friends. They had thought it would be fun to be pregnant at the same time. Later, they had been even more thrilled when they went into labor and gave birth on the same day: Diana to Luke, and my mom to me and Rose. After a childhood spent as inseparable best friends, we fell in love. We graduated from high school, and he joined the Army while I went to college in Tacoma, near where he had been stationed. Deployments had been hard, but we'd loved each other, so we'd made it work.

Until one day it stopped working. He went back to Afghanistan, and I never heard from him again. Luke was Dylan's father. Even me being pregnant hadn't made him come back. I still couldn't understand it; it went against everything I had ever known about him.

Dad's voice shook me out of my thoughts. "He was injured and discharged from the Army. Lily, honey, he never knew you were pregnant. The officer who was supposed to tell him died before he could give Luke the news. Jed told him about Dylan the second he returned to town. They came to the house and talked to me and your mother."

Violet smiled softly at me. "We were afraid you wouldn't come back if you knew, so we didn't tell you until it was too late for you to change your mind. Don't be mad, Lily. We all love you and wanted you here with us." Tears shimmered in her eyes.

I stared at her, too shocked to say anything. Will and I had decided that Dylan should know who his birth father was, but Will had been his father in every other way.

"You should have told me. What if I'd driven past him or something? What if Dylan had seen him out the window? He's seen pictures, you know," I hissed. "What were you all thinking?" I threw myself back against the couch and crossed my arms. I glared at Violet, but she didn't notice. She was busy spoiling my baby. Calla would be totally rotten by the time this day was through.

"You won't recognize him. He looks a lot different," Violet answered distractedly, too wrapped up in Calla to pay any attention to me.

Dad reached for Calla, but Violet shook her head and turned in her chair, so he couldn't get to her. He shrugged and laughed.

"Violet!" I hissed. "Different? You've seen him?" I asked after I finally got her attention.

She looked at me for a second and waved her hand around. "I see him all the time. His office is right across the parking lot. He came to Sunday dinner a couple times with Jed. He stops here for coffee most mornings," she helpfully added, and I glared at her.

"You are not taking this seriously enough, Violet," I gritted out, still in shock.

My mind reeled through all the possible scenarios of how we would end up seeing each other. I closed my eyes and rested my head back against the sofa. An epic headache was imminently approaching. I needed a cookie, or a brownie, or something sweet so I could eat my feelings. I looked up in gratitude as Finn tapped me on the shoulder and handed me a scone and an iced tea.

"Sweetheart, he was devastated when he found out about Dylan," Dad said gently, and patted my knee. I spared him a glance out of the corner of my eye.

I took a deep breath, trying to process this information. "How long has he been home? The way you're talking about this says it's been a while."

"Only about three months. His injuries kept him in bed when he first got here."

"Why hasn't he contacted me? Doesn't he want to see Dylan?" *Or me?*

"Of course he does. He has PTSD. He chose to seek treatment and get his life in order before contacting you and meeting Dylan. I supported him in that decision, Lily. He was a mess when he got home," Dad explained.

"I can understand that. I'm pretty much the walking, talking definition of a mess." I let out a small laugh and hoped my nerves and hurt feelings were adequately hidden inside my lies. "It would have been terrible timing for all of us." I sat up and sat sideways on the couch. I waved at Calla. She waved back and babbled at me.

"Mom invited him to dinner tonight, hoping to break the ice for you, but he said that would be too much pressure for you and Dylan," Violet informed me.

I scoffed, feeling incredulous. That was too much, even for my mother. "Pressure? Ya think?" I responded in my second language—sarcasm.

"Lily, please don't be mad. We're just trying to help." She glanced at me before Calla twisted and pulled her hair again, adding levity to this conversation and preventing me from losing it completely.

"I'm not mad exactly. I just forgot." I sighed and reflopped back on the couch. "I forgot what it's like to be here in the thick of it with all of you. I forgot what it's like to have you all in my business every day."

Dad laughed. "Lily-girl, we missed you. You've been gone a long time, and you'll be the focus for a while."

"How am I going to tell Dylan that his birth father is here in town?" I said, letting my frustration at this impossible situation go. For now, anyway.

Dad smiled at me and hugged me into his side. "You've been honest with him his whole life about who his father is. Just stick with that and tell him straight out. That kid is smart beyond his years. He can handle it."

"You make it sound so simple." This would not be simple. I was already flipping out about the possibility of seeing Luke again.

"Being honest makes things simple," Dad said with a smile and stood up. "But it won't be pretty if we're late to dinner. Let's head out. Girls, don't take too long." He winked at me and Violet, then went over to Dylan's table, ruffled his hair, kissed his cheek, and headed for the door. He climbed into his police SUV—Dad was the chief in Sweetbriar—and drove off.

"Lily, I have to close up. We'll meet you at the house." Violet finally gave me my baby back with a longing look then headed to the counter.

"Come on, Dyl. Let's go to Grandma's. Later, guys!" I called to Finn and Nick.

Chapter 3
Lily

I knew the exact moment that this place had stopped feeling like home. I had come back for Christmas break right after Luke had broken our engagement and gone back to Afghanistan. That day, I'd looked around and seen nothing but memories of a life I'd still wanted but could no longer have. Every time I came home after that all I could see were ghosts of the past.

The thought of driving all day, then seeing my entire family was exhausting. I wanted to go home, take off my bra, eat ice cream, cuddle my kids, then go to bed. But I had missed my family, so I agreed to dinner. It only took about ten minutes to get from Violet's shop to my parents' house, but that ten-minute drive was like traveling into another world. The road snaked out of a small town full of shops and activity and into mountains dotted with pine trees and covered in mist.

"Mommy, it smells clean. Like the tree hanging in Papa Jed's car but way better. I think I can smell the sun and the sky up here. Can you smell it too?"

"Yeah, baby, I can. It smells like home to me." I had grown distracted by the memories that started to rise in my mind, just like the misty sunshine we were driving up into.

"I can't wait to see Grandma. She's making me a chocolate cake. She told me she's going to set the world record for the number of layers. It might even reach the ceiling. Don't tell her I already ate snickerdoodles. I don't want to hear the words, 'Too many sweets will give you a tummy ache.'"

I smiled at him in the rearview mirror. "I'll keep your secret. But just this one time. After tonight, the 'too many sweets' rule is back in effect. Deal?"

"Deal. Too bad Calla can't eat the cake. When will she be able to do stuff? She's so boring. She just lies there and poops and burps and gets drool everywhere. She's sort of gross."

"Aw, she's cute too. Admit it," I teased.

"I guess so. I like it when she smiles at me. It's too bad she doesn't have a dad anymore."

I froze in my seat. "Are you okay, bud?" It had been over a year since Will died. Dylan's grief was no longer as overwhelming as it had been in the beginning. But it still popped up in random observations that made him realize the finality of Will's absence. Sometimes it still hit us both hard.

"I miss Daddy Will, and I was remembering when he showed me how to ride a bike the last time we were here. Then he put me up on his shoulders and I could touch the bottom of the super tall trees in the yard. Who's going to teach Calla?" *Daddy Will?* Not just *Daddy?*

"We can both teach her. We're great bike riders."

"Yeah, but you're really short. No way you can help her touch the trees."

"Grandpa will be there. And you have four uncles who can reach them. They used to climb those trees all the time. We'll make new memories together, Dylan."

"Okay, but I *remember* Daddy. Calla won't ever be able to remember him like I do. It's not fair." His voice trembled like he was close to crying.

"It will be our job to tell her all about what a great man he was." Now I was about to cry. At this point, thinking of Will was mostly bitter and hardly ever sweet. As time moved on, hopefully, the balance would shift.

"Okay, I can do that. Mommy, is my dad Luke back in this town now?"

I had been racking my brain trying to figure out a way to broach this subject with him. He must have overheard us talking at Violet's. Sometimes he was way more observant than I gave him credit for.

"Yes, he is. He got hurt and can't be in the Army anymore," I answered, deliberately vague so I could see where he was going with his questions.

"Did he want me?" I took a quick look in the rearview mirror; tears shone in his eyes.

"Oh, sweetheart. If he had known about you, he absolutely would have wanted you. He wants to get to know you now."

"But does he want a baby too?"

"I don't know. I haven't talked to him since before you were born." *He used to want babies with me. We had decided on four.*

"Will he be my dad like Daddy Will was?"

"He wants to try. Is that okay with you?"

"Yes. But Calla needs a dad too. I want to share him with her. Can I?"

"I don't know bud. It's not that simple. I haven't seen him in years. All I know is he wants to meet you and explain why he was gone."

"I want to meet him right now."

"Are you sure you're ready for that?" Thank God I had listened to my dad when he said I should tell Dylan the truth about Luke and Will.

"I'm ready," he insisted. Voice firm, tears gone.

"We'll go to his house. I don't know if he'll be there, but it won't hurt to check."

What am I doing?

Instead of heading to my parents' house, I turned onto the

road that led to Luke's place. The narrow road was nothing but twists and turns staggered with steep drop-offs that used to scare me when I was a kid. It was as familiar to me as the road I had grown up on, and it hadn't changed much over the years. We used to camp at the rear of the property, near the creek that fed into the Sweetbriar River. So many hours had been spent here—Luke, me, and my siblings—running around, exploring, and playing make-believe.

I handed my phone back to Dylan. "Call Aunt Violet and tell her we'll be late," I instructed. I couldn't help but think getting this meeting over with would be best. Like ripping off a Band-Aid or diving into a cold swimming pool.

Dylan's voice on the phone rang in my ears. I was lost in memories that I'd buried alongside my childhood dreams. He was ready to meet Luke, but I wasn't so sure about myself. I knew this was long overdue, but the anticipation was about to kill me.

"We'll be there soon, Dylan. I won't be mad if you change your mind. We can turn around any time you want."

"I don't want to turn around," he insisted.

"One more turn and we're there." My breath grew shallow as we approached. Tall pine trees dotted the land to the left and right of the long gravel road that led to the house.

My mouth opened in surprise at a new opening amongst the trees. The gravel path eased into gray slate pavers to form a long driveway that widened into a huge roundabout. There were carved wooden bears and evergreen shrubs decorating the center. I stopped the car and looked ahead. With stacked stone pillars, balconies jutting out here and there, and a massive deck, this was the biggest, grandest log cabin I had ever seen. I marveled at a garage that looked like it could hold at least five cars off to the left of the house and the huge fire pit and seating area in a clearing in the trees to the right. In the days when I spent time here, it had been a regular log cabin family home—modest and cute. Luke's dad must have gone crazy expanding the company in the years before he died. This place was something else.

"This is even bigger than Grandma's house. It might be the biggest house I ever saw," Dylan exclaimed in wide-eyed awe.

"It sure didn't look like this when I used to come here. Do you want to get out? You can change your mind, you know."

"Mom, do *you* want to get out?" he asked a little too observantly for a six-year-old boy.

"I want what you want, Dylan." He didn't answer; he just opened the door and hopped out. I hurried to follow him. "Dylan, wait for us," I called.

He stopped at the bear carvings to wait while I unbuckled Calla, then caught up to him. We stood there and stared at the massive house, startling when we heard barking.

"He has a dog!" Dylan got excited as a golden-brown and white blur came barreling out from behind the garage, its tail wagging furiously and tongue lolling out of the side of its mouth. The dog stopped, rolled over, got up, and came a little bit closer to us. Then he did it again: stop, roll over, get up. And again. Each time, he came a few steps closer to us. I grabbed on to Dylan's hand and started pulling him back to the car with visions of *Cujo* dancing in my head.

"Rocky!" a deep voice yelled. "Rocky, come." That wasn't Luke's voice. I'd spent my entire life hearing Luke's voice and I would know it anywhere.

A man jogged out from behind the garage. He was tall, broad, and covered in muscles, with a black buzz cut and a huge smile that got bigger as he approached us.

"Is he a giant?" Dylan whispered to me as Rocky rushed over to the man, then walked at his side back to us.

"I think he's just really tall," I whispered back.

"Hi, mister. I'm looking for my dad. Are you a giant?" Dylan yelled.

"Dylan!"

"Nope, I'm just tall," he answered, before addressing me.

"And you're Lily. You look just like Rose." His gorgeous smile warmed as he spoke to me. "I'm Liam, and this is Rocky. Luke is in the back."

Rocky seemed to take Liam's greeting as permission, because he rushed over to Dylan, licked his hand, then sat by his side. Dylan patted his head and Rocky leaned against him with a cute doggie groan.

"Yes, I am. Uh, I am Lily, that's me. Hi, Liam." I nodded as I shifted Calla to my hip and stuck out my hand. Liam shook it with a grin. "We were hoping to talk to Luke today. Obviously, Rocky is friendly, so I'm going to stop worrying about that and focus on worrying about other stuff. I don't have Luke's number anymore, so I couldn't call first. I'm sorry about that. I don't have a plan. I don't know what I'm doing. I—"

Liam cut me off in the middle of my nervous ramble with a laugh. He shook his head and gave me a look that said he knew me even though we'd never met. "Listen to you! You're exactly like Luke described. This is so great. Relax, Luke will be thrilled to see you. I'll go get him. Dylan, it's good to finally meet you." He turned to Dylan and shook his hand before gesturing to the trees closest to the mountain near the back of the property. "He's picking out trees to carve for a build, so it will take a few minutes for him to get up here. You guys are welcome to go sit by the fire pit and wait. Just please don't leave. Okay?" He was so open and friendly, it put me at ease. Well, sort of. Like, how much ease could I possibly have right now? I was about to see the long-lost father of my first-born child, for goodness sake.

"We won't leave," Dylan promised. He veered down the path to the seating area while Rocky trotted along at his side.

"We'll be here. Don't worry." I'd come this far; it would be silly to run away now, even though I was nervous as all heck and might throw up in that beautiful fire pit. "It's nice to meet you, Liam."

"Nice to meet you too. Thank you for coming. Seriously." He turned and jogged off.

"Look at these chairs. They have fairies and little wolves carved all over them. I bet my dad did it. I bet he made those bears too. He's picking trees to carve up right now. How cool is that? I wonder if he'll teach me to carve up trees too. I want to chop one down. Can I? I want to chop down trees like a lumberjack."

He started miming chopping with his arms and an imaginary axe. Dylan was a walking contradiction. He could act so grown-up that sometimes you forget he's a kid, then turn around and start chopping down imaginary trees. He started running around the fire pit with Rocky chasing him. Or maybe Dylan chased Rocky. Either way, they were having a blast.

"I don't know about chopping down trees. That sounds dangerous. Let's just take this one step at a time. Let's start by sitting down." It was a beautiful summer evening. The sun still peeked through the trees to shine on some of the chairs. I chose a bench swing in the shade and sat down. Dylan sat on the ground in a sunray. Rocky crawled into his lap and started licking his cheek. Calla started to fuss, so I tugged down my nursing tank to feed her.

"Even though we told Liam we would stay, you are allowed to change your mind whenever you want," I reiterated for the bazillionth time. "We can get in the car and leave right now."

"Mom, you're more scared than me. I'm not scared at all. Don't worry. I'll talk to him. You just take care of Calla."

He was right. My nerves were getting the best of me. I hadn't seen Luke since that disastrous visit in the hospital over six years ago. I should have taken more time to think this through before just driving over here. I either planned everything to death or rushed headlong into things, then regretted it later. Much to my consternation, I had yet to find a balance between the two.

"I love Rocky. He's the best dog I've ever met. What kind is he?" Dylan asked as he continued to play with the adorable dog.

"He's a boxer, I think. He seems pretty nice," I observed. "Hi, Rocky. You're a good boy, aren't you?" I couldn't help but laugh as he ambled over to me, tongue hanging out of the side of his mouth, tail wagging like crazy, and raised his paw for me to shake. I shook it, and he licked my hand. Was it crazy to be put at ease by a dog?

The nerves surged right back when I caught sight of Luke out of the corner of my eye. I turned to watch as he strode determinedly out from behind the garage. He had a slight limp, but it looked like he was refusing to give in to it.

And, oh *damn*, Violet was right. He looked different. Gone was the sweet-faced boy-man I'd fallen in love with. In his place was this . . . *hot guy*. He was broad shouldered and solid, like he went to the gym but still ate dessert. Or maybe he just tossed heavy logs around all day after he chopped them down for his carvings or whatever. A thick, dark beard covered the beautiful face I used to love. The rolled-up shirtsleeves of his dark blue work shirt revealed tattoos traveling up and down his forearms.

The Luke I had loved had been clean shaved with a head of hair he kept buzzed military short in accordance with his life-long goal to join the Army, like his grandfather Jed had done. My eyes started to glaze as I took in the gorgeous dark brown hair sweeping back to curl around his ears and down to touch the collar of his shirt. I wanted to touch that hair, to run my fingers through it and get a good solid whiff of it.

He was bigger too. Did people keep growing into their twenties? I could swear he was taller. Or maybe it was an optical illusion because his shoulders were so much wider, and his muscles were bigger and more prominent than they used to be.

Must. Stop. Staring.

My sweet Luke was gone. The man headed my way right now came straight off a romance novel cover or a documentary about lumberjacks.

Meanwhile, I was stuck sitting here like a stunned fool in my messy bun and nursing tank. I should have at least put on some dang lip gloss.

I glanced down at Calla. This was just great—my ex-fiancé, the former love of my life, the father of my son, was headed my way, and the top part of my boob was out. If Calla pulled away, we would be in nipple city.

My almost six-months-postpartum body had not yet recovered to the state it had been in the last time I'd seen him. Which was almost seven years and at least ten pounds ago. *Gah! That doesn't matter*, I reminded myself. I was not here to get him back. I was here for Dylan. I needed to get my priorities straight, or at least figure out what they were before I started beating myself up.

"Jeez, Louise," I whispered to myself.

"Who's Louise? Look, Mom! There he is," Dylan whispered, wrenching me out of my impure thoughts about his father.

"I know. He looks different than when I knew him," I muttered bitterly.

He helpfully whispered back, "Don't worry, your boob isn't showing."

"Thanks, bud." I was afraid I would say something dumb when he got over here. Or worse, not say anything at all.

"I'm going over to him. I can't wait." Dylan got up and excitedly ran off to meet Luke.

"Dylan, wait." I started to get up too, then changed my mind and sat back down. I decided that using my baby as a shield was a great idea.

No handshake. No, '*Oh wow, it's been a long time, you haven't changed a bit*' bullcrap hug. And absolutely no kiss on the cheek or elsewhere, no matter how much I found myself growing curious about whether it would feel the same to touch him.

All contact would be blocked by the baby nursing heartily at my breast. Rocky sighed, headed over to me, spun around a few times, and then crashed on my feet, providing me with a canine shield. I knew I liked this dog.

Dylan and Luke were frozen near the bears at the roundabout. Luke's eyes, so much like Dylan's, filled with tears he quickly blinked away as he gazed reverently at our son, searching his face for a clue on how to address him.

"Dylan. I have waited so long to meet you," he finally murmured.

Nine words. That voice.

I closed my eyes as memories crashed into my mind in wave after wave, enough to drown in. His voice echoed in my head as a lifetime of words skipped through my thoughts like stones over the surface of a river. I heard us laughing and playing together as children, him calling me beautiful when we lost our virginity to each other in the back of his truck. Tears pricked behind my eyes when I recalled him telling me he would love me forever as he asked me to marry him. Then years later that same voice sobbing when he realized what he had done and screamed at my mother to take me away . . .

There had never been a moment in my life when he hadn't been *mine*. But I didn't know him anymore. Too many years had passed between us.

I needed to get a grip. *I* didn't matter right now. Dylan mattered. And Dylan wanted his father. I would do anything I could to give him that.

"Let's go talk to your mom," Luke said.

Shoot! They were coming over here. Calla, the baby shield, was still in place, and Rocky was snoring on my feet. *Now or never.* Rip it off, like a Band-Aid.

"Lily, thank you for coming over."

"You're welcome. I figured it was silly to wait, to drag this out. Dylan was so determined to meet you." I shrugged and that same liar's laugh escaped me like it had earlier with Violet and Dad.

His gorgeous chocolate brown eyes gazed at me like they always had—possessively, protectively, like I was the only thing he could see—and I fell under his spell, drowning myself in the memories his presence evoked.

It had been almost seven years, yet my heart felt like no time had passed. But looking at him made it obvious every-thing about our circumstances had changed drastically. I couldn't reconcile the two feelings. Everything I had ever felt for him rapidly resurfaced, and I was confused about how I should react.

The old Luke and Lily would be affectionate and at ease with each other. But I couldn't be myself around him anymore; I didn't know how. I remained tongue-tied and waited for him to say something.

"You have the same eyes as me," Dylan observed as Luke sat in the chair across from me. Dylan sat on the edge of the fire pit between us staring at his father. It was true; every time I looked at Dylan, it was hard not to think of Luke. They had the same hair and build. Dylan would probably be tall like Luke, who was a foot taller than me. I always used to wear heels so I could reach his mouth to kiss it whenever I chose. And I used to choose to do it often.

Why can't I stop thinking like this?

Luke grinned at Dylan and said, "Chocolate-covered eyeballs." That grin had always given me a swoony belly whoosh, and this time was no exception. My physical reaction to Luke was disconcerting, to say the least. It was freaking me the heck out, to say the most.

"That's what Mommy always says!" Dylan laughed. "What else do we have the same? Do you like to read? I do. I'm reading *Harry Potter* with my mom. I like to draw. Do you? Did you carve those bears up? Will you teach me how?"

Luke waited a beat before he answered, probably to see if Dylan was done talking. Sometimes it was hard to tell. "When I was a kid, your grandma used to babysit me after school, and your mom and I read *Harry Potter* together. I like to draw, and I made the bears. If it's okay with your mom, I will teach you whatever you want to learn." He looked at me with a nervous smile.

"Awesome! My baby sister looked like Dobby the house elf when she was first born. I want to make a baseball bat out of a tree. Then we can play baseball. We can get my uncles and your giant friend Liam and my cousins and play all day! Your yard is even huger than my grandma's. It will be so fun." He stood and started swinging an imaginary bat while Luke chuckled at his antics.

"Dylan, Calla did not look like Dobby," I insisted. This was a play argument that Dylan and I had often. I couldn't remain quiet with Dylan looking at me with such joy.

"Her ears did, and she was all wrinkly and scrawny like Dobby." Dylan laughed, then a serious expression came over his face and he turned back to Luke. "Do you like babies?" he demanded.

I froze, my lips parted as I waited, with far too much interest than I thought I should have, to see what he would say.

"I do like babies," Luke answered. They both looked at me —Dylan with a satisfied grin, and Luke with a hopeful smile.

I remained frozen in my seat as I dipped my head low to snuggle Calla and avoid Luke's eyes. He kept attempting to catch my sight. To connect? To discern my feelings?

"Good. Even though she has huge ears and smells like poop sometimes, my sister is cute. She smiles a lot and hardly ever barfs all over my mom. If we're going to get to know each other, then you need to get to know her too. It's not fair if I'm the only one with a dad now." He eyed Luke with a determined expression.

"I would be happy to get to know your sister as long as it's okay with your mom." Luke glanced up at me with a soft look that I caught out of the corner of my eye. "Whatever makes you comfortable, Lily. Anything you need."

I was too busy trying not to cry to give an answer. As I looked away my lower lip trembled. I bit it to regain control. *Too hard. Ow.*

"Should I call you Dad? Can I?" Dylan asked, breaking the awkward silence with a potentially awkward question.

"I would love that." Luke smiled hugely at Dylan and repeated, "As long as it's okay with your mom."

The hope shining in Luke's eyes blinded me as he searched my expression with a faint smile on his face. And oh, how I had missed his smile. I shut my eyes briefly against the sight of it before steeling myself so I could respond. "You can call him Dad if you like, Dylan. It's up to you." I tried discreetly switching Calla to the other breast to nurse. Luke quickly averted his eyes back to Dylan. I guess I failed at being discreet. My face flamed with embarrassment.

"Do you think it would hurt my dad Will's feelings?" Dylan asked, finally showing a little uncertainty.

Luke answered before I could. "I'm not trying to take Will's place, and I don't want you to forget about him. Love makes a father, not blood. Will loved you and took care of you when I wasn't there to do it myself. He was a good man, and I liked him a lot."

"I didn't know you knew my dad. Why weren't you there? Why have I never met you before?" Dylan asked.

"I met him a few times when I visited your mom whenever I was on leave. She lived with your aunt Jane then, and Will would come around and visit."

I had never talked about this part of my life with Dylan. It was too painful. What would Jane think of Luke being back in our lives? Jane was Will's little sister and my college room-mate; we'd been best friends ever since we met. After Will died, she took a leave of absence to move in with me. We grieved together and she helped me care for Dylan while I was on bed rest, pregnant with Calla.

Luke continued, "I am so sorry I wasn't there for you." He closed his eyes briefly, before looking intently at Dylan as if willing him to understand his words. "Have you ever felt lost? Not like you can't find the right turn to take or the right path to follow, but lost inside your mind. Maybe so sad you thought you would never be happy again. Or so bad about something you had done that you thought no one could love you anymore?"

My heart cracked wide open at his words.

"I felt sad like that when my dad Will died," Dylan answered. His expression was one I'd never seen. This was serious to him. He was growing up right before my eyes. I took a deep breath to abate the tears that filled my eyes.

"I felt that way for a really, really long time. I'm just now starting to feel better. Your Grandpa Jed told me about you when I got home, and at first, I felt guilty for being so stubborn and stupid for not letting your mom or Jed talk to me. Years had passed and I missed everything." He stopped talking; perhaps he was lost in his memories. He blinked, shaking it off, and refocused on Dylan. "Grandpa Jed made me see that I have one chance to make it right. He told me I had to fight for you by getting better, so I could earn your forgiveness. When I was in the Army, I got hurt really bad, Dylan. Most people understand that we need to take care of our bodies. When our bodies get hurt or sick, we go to the doctor or we rest so we can heal. But sometimes our minds get sick too. I had to heal my mind, so I could be the dad you deserve. And I would like to try. Is that okay?"

"How did you hurt your mind?" Dylan asked.

It was one thing to know that Luke was suffering from PTSD. It was something completely different to hear the words coming directly from him. I could feel his pain and guilt like something tangible. The wall I had erected in my heart to keep him out began to crumble. And it terrified me.

"When you are in the Army, you see things that are scary. Sometimes people you like get hurt or even die, and it makes you sad. Every day is busy and sometimes dangerous. It's hard to stop and think. So, sometimes, you just quit thinking because it hurts too much." He stopped talking and ran his hands over his face and into his hair, leaving his palms covering his eyes. Dylan got up and placed his little hands against Luke's cheeks, forcing Luke to look at him.

"I forgive you Dad," he stated firmly.

Luke inhaled sharply and clenched his jaw before issuing a solemn promise: "I will prove to you every day that I deserve it."

I needed to get out of here before the tears burning behind my eyes spilled over and showed Luke just how much he still affected me. I wasn't ready to be vulnerable like this. One more word from his lips and I would lose the grip on my tenuous control. Hastily, I stood up. Rocky looked up at me plaintively before hopping to my spot on the swing.

"I have to go. It's time," I announced a little too brightly. "We can make plans for you two to get together. Let's exchange numbers. Dylan has my phone." Calla started to fuss as I popped her off and righted my shirt. I hugged her to my chest and rubbed her back. I was not sure who was comforting whom at this moment.

"Okay, but I would like to talk to you too, Lily," Luke answered softly.

"Sure, we can make plans to talk soon, but I'm supposed to be at my mom's house right now for dinner, and I need to put Calla down for a nap."

Luke took his phone from his pocket and they exchanged numbers.

"Come on, Dylan, let's go to Grandma's. They're probably

waiting for us. We'll get you together with Luke soon. Promise."

Dylan threw his arms around Luke's neck. Dylan whispered in his ear, "I'm glad you came home." I felt my heart break and mend at the same time at the sight.

As Dylan ran to the car, I offered a small smile to Luke and said, "I'm glad you're back, too." I turned away and followed after our son.

"I'll see you soon," he said as I buckled Calla in. I chose to assume he was addressing Dylan and didn't answer. I needed more time to think.

Chapter 4
Luke

I was rooted in place next to the fire pit, unable to look away as I watched our son hop into the back seat of Lily's car and wave to me from the window. My heart seized as I watched Lily put her baby in the car seat and buckle her in. Her hair was fiery red just like Lily's and she was tiny and adorable in her flowered pink pajamas.

That should be my baby. The thought barreled into my mind before anything rational could form. I didn't want to rush, but seeing her again made me want things I shouldn't— things I knew I wasn't ready for. I'd only been back a few months. I still had a lot of work to do on myself.

Lily was more beautiful than ever. I only managed to catch her eyes a couple times and I was saddened that the bright hazel happiness I'd taken for granted when we were younger had dimmed. I knew I was a large part of her sorrow, and it broke my heart. She seemed tired, or maybe just emotionally exhausted from all that had changed for her recently.

I had liked Will. He had been a good man, but he was gone. This was my chance to take care of Lily and Dylan. I looked up, to thank him or somehow acknowledge what he had done. But it was impossible; the only way to show my appreciation was to take the action I had already planned on taking. He had taken care of Lily and Dylan when I was gone, and now it was my turn to do the same. But it wasn't doing it for him, just like I knew he hadn't done it for me.

Back then, I knew Will had wanted her. And I had respected him for never crossing the line. He was her best friend's brother, and he had never acted as anything beyond that toward her.

She hadn't seen what I had—the desire in his eyes and the longing. I saw it because I felt the same way he did. But she'd been mine then, not his. Not until I'd been so damaged, so blinded by pain I'd lost her from my sight and let her go. My vision cleared just as his life had ended. Was it tragedy or fate? Who knew? I wasn't going to bother trying to figure it out. I had only one objective: to win my family back. Lily. Dylan. And now Calla.

Lily and I were born knowing each other. Our mothers said we met in the womb. They'd been best friends, pregnant at the same time, so maybe we did. But she had always been special to me.

Never once did I imagine that she wouldn't be my friend— not until the day I realized what love really was and started imagining her being so much more. When I learned what a kiss was, I wanted to do it with her. When I was curious about sex, I imagined it with her. When I pictured the family I would have someday, she would be my wife. I wanted to be with her always. I wanted to live with her, die with her. Just *be* with her. There had never been anyone else for me, not ever.

I continued watching them, though I did sit down and absentmindedly pet Rocky so I wouldn't seem like a creeper just standing and staring. My years of celibacy suddenly became too much as my body reacted to being near hers again. Her red hair shone in the sun, as gorgeous as ever. I imagined what it would be like to have it wrapped around my hands again, draped across my chest, tickling my skin as I held her close. Her body was lush with curves and her face was straight out of my dreams. She looked the same, but there was a new depth to her beauty. She had grown; maybe she had changed just as much as I had. I was dying to know her again.

She was the love of my life. She was the beat of my heart, and I had been living without her for too long. As I watched her drive away, I felt torn in two. I knew I wanted her back in my life, but I didn't want to push too hard too soon and drive her away or scare her off. My feelings were rapidly running out of control.

"Heads up!" Liam called as he tossed me a beer, sprawled out on one of the chairs, and propped his feet up on the fire pit. "I heard her drive off. How did it go?" He cracked open his beer and took a long sip. Rocky jumped off the swing and sat next to his feet.

"It went fine. I mostly talked to Dylan. He's funny and curious, and so smart, Liam," I said with a laugh.

"And Lily?" he prodded.

"We didn't talk much. She said she was glad I was back, we exchanged numbers, and that's about it. Dylan and I did all the talking. I doubt she would have even spoken to me at all if he wasn't here." Disappointment filled my heart. I had a lot of hope built up and not really talking to her at all shook me.

"Sorry, man. She'll come around."

I popped open my beer and sipped it. "Dylan forgave me. But I didn't hurt him like I hurt her. I wasn't there for him, but he didn't know the difference because he had Will. I could see the hurt in her eyes. She gets this look, like she wants to run away. Then she kind of did run away. After Dylan said he forgave me, she couldn't get away from me fast enough."

"You know it's not just you she's running away from. She's been through a lot. Coming back here must dredge up just as many memories for her as it does for you. Bottom line, you regret letting her go. Make her believe it," he advised.

I quirked an eyebrow in his direction and said, "I didn't

know you were such an expert on relationships, Liam," making him laugh.

"I'm not. But if you're not decisive and clear about your intentions, she'll think you don't mean it. This is important. This is your woman, your family. You have to be all in. It's the only way you'll get anywhere with her."

"She's not my woman anymore," I argued. "Today proved it."

He sat forward and pointed at me. "Bullshit. You've talked about her so much I knew it was her an not Rose was the moment I saw her. And she was nervous. If she didn't care, she wouldn't have acted so skittish."

"She's worried about Dylan," I said.

"And seeing you again," Liam insisted.

"I doubt that." Rocky always sensed when I was feeling down. He came to me and put his head on my leg. I scratched behind his ears, then he jumped on my lap and licked my cheek.

Liam shook his head. "Keep arguing, Luke. Argue yourself right out of getting your family back. You want them? Earn it. You have a child together and that's a bond that will never break. That's your way back to her. You all need each other, and that boy needs a father—and a good one at that. That's something neither of us ever had. This is your chance. Don't waste it."

"You're right. This just didn't go as I wanted it to. I should have expected her to be like this. I know her. She's got to be questioning everything right now."

"You've got this. Be the strong one for both of you."

Liam was right. If I had doubts and let them show, it would only hurt us all. For all these years, I could have had my family. Terrified of physically hurting her again, I'd cut off all contact. I'd allowed myself to succumb to my fears and remained alone. I'd ended up hurting her far worse than my hands ever could have done. I'd abandoned her when she needed me the most, violating a lifetime of trust we had built effortlessly between us over the years. I hoped like hell I could find a way to repair it. She didn't need me to take care of her; she had her family, and she was more than capable of doing it herself.

I was the one in need.

Chapter 5
Lily

I groaned as I drove up my parents' long brick driveway. I counted the cars parked neatly along the side and realized that I was the last one to show up. The house I'd grown up in had changed a lot through the years. It started out as an average two-story, three-bedroom and two-bathroom ranch house with white clapboard and dark blue trim set on fifty acres of land backed by forest and foothills. It was still white with blue trim, but now it was a sprawling eight-bedroom, five-bathroom monstrosity with a huge pool, a pool house, an apartment over the garage that my Grandma Rosemary had just moved into, and an office retreat in the backyard for my mom to write her books in.

Mom was a novelist who wrote under the pen name Dahlia Lake. She wrote romance. She was a firm believer in true love and she was an unapologetic matchmaker. She was slightly nuts, but her heart was in the right place. She loved kids—there were eight of us, after all—and she was always begging us for more grandchildren.

Instead of moving every time my mother popped out another baby, Dad would just add on to the house. In addition to his job as Sweetbriar's chief of police, my dad was the ultimate do-it-yourselfer. He had just finished adding a massive great room to the house so we could all fit for Sunday dinner. This would be my first Sunday dinner with the family, and I was already off to a bad start, seeing as I was late.

I cut the engine and turned around in my seat. "Dylan, we're late. I might get grounded," I joked.

"Ooh, you're in trouble." He laughed at me. "I'll tell Grandma it's my fault. She never gets mad at me because I'm so cute."

I hopped out of the car and opened the back door. I gave him a grin as I unbuckled his seatbelt. "True, you are cute. But we'll be living in town and Grandma is going to babysit you all summer when I work at Violet's. Cuteness is only going to get you so far when we're here all the time. Keep that in mind."

He considered my words. "Okay, you're on your own, then. I'll save my cuteness for when I spill milk or break a window."

"Solid plan." I held out my fist for a bump. "Let's go in."

He jumped out and started running for the front door.

"Lily Elizabeth Barrett-Sullivan. You are late," Mom shouted from the huge brick porch. "Tell me you did not stop for snacks. You'd better not be full after I've been cooking all of your favorites all day," she said as she headed for my car. Rose was hot on her heels and headed for the back seat to steal my baby.

"Hi, Lily," Rose said as she unbuckled Calla and gave her a snuggle. Calla pulled her hair and "kissed" her cheek. Calla kisses consisted of an open mouth and copious amounts of drool.

Deliberately not mentioning the fact that we'd stopped at Violet's for a snack, I informed her about my visit with Luke. "Dylan wanted to meet Luke, so I decided to get it over with." I was hanging by a thread; so much was going through my mind. I needed to sit down or have a drink or take a decade-long nap.

"Oh my goodness!" She put her arms straight up in the air. "Yay! Rose, she went to Luke's! How did it go? Is Dylan okay? Mark and Mara grabbed him as soon as he crossed the doorway. I didn't even get to say hi or get a hug." Mark and Mara were the children of my oldest brother, Asher, and were twins the same age as Dylan. There were a lot of twins in my family, but Rose and I were the only identical pair.

"Well, we're here for good. Plenty of time for hugs now," I said and hugged her for emphasis. My mother was a tall, willowy woman. I had been looking up to her literally and figuratively my whole life. She was a force of nature with long, wavy silver hair and blue eyes framed with black, cat-eye glasses. She was always dressed stylishly, even when she'd had all of us kids running around. I didn't know how she managed it because I could barely find time to brush my hair. In fact, I usually just threw it up in a bun without even touching a brush. *Slob, thy name is Lily.*

"I'm so excited." She looked first at me and then at Rose holding Calla as tears filled her eyes. "I finally have my little fairy babies back together! And a tiny redheaded fairy grandbaby too." Mom called us her little fairies because Rose and I had been so small when we were born, and we'd stayed small and short into adulthood. Our other siblings were tall, even the girls. Mom took Calla from Rose just as Dylan ran up to us. "There you are, Dylan."

"I'm here, Grandma, but I'm not a fairy," he said and hugged her around her waist.

"What do you want to be, darling?" She squeezed him back and kissed the top of his head.

"I'm a lumberjack like my dad Luke." He laughed and ran back inside the house.

Mom beamed at me as we started walking to the house. "You had a good talk with Luke, then?" She snuggled Calla close and kissed her chubby cheek. Calla did not pull her hair.

Even though it was long and shining silver in the sunlight, she just stared at it, watching it sparkle in the sun.

"Dylan did the talking. I didn't know what to say, or maybe I have too much to say." My eyes burned and my lips trembled, each a sign I was about to burst into tears. What was it about being near my mother that made me so emotional?

"Oh, honey—"

Rose interrupted her. "Mom, give me the baby and take her upstairs to talk. I'll check on Dylan and get him some dinner. Go on upstairs, Lily." I loved my sister so much. She always knew what I needed. She headed out of the entryway and into the living room where she was accosted by Violet, who demanded to hold Calla again. I rolled my eyes and followed Mom up the stairs to the upstairs sitting area.

"Shoo, Levi, Jude. Go down and get something to eat. Lily and I need to talk." My youngest brothers were lounging on the giant sectional playing a game on the Xbox. They took one look at my expression, and each gave me a hug before practically running down the stairs. They were allergic to female tears and emotions of all kinds. I turned to plop onto the over-stuffed couch and snagged a pillow to hug.

"Stop hugging pillows, Lily," Mom demanded. "You have your mama to hug now." She sat next to me and pulled me sideways into her arms. "Tell me what happened. Luke seemed so determined to make things right with you. I'm surprised it went badly."

"It didn't really go bad." I sniffed as I rested my head against her shoulder. "I just couldn't talk. I took one look at him and it was like going through a screwy time machine. Being near him again felt familiar. But I also couldn't stop remembering how much it hurt when he left me. And I was attracted to him even though he looks different. It was so confusing."

"How was he with Dylan?" she prodded.

"Perfect. He said everything right. Dylan is going to love him, which makes me happy, but I also can't help but think of Will. Dylan was so natural with Luke, and it made me wish we'd all been together all along. Then I felt guilty, like I was betraying Will. I loved Will very much and I still do, just not like . . ." I covered my face with my hands. I couldn't even say it out loud.

"Not like you have always loved Luke," she finished for me.

"Yeah," I whispered.

She reached out and brushed the tears from my cheeks. "Honey, we all love Will. But he wasn't Luke. Luke is the *one* for you. He was your first love, your first everything. Diana and I used to dream of you two getting married." She smiled sadly as she remembered her best friend who died in a car accident when Luke was eight. "Even as babies, you gravitated toward each other. You have an identical twin sister, and sometimes it seemed like you were closer to Luke than to Rose."

"This is just too much. I didn't expect to feel this way. I shouldn't have gone over there so soon." I shook my head to clear it. "I'm done with being upset. I'm just going to quit thinking about it."

"You have to talk about it, Lily. You can't just stop thinking about things." She was incredulous. My mom was a thinker, an analyzer, and a problem solver. I tended to ignore things until they slapped me in the face.

"Why? I have more important things to focus on." I pulled out of her arms.

"Like what?" I could feel a lecture coming on, and I didn't want to hear it.

"My kids, for one. Getting settled at Gram's house, working with Violet, my job at the school when it starts in the fall, being on my own with two kids." I shrugged. "Take your pick."

"You are not on your own. You have me, you have Daddy, you have brothers and sisters who will help you whenever you need it. Even Levi and Jude will help. Those two jokers helped you today by driving your stuff down. See? We're all here for you," she pointed out. I knew they would help me whenever I needed it, but I wanted to feel like I could handle my life on my own for once.

I hesitated, looking for the right words so as not to offend my well-meaning mother. "I'm a grown woman. I'm a mom. I need to be able to do this on my own."

"Once upon a time, you were my responsibility. One day you'll see that a mother never lets that go. I am overjoyed that you're back home and I am finally able to be there when you need me. And Lily, you need me. Let go of this tight leash you have put yourself on."

"What if I let go and I fall apart?" I choked out. Talking through the lump in my throat hurt. I had to end this conversation before I turned into a blubbering mess.

"Then I will be here to help you put yourself back together."

"I've never been on my own. I'm talking about true independence. Being an adult. Not a child. Not a girlfriend. Not a fiancée. Not a wife. Just Lily."

"You are already strong and independent. Standing on your own does not mean you have to actually *be* alone," she insisted.

"You want me to be your child and I need to be a grown-up. Do you understand? Please understand." Right when Mom was about to answer, Violet walked in. She always did have perfect timing.

"Rose is hogging Calla. She won't let me hold her." Violet pouted and threw herself down next to me. "How're you doing, Lily?" she asked as she rested her head on my shoulder.

"I'm fine. Did I miss dinner? Or is everyone grazing tonight?" I asked.

"Since you pulled a disappearing act, we've been grazing. Gram ate early, of course, and she's left already. I mean, it's seven o'clock. *Jeopardy* isn't going to watch itself, is it? She'll see you another time."

Gram had started having trouble taking care of her house and the huge yard by herself, so Mom insisted she move into the garage apartment to be closer. It worked out for me too, as it gave me a place to stay. Dad had cleared out one of the bedrooms in her house and put Calla's new crib together. Mom had redecorated one of the other bedrooms for Dylan and probably decorated Calla's new nursery as well. Levi and Jude had driven all the boxes of our clothes, books, and toys down today.

We'd all left at the same time, but they drove at single-man-in-a-car speed, and I drove at mom-with-kids speed, so they got here first and unloaded my stuff for me. Thanks to my family, when we left after dinner, we could just go to Gram's and get into bed. With that thought came the realization I had a lot of work to do to be completely independent. My family had done too much for me. I sighed in frustration, contemplating how to make them understand what I needed when I wasn't even sure how to explain it to myself.

I had no idea. So I ended the conversation instead. "I'm starving. Let's go eat."

"Okay, Lily. But we aren't finished talking about this," Mom said with audible impatience.

"Oh, I interrupted something heavy. You're welcome." Violet laughed as we headed down the stairs then through the great room toward the kitchen. Rose was at the counter attempting to make something.

"I smell cinnamon. What are you making, Rose? And where is my baby?" I sat on one of the barstools at the massive butcher-block island counter in my mother's kitchen. There were all sorts of hors d'oeuvres set up for everybody to munch on. My mother loved to entertain.

"Apple crumble, and Dad stole her. She went willingly though, the little traitor. Dylan is playing catch in the yard with Mark and Mara, Finn and Nick, and the brothers." Violet took off, probably to try to steal Calla from Dad. Calla was adorable, but this was getting ridiculous.

"Where are the apples, Rose?" I saw nothing but crumble, nary an apple to be seen.

"I can sense your judgment." She glanced at me with a smirk. "I am doubling the crumble because it's the best part, and I halved the apple portion because I'm not in the mood to be healthy. I have ice cream to go with it. We can talk and eat, and you can tell me all about the drive down. I've missed you, little sister." She opened the oven and shoved the apple crumble in.

"Rose, I am ten minutes younger than you are. Get over the little sister stuff already." I laughed as Dylan ran up to me and handed me my phone. Rose snatched him around his waist and swung him up in a huge hug.

"Your phone rang, but no one talked when I answered," he said, laughing as Rose blew raspberries into his neck. She put him down, and off he went back outside.

"That's weird. Probably just a wrong number." I shrugged and put my phone in my pocket. "Okay, Rose, I'm not judging your attempt at baking. It actually looked good."

"I know, weird. Help me make sure it doesn't burn. So, want to talk about Luke?" she asked, opening the fridge to pull out a soda.

"Nope." I stuffed a ranch-dressing-covered baby carrot into my mouth.

"I didn't think so. But I've talked to him, and I think you should give him a chance. He thought he was doing the right thing. None of us will give you any crap after you forgive him and get back together and get married and have more cute babies."

"Why are you all so sure that we'll get back together?" I was kind of freaked out that my family had not only forgiven Luke so quickly, but they all seemed to think it was inevitable that we'd get back together. I got up and headed to the fridge in search of something to drink.

"Duh, because it's Luke. Luke and Lily are like peanut butter and jelly. And I was always the pickle on your sandwich." She stuck her tongue out at me when she caught my eye.

"You're not my pickle, Rose, you're my best friend, and I've missed you so much." I hugged her around her neck, swinging her side to side, and she hugged me back, wrapping her arms around my waist like she always did. We pulled apart just as our brothers started filing through the door at the rear of the kitchen.

I grabbed Rose's hand. "Aw, back inside so soon? Rose and I wanted to play catch with you guys."

"Yeah," Rose added, "we wanted to play too."

Then we said in unison, "Forever and ever and ever." Suddenly our four tall, macho brothers turned around and ran back outside. We high-fived because we still had it going on.

Mom, who had just entered the kitchen from the living room, got mad. "Rose, Lily, stop scaring your brothers. I never have all my babies together, and you just ran them off with your scary twin act." We used to go all *Shining* twins on them regularly, and they would always run off, much to our amusement.

"You have to get over it because we're not all here." Rose laughed. "Woman, do you have so many kids that you can't tell when one is missing?"

"You're all here, aren't you? Violet, Asher, Caden, you two brats." She pointed at me then Rose as she went down the list, naming us all. "Levi and Jude. Shoot, I did forget about Holly. Don't tell her," she mumbled as she turned around and left the kitchen.

"She's a crazy woman." Rose rolled her eyes. "Hey, do you want some of this lasagna?"

I headed back to my barstool and sat. Rose was by the

chafing dishes my mom had set up on the counter making room on the table for the crumble.

"I'm waiting for the apple crumble," I said as I stuffed my face. I was stress-eating my way through the hors d'oeuvre platters. When one is stress eating, bite-sized food is a must, along with dessert of any type. "Where is Holly anyway?" I asked through a mouthful of quiche. They were tiny, perfect for stuffing the whole thing in.

"Check her blog or her Instagram. She posted this morning. She's in Washington, hiking the Pacific Crest Trail."

I shuddered. My younger sister Holly was athletic. She loved running and climbing things and going on long hikes that lasted for days with zero opportunity for a shower. I basically hated all that stuff. I required frequent access to snacks and a television to properly function.

"All that walking? Yuck. I'm tired just thinking about it." I stuffed a blanket-covered pig into my mouth. "Though, I'm tired all the time lately. Calla is against sleeping more than three hours in a row."

"Want me to come stay with you tonight?" Rose offered as she sat in the stool next to mine.

"No thanks. I don't want to get used to that kind of thing."

"I don't mind helping. I'm off all summer too, remember? Being a kindergarten teacher is the best thing I ever did. Summers off!" She took a bite of lasagna and reached out a hand for a high-five.

Laughing, I smacked her palm. "No thanks. We have to get used to it being just the three of us."

She sighed. "It's not just the three of you and it never will be. Why are you so stubborn? Just let me help you."

"You've helped me enough. You were there for my bed rest. Between you, Jane, Mom, and Violet, and Trevor stopping by and helping, I was never alone." Trevor had been Will's partner on the police force. His son Mikey was Dylan's best friend. Hopefully, he would drive down sometime over the summer, and the boys could get together. Trevor was from this area anyway, somewhere near Portland. The boys could have visits whenever Trev visited his family.

"Lily, I heard you talking with Mom and it's all a bunch of crap. You don't have a problem with us helping you. You want to learn to do everything by yourself because you're scared. Luke left you, then Will died, and you lived far away from all of us. But now you're back, and let's talk odds. You have two parents and seven siblings. Plus, Gram, Jed, Auntie Delphine, and our cousins, and of course, there's Jane, and don't forget Luke is back. Unless the house blows up during a Sunday dinner or something wacked like that happens, we won't all be taken out at once. You'll always have at least one of us to lean on. Think about that and chill out a little bit."

I knew I was being ridiculous, but I couldn't help it. I felt anxious when I thought about all that I had lost. "You're probably right," I conceded. "But I don't need you to spend the night. We'll be okay." Telling Rose she was right was the best way to end a disagreement. She could go on and on and on until she got her way.

"Have it your way. But promise to call if you need me, no matter what time it is. You are nightmare prone, and I don't want you freaking out in the middle of the night when Gram's house starts all that weird creaking and her neighbor's asshole dog starts howling at the moon."

"Fine. Deal," I agreed. "I need to leave now anyway. If I can find my baby and wrestle her away from Violet. It's almost bedtime."

"What about my apple crumble?" she pouted.

"I'm full of all these snacks. Tell me how it turned out."

I yelled for Dylan and went off to search for my baby and distribute goodbye hugs and kisses to my family.

Chapter 6
Lily

The sun had just begun to set behind the tallest fir tree in Gram's front yard when we finally made it home for our first night as a family of three. Jane was already home in Portland, finally back at work after her leave of absence. This was the first night since Will died that it would be just me and the kids.

I had always loved Gram's house. It was a cute little cottage painted a creamy white with dark green shutters and trim. It was right in the middle of town on a street lined with other old houses. Picket fences surrounded yards with lush green grass, abundant flowers, and tall trees that created an arch over the street. As kids, we used to pretend the house was haunted because it would creak and settle all night long making noises that we were sure had to be ghosts and zombies. So many memories lived in this old house. It was strange to think her bedroom would now be mine.

Shaking off my sudden nostalgia, I stopped my Expedition and climbed out to get the sleeping kids. I dreaded waking Dylan; if I had let Rose come home with me, we could each take a kid and let them both sleep.

"Hey, sweet boy, can you wake up so we can go inside?" I

rubbed his cheek softly and smiled at him to take the sting out of having to wake him up.

"Mommy, where are we?" His sleepy eyes examined our new home in confusion.

"Grandma Rosemary's house. It's ours for now, remember?"

He didn't answer as he jumped down and ran to the wrap-around porch to wait for me. Luckily, Calla didn't wake as I took her carrier out of its base in the back seat.

"Lucky girl. I hope I'll sleep this well tonight," I whispered.

I unlocked the front door. The house was still decorated in grandma chic—homemade quilts and doilies, Hummel figurines, and family pictures. I made a mental note to pack up the breakables; Dylan could get rowdy. Gram's tiny bookshelf in the corner was still filled to overflowing with the books my mother had written, along with her other favorites. I hoped my kids would feel as comforted as I did by the familiar surroundings.

I carefully walked up the narrow wooden staircase and down the hall to transfer Calla to her crib in my mom's child-hood room. I had guessed right. It was newly decorated with a mermaid theme, all greens and aqua blues with hints of pink and coral. Calla stirred for a minute as I slipped her into her pink blanket sleeper in the crib, but luckily, she went right back to sleep. Sometimes it seemed as if she knew what was going on and tried to help in her own way. I turned on the nightlight, snagged the baby monitor off the dresser, then walked down the hall to find Dylan.

I found him standing in his new bedroom looking around. Mom had decorated it in shades of dark blue with cute pops of red here and there as an accent. Jude and Levi had unpacked Dylan's toys and set them up on the shelves and dresser top and filled the bookcase up with his books. They acted like they were so tough, but deep down they were big softies. I started to tear up as I thought of all the things my family had done to make the transition to our new life as smooth and easy as possible. "Let's get you tucked in," I whispered, then picked him up to get some cuddles in before I took him to bed.

"This used to be Aunt Delphine's bedroom when she was a little girl." I found his pajamas in the top dresser drawer. Wow . . . Levi and Jude had even unpacked his clothes. "Get changed, little bug, then I'll tuck you in."

Once he was snug as a bug, he asked to talk to Luke. "Mommy, can I say goodnight to Daddy Luke? I think he lives by himself in that huge house. Someone should tell him goodnight."

"Sure, I guess so." I found his name in my contacts and passed my phone to Dylan. My heart kicked up to a nervous beat once I heard it ring.

"Hi Dad, it's Dylan. I wanted to tell you goodnight." My heart lurched when he called Luke "Dad," and I tried hard not pay attention to Dylan's side of the conversation. My brain could only handle so many feelings in one day.

How was this real?

Dylan finally said his goodbyes, hung up, and put the phone down on the night table. "He said to tell you goodnight for him. He wants you to have sweet dreams, and I should remind you that there are no zombies in the basement. Did you think there were zombies down there?" Dylan laughed at me.

I smiled. "I used to. Luke used to laugh at me too, you little stinker." I sat on the edge of the bed and pulled him into my arms for another hug. "Good night, my sweet boy. I love you." I snuggled him closer and kissed the top of his head.

"I love you too, Mommy. He said there were no ghosts in the backyard either." He burst out laughing as I turned off the light and headed down the hall to get ready for bed.

I crossed the threshold to Gram's old room to find my suitcases and boxes piled up in the corner. I guess Levi and Jude had reached their helpful limit with Dylan's room. I laughed to myself as I dug through the boxes until I found my pajamas and toiletries and headed into the bathroom. Mom had left a basket on the white marble-topped counter filled with bubble bath and other girlie fun things, along with a card to welcome me home.

I couldn't help but feel like a brat for the way I had acted earlier. I craved independence, but I should have been nicer about it. I placed my phone and the baby monitor on the edge of the counter near the old claw-footed tub and started the tap, adding a huge amount of the sweet-smelling bubble bath. I had always loved this tub. I twisted my ponytail up into a bun, stepped in, and let myself drift down into the warm, bubbly haven of relaxation. The stress of the day washed away as the water got higher.

My phone pinged with an incoming text. I shut the water off with my foot and reached for my phone.

Luke: *There's so much I need to say to you. Can we talk soon?*

My heart raced and my stomach swirled. I felt ridiculous because it was just a text message and still my body reacted like a hormonal teenager in the throes of a crush. Which, in all honesty, had been how I'd used to react to Luke every time I was near him. But I hadn't seen him in years, and there was this huge hurtful history between us that had yet to be addressed. I had come in here to relax, and one ping of my phone had ruined that.

I should suck it up and be a grown-up about this. The water swished around me as I sat up and grabbed a towel to dry my hands so I could text back.

. . .

Lily: I'll be working at Violet's shop tomorrow. We can talk there. Will that work?

Luke: Works for me. Sweet dreams.

Lily: See you tomorrow.

So much for relaxation. I tossed my phone onto the bathmat and blew out a sigh. I tried to relax again but it was no use. Luke had me keyed up and I couldn't calm down. Visions of his gorgeous face and super-sexy body danced through my mind and I decided being naked in the bathtub was not a good idea anymore. At least I'd managed to wind down for five minutes before getting all twisted up in a knot again. I pulled the plug and got out, quickly dressed, and headed for bed.

Hours later, I woke up with a start in a tangle of sheets with Gram's beautiful quilt tossed to the floor. Rose was right about me and my nightmares. My heart pounded hard, and my mind raced with jumbled thoughts of Luke and of Will and how to deal with being stuck in this town full of memories. I got out of bed and headed into the hall to check on the kids. The floor creaked with every step I took along the old dark wood. I peeked into Calla's room to find her sleeping. With a quick glance at the clock, I smiled at the time. A new sleep record—yay! I crept into Dylan's room. He was asleep too. I should be asleep along with them.

I was wide awake and in the aftermath of a nightmare. My history told me that going back to bed and trying to fall asleep would be pointless. I descended the stairs for a change of scenery, turning on every light as I passed. Being in the dark after a nightmare freaked me out. Honestly, being in the dark freaked me out, period.

I should have never encouraged my kids to start sleeping through the night. I hadn't been doing so well with my own thoughts lately. Was it wrong to wake a sleeping baby? Right now, I needed my kids more than they needed me, and it made me feel weak. There were so many things I didn't want to think about, and now that my life had begun to settle down somewhat, those things long buried were rising to the surface.

At one point in my life, this hour would not have been late. Now that I was a mother, this was definitely past my bedtime. I got a Diet Coke out of the fridge, but it was caffeine free. Yucky, but better than not having a Diet Coke. I headed out of the kitchen and into the living room, filling the house with light as I went.

I sat down on the sofa and covered myself with one of Gram's quilts. It was almost as good as a hug. I stared out the front window and tried to stop my racing thoughts. Sitting in this familiar place, surrounded by the night sounds I hadn't heard since I was a kid, made my mind wander to places I didn't want it to go. Luke had been in this house just as much as I had. I could look anywhere in this place and find a memory. I propped my feet up on the coffee table and tried to rein in my anxiety. I was tempted to call Rose, but I was not ready to admit defeat.

Since Will died, I had been stuck in a whirlwind with no time to think. With so much other stuff to focus on regarding his death and finding out I was pregnant, it had been easy to bury my grief. Later, after I'd developed pre-eclampsia and had gone on bed rest, I'd had my pregnancy to focus on. I had been so afraid I would lose Calla—the only part of Will I had left—that I had forced my mind into a state of blankness to keep my blood pressure under control. I hadn't been alone like this since he had died. I had nothing to distract me, no funeral to plan, insurance company to call, clothes to donate, or newborn baby waking up every hour or two. Jane, Mom, or one of my sisters weren't here to check on me and keep me company. I mean, my kids were here, but they were asleep, so they didn't count right now. Right now, I was stuck in this dark quiet house alone . . . and losing my freaking mind.

I got up again to check on the kids. Both were still asleep.

I can't stand this.

Tension built in my chest. Had I drank too much coffee today? God, I hadn't had any coffee since I'd found out I was pregnant. I felt like I could run a mile in a minute or jump up in the air and fly. I was about to burst out of my skin. I continued down the hall and descended the creaky staircase once more to head into the kitchen. I dumped my Diet Coke, turned on the tap, and filled a glass. I sipped and squinted against the beam of light that shone through the window. It looked like a flashlight beam shining in the distance. The glass I held crashed to the floor and shattered. Gram was going to be so pissed!

I fumbled and flailed, slapping my hand against the light switch and plunging the kitchen into darkness. I spun wildly around in circles once I reached the living room until I spied Gram's baseball bat in the umbrella stand. I dashed to it and held it at my side with a trembling hand as I fumbled for my phone in the pocket of my robe to call my father.

I jumped when I heard ringing from outside on the front porch. I took a breath and put my eye to the peephole. I had never been so glad to see my big brother. Cade stood there with my father at his side. Cade was a cop, too. I sighed with annoyance as my heart rate slowed. It was probably one of their flashlights I had seen. I opened the door. "Dad, I saw a flashlight from the kitchen window. Was it you guys checking up on me?"

They pushed past me to enter the house and rush through to the back door.

"Uh, come on in," I muttered.

A few minutes later they came back inside.

"No one is back there. But Dad is still checking it out,"

Cade said. "We just left a scene. You have all the lights turned on, so we stopped to check on you." He gestured to the baseball bat I still gripped in my hand. "It's okay now, Lily."

I put the bat back in the umbrella stand and crossed my arms over my chest. "I was getting a drink of water and saw a flashlight out in the yard. It startled me. I dropped a glass in the kitchen," I blurted. I was definitely rattled.

"I'll go sweep it up. You're barefoot. Go sit down," Cade ordered. He hugged me quickly as he walked past me to enter the kitchen. I curled back up in my quilt on the couch.

Dad reentered the living room and crossed it to sit in one of the wing chairs. "Did you have a bad dream? Is that what woke you up?"

"Yeah. I just woke up a few minutes ago. I won't be able to go back to sleep."

"I'm sleeping on the couch tonight," Cade said from the kitchen. He came back into the living room with a bag of Oreos and a glass of milk.

"Violet stocked your fridge earlier and I haven't been to the store in days. You'll be doing me a favor. You have all kinds of breakfast stuff in there. I'll cook in the morning." Cade had a way of getting what he wanted by which you didn't realize you'd been steamrolled by him.

"Oh, sure. Thank you." I agreed, grateful that I would be able to sleep since he would be here.

Cade sat on the other side of the couch and carefully placed his glass of milk on a coaster on Gram's old coffee table. He handed me an Oreo. I stuffed it into my mouth whole. He laughed and passed me another. I stuffed that one in too. Stress-eating was kind of my thing. He grabbed a handful, then gave me the rest of the package with a grin.

Cade was the best big brother. He'd been a grade ahead of Rose and me in school, and all our friends had had crushes on him when we were growing up. Even though he was my brother, I could admit he was a catch.

"Tell me about the flashlight," Dad said, snapping me out of my wandering thoughts.

"It was out back, in the trees. Should I be worried? I thought maybe I imagined it. I was kind of spaced out." I stole Cade's glass of milk and took a huge gulp. He rolled his eyes and took a bite of cookie.

"No one was there," Dad replied. "There are footprints, but gardeners were just here yesterday doing some clean-up. Has anything out of the ordinary happened?" He nodded at Cade, who tossed him an Oreo. Cade looked at me to give him some more.

I sighed and gave him another handful. "My whole life is out of the ordinary right now. But nothing scary or threatening. I had a wrong-number call earlier, that's it," I added after swallowing a mouthful of cookie goodness.

"Just be aware. Let me or Cade know if anything freaks you out. Even if you think it's your imagination" Cade nodded his agreement.

"Okay, Dad." The power of the Oreos started to wear off as I worried that I hadn't imagined the light in the backyard.

Chapter 7
Luke

After texting Lily, I set my phone down with my heart soaring. All I needed was a real chance and it looked like I had one. I picked the phone back up when my text notification went off.

Rose: *Are you coming tonight?*

Luke: *Meet you there.*

Rose and I had always been close; she'd been my best friend growing up, just like Lily. But there had never been anything romantic between us, ever. I used to wonder how I could find Lily so sexy and irresistible and Rose so . . . not. Rose wasn't even like a sister to me. I had always imagined her more like what a brother would be. She was always in my face with a joke, we teased each other, and watched football together. But as an only child, I could never know for sure.

She was the first of her family to visit me when I got back

to town, full of suspicion but willing to listen. Sometimes I took Rocky and met her at the Sweetbriar High School track for a run. I parked my truck next to her VW Bug and got out, Rocky bounding out behind me. He loved Rose, but he loved running the track even more.

"Did you text her like I said?" she asked without preamble.

"Hello, Rose," I deadpanned.

She rolled her eyes and bent to pet Rocky. "Yeah, yeah, hi. So, did you?" she demanded. "You're the best boy, yes you are." She baby-talked him and scratched behind his ears. Then she sat down and let him crawl over her and lick her face.

I had to ask, even though it made me feel like we were back in high school. "Did she talk about me at dinner?" At least our location was appropriate.

"Of course she did. But I can't tell you anything about that. Me and you are besties, but as my identical twin, she outranks you. Don't worry, I didn't tell her anything about you either." She mimed turning a lock over her lips and smirked. "Did you text her?"

"Yes, I'm meeting her tomorrow morning at Violet's."

"Ouch, you'll have to wake up early for that."

"Worth it. All right, let's go." She got up and we took off, the evening breeze cool against my face as we ran. As always, Rocky had a hard time staying by my side. He wanted to go faster than I was able to. I was supposed to keep my pace at a light jog due to my injured back and he wanted to sprint.

"She's having a hard time. Obviously." Rose huffed as we rounded the track for the second time. I was appreciative for the information, but I already knew she would be struggling.

"Yeah. I know how she is. Or how she used to be, anyway." Lily had always been a worrier and an over-analyzer. I used to be the one to unwind her and help her relax. I hated that I was now one of the sources of her stress.

"Oh, she's totally the same. You should have seen her at Mom's snack platters. And how are *you* doing? Spill." As kids,

Rose had never been the type of friend to push for information, but that had changed during the time I was gone. She was up in my face to talk to her every time we got together. I didn't mind it though. I was happy she cared enough to pry, and it felt good to get things off my chest with someone who I had known forever.

"I don't know how to feel like this anymore. It's been a long time" I wasn't trying to be cryptic. Being cryptic around Rose got her curiosity piqued. I sped up, as if I could outrun my answer to her question so she wouldn't press for more details.

"Feel like what? *Gah!* Slow down, you're running too fast. My legs are too short to keep up with you, damn it."

I stopped short, earning myself a look from Rocky. "Sorry. Uh, well, I hadn't been home in so long. Everything is so different now. My dad isn't around anymore to give me shit. The house is different . . . I feel different about everything."

She caught up and stopped next to me, huffing and puffing as she rested her hands on her knees. "Good. Your dad was a dick. Fuck him. I mean, I'm sorry he's dead and all that, but he was a total asshole to you after your mom died."

Her familiar words shot right into my heart, reminding me of when we were kids and she and Lily would comfort me after one of my dad's ranting outbursts about how much I disappointed him. It was always Lily with hugs and soft words, and Rose making jokes to make me laugh while she cursed him. I turned away, not ready to feel this vulnerable. I had spent years burying my feelings; being back home was driving them all to the surface and sometimes it was too much.

"Hey, it's okay, Luke." She took my hand. I squeezed it gently, grateful for her support. "I'm done with running, let's get tacos at the food trucks."

I glanced at her, grateful for lightening the mood. "This is why I like running with you. Liam never wants to quit for tacos." We started back toward the parking lot.

"Dude, he is so ripped, it's crazy. I can't live like that. I need tacos—they're necessary for stress relief. Nobody realizes how hard being a kindergarten teacher really is. It's not all coloring and sing-a-longs. I've seen some shit, Luke."

"I believe it. I saw how much energy Dylan had when they were at my place."

Her smile was knowing. "He's a good boy. All he could talk about earlier was you."

Feeling dumbstruck, I just blinked in response. I didn't know what to say. So much was changing in my life and, so far, all of it was good.

She studied my face with a smile as I contemplated her words. "I didn't end up eating at my parent's house and I'm starving. Let's get out of here," she finally said.

We got into our respective vehicles and re-met at the food truck lot in the center of town. Luckily, we were able to score an empty table after grabbing our tacos.

"So. What did you mean before when you said it's been a long time?" she eyed me with a sly grin.

My mouth opened, but I didn't answer. I took a gulp of my Coke and looked everywhere but at her.

"Thought I'd forget about that, did you?" Her eyebrows raised expectantly as she took a huge bite of her taco, cursing when half of it fell on her plate.

I shook my head. "I can't talk about this with you. I didn't mean to bring it up."

"You can talk about anything with me, like always. Pretend I'm a guy if you have to." She snatched the baseball cap off my head and put it on backward. "There, hit me with it. Should I burp or scratch myself somewhere inappropriate? Would that help loosen you up?"

I shook my head, trying my best not to laugh at her earnest face. "I can't—"

"Fine." She looked around the seating area before whispering. "You haven't had sex since Lily. That's it, right?"

"Uh . . ." I turned bright red. I could feel my cheeks burn above my beard. Rocky let out a sharp bark at my feet and nudged my leg. Damn, even he noticed I was embarrassed.

Her grin was smug. "Nailed it. It's okay to be nervous. I think it's sweet. What I wouldn't do for that kind of loyalty—"

"I can't even think that way yet. Come on—" I *shouldn't* think that way yet, but it hadn't stopped me. Ever since seeing Lily at my house, she had been the only thing on my mind.

"Fine, moving on. What was it like for you? I mean, over there. Not having sex with my sister, because *ew.*"

A startled laugh escaped before I could stop it. "You're chatty tonight. Maybe I should ask you some personal questions."

"Do it." She raised an eyebrow. "I have nothing going on. I haven't gotten laid in over three years and I'm not ashamed of it. I have no news to share other than stuff about work and jogging with you. How can I be here for you if you don't tell me about anything other than your back hurting or your job? Tell me something real."

"Fine. Sometimes therapy makes me feel like two different people and I'm trying to put myself back together. Now that I'm home it's like my time in the Army went by in a blur. But while I was there it felt like an eternity because it was all I had. Is that real enough?" I didn't mean to be sarcastic, but I had to cover how raw my words made me feel. Brutal honesty was too damn hard.

Her eyes softened. "I could see feeling that way. Actually, it makes a lot of sense. But listen, I'm glad you're *feeling* now. When I first saw you again—" Hesitating, she looked away.

"It's okay, say it. I know how fucked up I was."

"Your eyes were dead, Luke. Like you weren't even there. Was it always like that for you?" Her words hit me physically. I flinched.

"Sometimes I wish it had been. Then I wouldn't remember anything."

"You're safe now, you know. And we're all here for you. I know I'm being pushy, but it's because I want you to be okay. You can tell me to back off any time and I will."

"I know and I appreciate it. But I'm not so broken I can't be here for you too. You know that right?"

"I know." Her lips tipped up in a smile. "But you're not broken, Luke. Not at all. You've always been one of the strongest people I know."

I swiped my hat from her head and put it back on. "Thanks for saying that. I'm trying."

"I know you are, and don't take this as me being condescending—I'm proud of you."

Touched by her words, I smiled at her. "That means a lot to me. Thanks, Rose." We finished our tacos and I walked her to her car, just like I did in high school. On my way home, I drove past Lily's house to see if everything was okay.

Every light in the house was on.

I had known her forever. I knew she was scared of the dark and alone with her kids in the house. She was probably trying to be brave. But fuck that. She'd been through too much lately and she needed her family. One thing that therapy taught me is to reach out when you need help, and I knew she wouldn't do it. I sent a text to her dad to go check on her and waited by the curb until he pulled up in his police SUV. Maybe it was presumptuous and not my business, but if no one had butted into my life, I wouldn't be here right now.

I waved to her dad and brother as they exited the vehicle and headed home.

Chapter 8
Lily

I woke up to the smell of bacon and coffee and the knowledge that my first night alone with my kids had been pretty much a failure. After Dad left and Cade crashed on the couch, Calla had woken up. She'd beaten her sleep record last night, but not by much. She was up for hours nursing and cooing at me. She finally went back to sleep at three thirty this morning. It was five now and I needed to get ready for work.

I was not in the mood to be awake, so I threw on a pair of jeans and a T-shirt, found some shoes, and put my hair up in a bun before heading downstairs. Cade and Mom were in the kitchen sitting in mismatched painted chairs at Gram's battered wood farm table. Mom held Calla while Cade stuffed his face with bacon and eggs. He gestured to a filled plate on the table next to him. I lifted my chin in thanks and sat to stuff my face too. Dylan was still asleep, as one should be at five in the morning during summer vacation.

"Morning," I grunted after swallowing my eggs. "Let me nurse her. I'm full." I took Calla, so I could feed her and get some cuddles before I left.

"You're wearing that?" Mom asked me.

"She's fine, Mom," Cade told her. "Lily, you're fine."

"I don't even care if I'm not fine." I stole a piece of bacon from Cade's plate. I couldn't reach my own while holding Calla. Cade laughed and took a piece from my plate. "I'm just glad I remembered to put on a bra. I'm not going back upstairs." I did not have enough energy for any more stairs today.

"Well, that's okay, I guess." Mom gave up on making me change clothes a little too quickly, but I was too tired to worry about it.

"I'll wait until Dylan gets up, then take them back to my house. Mark and Mara will be there soon. Jude is off so he's going to swim with us today." She pointed at me and said, "Don't worry. I won't take Calla in the pool. She's still too little."

I smiled at her. She already knew all my parenting rules because I got them all from her.

She winked, then continued, "You can come pick them up whenever you're ready. I packed the diaper bag. There is no need for you to do a thing. You have a great day, honey." She gave me one of her million-watt smiles, then started texting on her phone.

I smiled back and reached out to touch her hand. The kids would have a blast with her. "I will. I'm turning over a new leaf today. I'm going to be fearless." I passed Calla back to Mom. I had already kissed Dylan goodbye before I came downstairs and was ready to go.

Cade handed me another piece of bacon and gave me a chin lift. "Good luck, Lil."

After kissing my baby goodbye one more time, I left. I grinned when I spotted Violet smiling and waving at me from the back door of her shop.

"Are you waiting for me?" I hollered as I got out of my car. She laughed at me as I climbed out of my Expedition. I was so short I had to use the running boards along the side to get in and out of it.

"Yes, I'm waiting for you, silly. Here, put this on when you get inside." She handed me a tiny, fitted, black T-shirt, one that was cuter than the one I was wearing and didn't have spit-up on it. It said, "First, I drink the coffee. Then I do the things." Violet's said, "Death before decaf." Our ensembles would be completed by purple half aprons.

"You were the one texting with Mom earlier, right? Fine, I'll change." I huffed and stomped toward the back door of the shop. I knew I was cranky from lack of sleep and needed to shake it off. I sighed and smiled at Violet to make up for my attitude.

"I brought lipstick and mascara too. And a hairbrush. My God, Lily. You're lucky you have me," she said with a smirk.

"I was up all night with Calla and basement zombie night-mares. Give me a break. And what's wrong with my hair? You don't like my mom-bun? I'm stealing this look back from the hipsters." The crankiness surged back through me. I was mouthing off to Violet and that took balls. I took a deep breath and tried to settle down.

"You have two different shoes on. Have you no pride?" Vi's teasing smirk helped to calm my sass.

I looked down. Hmm, so I did. One pink and one black sneaker. I was just glad I'd chosen the right feet. "They're both Converse. Lay off."

"Grouchy, too," she muttered under her breath.

I sagged against the side of the building as she unlocked the door. "I'm so tired, Vi. I feel like I've been tired for the last two years. I apologize in advance for every rude comment that comes out of my mouth today."

"Don't worry, I get you. I've been there. We'll go in, you'll change, and I'll make you some coffee to wake you up," she offered as we walked into her back room. I paused for a moment and took a deep breath. It smelled like heaven in here, like sugar and spice and everything nice—and coffee. So much coffee. We passed a restroom, a big walk-in storage closet, and a staircase that led to a tiny loft before we got to the kitchen area.

"I can't drink it because I'm nursing. I haven't had coffee in over a year. I'll be surrounded by delicious, caffeinated beverages for hours, and I can't drink any of it. What was I thinking coming here?" I almost shrieked the words—that's how sorry I felt for myself.

Violet looked at me with horror and pity. "When I was nursing the boys, I drank one cup of coffee a day. The doctor said it was fine. You can have one coffee," she declared.

"How did you survive on only one cup?" Violet was a coffee fiend, completely addicted. Owning this shop was her life dream come true.

"One cup of coffee a day, no sleep, and twin boys." She closed her eyes, held up a hand, and shook her head at the painful memories. "That was when I perfected my decaf roast. It won't give you all the feels, but it's not bad. You can try the decaf after I get you all fueled up on the regular." She winked and bumped my shoulder with hers as she passed me. I followed her through the swinging doors to the front.

"I am so ready for this. Real freakin' coffee. This is the best day ever." I beamed at her. "Hey, Rose." She had unlocked the front door and burst inside with a big smile aimed my way.

She flipped the *Closed* sign to *Open*, then waved a pair of shoes at me. I flipped her the bird and headed for the restroom to change. Her loud laugh followed behind me as I shut the door and looked in the mirror, which was something I probably should have done before I left the house. I cringed and splashed my face with water. I applied mascara and lipstick, then added a bit of the lipstick to my cheeks to give me some color. Good Lord, I looked like one of the zombies in Gram's basement—pale and dead. I decided the mom-bun could stay. Everyone loved a messy bun, right?

Rose knocked on the door, opened it, and passed me the high-heeled, strappy black sandals. I decided to play along with my sisters and changed. I was supposed to see Luke later. There was no need for him to see me at my slovenly best. There would be plenty of time for reality later.

"Lily, get your tiny booty out here," Violet bellowed. I exited the restroom and tossed my stuff into Violet's office.

She held out a cup of coffee. "You look pretty. At least you picked good jeans to wear today. Your ass looks nice." She nodded as she checked me out. I wasn't even looking at her. My eyes were on the coffee. She grinned. "It's my special of the day—vanilla bean latte. I made the syrup myself, with real vanilla beans. I don't fool around here."

I accepted the cup from Violet with reverence. This would be my first real, fully caffeinated cup of coffee in over a year. And not just any coffee, but Violet's coffee. I closed my eyes in blissed-out anticipation, then took a sip. It was delicious. Violet was a coffee goddess.

I opened my eyes to the *bing-bong* sound of the bell at the door signaling the arrival of the first customer of the day. I looked up and spotted big Liam, Luke's friend. We waved and smiled at each other as he headed to the counter to order from Rose. My eyebrows raised after he pulled out his phone and started texting. I headed to the cash register, feeling special because I was the official ringer upper for the day. I also got to fill the little purple bags with baked goods.

Violet had embraced her name and the purple lifestyle. There were purple accents all over her store. The sofa was a rich royal purple and the pillows on the leather club chairs were of varying purple patterns. The tables were dark wood, but the chairs had all been painted in different shades of lavender. I inhaled deeply. It smelled good in here, it was pretty, and my kids were being taken care of. I started to relax. This would be a great day. I could feel it already. Or maybe it was just the caffeine I was feeling. Either way, day one of being fearless was a success.

I rang up Liam's order: fat-free iced soy latte with no whip and an egg white and spinach breakfast sandwich on Violet's special no-carb cloud bread. He had huge, defined muscles popping out everywhere. I could see his six-pack through his shirt, and it was glorious. I guess his disgusting breakfast was one of the things that helped him get that hot bod. Aside from lifting heavy things and doing crunches or whatever.

He grinned. I think he caught me checking him out. I blushed. "Have a great day, Lily," he said.

I nodded and waved as he headed out, then cringed at myself. I had been cooped up on bed rest surrounded by family members and kids for so long that I had forgotten how to behave around regular humans. Whatever. I shook it off.

The door *bing-bonged* again, and Luke walked through, followed by a few other people I didn't care about. He smiled at me, then approached Rose to order.

"Hey, Rose," he said.

"Hey, Luke, you want the usual?" She offered with a smirky smile. She had been giving him crap since the day we were all born. If there was something to tease him about, she would be the one to do it. They had the quiet-brother-and-annoying-sister dynamic going on.

"Has Violet changed the name of it yet?" he asked.

"Nope, it's still called The Spoiled Princess. Do you want me to make the pink Barbie silhouette in the froth?" She laughed as she started to make his order. It looked like a type of cappuccino.

He sighed. "No, I do not. But I do want the sprinkles. And two of the raspberry scones, with extra clotted cream, please." Wow, I was right. Luke was a dessert eater now. I guess that was how he got that delicious hulky bulky quality to his body. I frowned as I busted myself staring at him again. *Damn it.*

I shook myself out of my Luke trance and reached for his

scones. I put them in the cute little lavender bag, then found the clotted cream.

He came to me to pay. "Hey, Lily. Did you have a good night?"

"What? Yeah, sort of. I think the zombies in the basement were extra active last night. I couldn't sleep." *Was I flirting?*

He grinned that adorable half-grin that always used to get me all swirly, then I realized who I was talking to, and my brain turned to mush. I was flirting with *New Luke*. Fine-as-heck, totally-pinnable-on-my-hot-guy-Pinterest-board, lumber-jack Luke.

He stared at me intently, searching my eyes. I didn't remember Luke ever being this intense with me. It was both scary and hot. I blushed bright red. I was cursed with super pale, typical redhead skin. I couldn't remember ever blushing or being uncomfortable with Luke before. I mean, we'd been born on the same day and we had literally known each other our entire lives, even in the womb.

"That'll be nine-ninety-five," I blurted. I took his ten-dollar bill. I made change and dropped it into his huge, manly hand. A hand that had been everywhere on me, and *in me*. I couldn't take it. The way he was looking at me freaked me out. I turned and made a mad dash for the kitchen.

I called over my shoulder, "Um, I'm going to work on an order for later. Be right back," and hurried through the door that led into the kitchen to squat down on the floor. I heard Rose talking to Luke out front as I huddled there like a total wuss.

Violet eyed me with a knowing look. "Luke here?" she asked as she poured blueberry muffin batter into muffin cups.

"No, why would you say that?" Who was I trying to kid? I couldn't play this off. These people knew me too well. "Okay, yes, he's here. Don't ask me what I'm doing. I don't even know. I am perplexed and you know I don't like being perplexed. I can't handle this, Violet. He was looking at me like he was on a mission or something. I am not mission material right now. I just had a baby. Women who have just had a baby can't be mission objectives," I rambled. I couldn't stop talking, or thinking, or saying what I was thinking.

Make it stop.

"Make it stop, Vi," I pleaded.

"Take a breath, Lily. You're going to stroke out or something." Her tone was soothing when she said, "You don't have to do anything you don't want to do." Then she snickered. "But you are coming off kind of crazy right now. You know that, right?" She raised an eyebrow at me, then shoved the future muffins into the oven and set the timer.

"I don't know why I'm freaking out. I texted with him on the phone last night. I knew I would see him today. I tried to mentally prepare for it. I shouldn't be reacting this way. It makes no sense."

"It makes complete sense," Violet countered in an annoyingly sensible voice. Now was not the time to be sensible. Now was the time to feed me chocolate and pat my head, damnit.

"Does not," I argued.

"Are we doing this?" Visibly exasperated, she sighed. "All the reasons why he was on our shit lists are invalidated. Explanations have been given. All the explanations are reasonable and have been accepted. Anger is no longer warranted even though he hasn't talked to you yet"—she pointed at me—"and you know it's true. Therefore, feelings that were buried beneath years of anger and hurt have resurfaced to mess with your head. Plus, he is absolutely smoking hot now. I mean, he was cute before, but damn, that man is sex on a stick now. That hair, those huge arms, those shoulders, that fine ass, not to mention those tattoos . . ." Her eyes glazed over, then her head jerked, and she refocused on me. "I could go on, but I see that you get me, so I'll go ahead and stop."

"Maybe I'll go back out there. I did say I would talk with him today. He wants to give me all the validated reasons himself." I stood up and took a deep, steadying breath before heading to the kitchen door. Fearless. *Right?*

"Good idea. Acting like a grown-up is always the way to go." I stuck my tongue out at her in response.

As I got ready to open the door, I felt the same tingly jolts throughout my body that I used to get whenever I was near Luke. After all these years, that boy still made me tingle, and it pissed me right off. I didn't have time for tingles, shivers, or swoony behavior of any kind. I quietly slunk back to the cash register that was now manned by Finn. Nick was busy helping Rose make the coffee.

"Hey, Aunt Lily. We got it. Take a break and finish your coffee." He handed me a bag full of scones and shooed me away. I loved this kid. Our mutual love of Violet's scones was only one of the reasons why.

I needed to fuel up my fearless mojo. I tried to think of all the girl power songs I had on my playlist. Help me, Pink! Help me, Katy Perry! But all I could hear was "Photograph," the Nickelback song we'd danced to at prom.

My feet were walking toward Luke's table, but my mind was taking a walk back through years of memories—the fond ones this time, not the bad ones. Luke noticed me heading his way and stood up to pull out the chair across from him for me. We both sat, then just stared at each other. I could tell our thoughts were similar. He had a wistful, sad expression on his face as he gazed at me.

"I don't know where to start," he finally said.

Feeling nervous, I blurted, "You don't have to get into anything heavy right now if you don't want to, Luke. I pretty much know what happened." I didn't want to push him into telling me anything that would cause him pain. The last thing I wanted was for him to bare his soul to me out of a sense of obligation. We could work up to it, if he was able. I had already accepted that he hadn't tried to hurt me by leaving, even though it was the most excruciating thing I had ever experienced in my life, at least up until Will died. I don't think you ever fully recover from your first heartbreak. You will never have the same open ability to trust again.

"You do?" He looked at me doubtfully.

"You have PTSD. That's the nutshell version, right? I know there's more and I want to talk about it with you, but I don't want you to open wounds right now if it's going to hurt your progress. I want you to get better and feel good about talking with me. When we're both ready we can discuss everything."

He took a sip of his coffee with a thoughtful expression. "It is the nutshell version. I feel like I have more to tell you though. The main thing is, if I had known you were pregnant, I never would have stayed away. I hope you know that."

Wow, that hurt. I unconsciously rubbed my chest, over my heart. I alone hadn't been enough to make him stay?

I leaned back in my chair and looked out the window. Violet was lucky. Her shop was at the end of a cute little strip mall designed to look like a bunch of log cabins strung together. She had windows on the front and along one side. Our table faced one of the side windows that overlooked the park across the street. We'd taken our prom pictures in the white, flower-draped gazebo sitting in the center of the park. Similar baskets of flowers were hanging from the hooks that lined the outside of the gazebo, and the rose bushes were in bloom, just like on that day. Prom was this time of year. Maybe that was why I kept thinking about it. Or, you know, the fact that my date from back then was sitting right across from me. We'd taken the pictures, and then later when we were alone, Luke had proposed to me. He had said he would love me forever, and back then I had no doubt that he would.

I struggled with what I should even say to him. What would possibly make him understand how much his leaving hurt me?

"I tried to let you know about Dylan, so many times, Luke.

I wrote letters—dozens of letters—and you sent them all back. I still have them somewhere at home in a box. I kept writing to you for a while after he was born, and you sent those back too. They're in the same box." I was beginning to realize that I had put a lot of things in a box. Memories, hurt feelings, fears, grief, sorrow—I had stuffed it all inside a box and shoved it into the recesses of my heart. It was about to burst open, and I didn't want it to happen right now, or maybe not ever, so I stopped trying to explain.

"Can I read them?" he asked tentatively. His crossed arms rested on top of the table. I could see pine trees, a whole forest full of them, tattooed on his arm. It reminded me of his back-yard, like it was a piece of home inked on his arm.

My eyes drifted up to find him leaning toward me, studying my reactions. "Maybe someday," I finally answered. I wasn't ready for him to read the feelings of pain and love and hope I'd poured into those letters, and I might not ever be. But I couldn't hold in the burning question any longer. "You would have come back for Dylan because I was pregnant. Why wasn't I enough, Luke?" I had to know.

He shook his head with a determined expression on his face. "That's not what I meant. You were pregnant. You needed me. You didn't need some crazy asshole who almost killed you, but you did need the father of your baby to stand by your side. Maybe that would have sunk in and pulled me through faster."

I looked away from him, back out the window.

"Look at me," he demanded. My eyes hit his, surprised at his assertive tone. "I won't leave again. I want to be a part of Dylan's life. I want to be a part of yours too," he said with a look almost defiant in its intensity. "I have learned why I behaved the way I did. Why I left and stayed gone. I got help. I'm still getting help. I won't ever hurt Dylan like I hurt you, and I won't ever hurt you again. I'm sorry, Lily, so sorry."

"I'm not the same girl you used to know, Luke. I've

changed. I was a wife. I'm a mother. I'm a widow too, for good-ness' sake. I grew up. When we were together, I was just a girl in love with a boy." I smiled sadly. "You were my whole life. I thought we were part of each other, like soul mates or some such nonsense. I couldn't believe how lucky we were to have found our other half the second we reached this earth . . ." I looked out the window again.

"We could be that lucky again, Lily. I believe it. I want to know you again." He grabbed my hand and held it in both of his.

I glanced back at him, then quickly away. To look into his eyes would be too risky. I could drown in them if I let myself. "I let all of that go. I don't want to feel that way ever again. It hurts too much when it goes away. There is no going back."

"I don't want to go back. I want to go forward. With you. I want a chance, to be your friend again, maybe more someday." His eyes held such longing. All the feelings we used to share shimmered in his gaze as if time had not left us behind.

He reached out to touch my cheek but pulled his hand back at the last second. I felt the warmth of that almost touch and regretted not leaning into it.

Gently, he tugged on my hand, forcing my eyes to drift back to his face. "Lily, I don't know how to be around you anymore but I want to. I remember when we used to walk down that path right over there." He pointed to the path that led past the gazebo where we used to make out after school let out. "God, Lily, I remember *you*. Everything we did and all that we meant to each other. Sitting with you now makes me wish we'd never left. We had everything, and we didn't even know it."

"I don't want to hurt you, but I'm not ready to walk down memory lane with you," I whispered. "It hurts too much."

"Can we be friends again? I can be patient."

I laughed softly at that. "You've never been patient."

"For you, I will be anything. I will do whatever it takes. I have been missing you for years, and you haven't been mine to miss. I only saw you in my dreams. But my eyes are open, and you're right here in front of me, more beautiful than ever."

"I have feelings and memories too, but I can't allow myself to get lost in them. This is too much for me right now," I told him, because he had to know the truth.

"Don't get lost. I'm not asking for that. I just want to talk to you, be friends with you again, to try—"

"You don't want much, do you?" I teased with a laugh. I needed to steer this conversation back into the realm of casual.

"Just you, back in my life," he replied, grabbing the proverbial wheel, and steering us back into Intenseville.

"Well, we're not starting with my heart on a platter, Luke."

"We can go slow. We can just talk, get to know each other again. I will explain everything to you when you're ready to hear it. I've learned a lot, Lily. I've changed a little bit too. We can go at your pace," he offered.

"My pace is going to be slow. Possibly nonexistent. Think snails and old ladies with walkers. I don't want to lead you on. I'm telling you upfront—get rid of all your expectations. I don't have much left in me," I warned.

"You have everything I want. I can still see it in your eyes." He dipped his head and looked up through his lashes at me. "When I can get you to look at me, that is."

My heart couldn't take this. "You can't say things like that. That is not going at my pace."

"I'll be honest about how I feel and when you're ready, you can be honest about how you feel too. But I promise not to push you." That half-grin was back. I could never resist it. Especially always knowing he would kiss me after doing it. And why did I get the impression he thought he knew how I felt? *I* didn't even know how I felt.

I spent the rest of our time together this morning trying to avoid his eyes as well as the ever-present memories. And after he said goodbye and left, I had to stop myself from rushing to the window to watch him walk back to his office. Instead, I watched him walk away from what I thought was a surreptitious position at my table. Violet's reaction when I turned around to go back to work told me I had been completely obvious instead.

"Whatever, Vi." I huffed as I made my way behind the counter.

"I saw you watching that booty walk away," she teased.

I laughed, but sensing my heart wasn't in it, Violet's expression shifted, and she hugged me. "You'll be okay, Lily. Don't you worry about a thing." She didn't tease me again for the rest of my shift.

Upon returning home I couldn't help but imagine what it would be like to let Luke back into my life. But I managed to shove those thoughts aside so the kids and I could spend a quiet evening together. I thought I would be okay until Luke's bedtime call to Dylan added another crack to the wall in my heart and shook the foundation.

I stared at the ceiling in my room for hours until finally falling into a fitful sleep. Dreams of Luke filled my head as I tossed and turned before being roused by Calla for a midnight feeding.

I stared out the window as I rocked her. How would I make it through tomorrow, let alone live in a town where Luke wasn't mine?

And how could I ever trust him enough to let him back into my life?

Chapter 9
Luke

I had never been to my office this early before. Four thirty in the morning was not my favorite time of day, especially when I had been too nervous to sleep the night before. But if I wanted to run into Lily and have any real chance at talking to her, I had to get to Violet's before she opened. The lights were on as I approached the door and I could see Lily removing the chairs from the tabletops and arranging them back on the floor.

She spotted me and opened the door before I could knock. "Hi. What are you doing out and about so early?" Damn, she was cute in her tight little coffee T-shirt, which read, "How you brewin'?" Her hair was up in another bun, and I was dying to see it down, to get my hands in it again, to tug her close and kiss the hell out of her. She used to love it when I would run my fingers through the soft strands and massage her scalp. It was hard to keep those thoughts out of my head, but I had to try. She hadn't even heard me out yet.

"I saw your car when I drove in, so I came over to tell you good morning. Did the zombies quiet down for you last night?" I teased.

"I barely got any sleep. I think Calla is going through a

growth spurt. She wanted to eat all night. She was a little fussy and a lot hungry. But when my mother showed up and took her, she went right to sleep against her chest, the little booger." Watching her closely, I saw her relax. The range of emotion on her face had gone from tense to smiling in the thirty seconds since I showed up at the door.

"She's beautiful, Lily. Just like her mama." Now she was red in the face. Was it embarrassment, or was she about to invite me in?

"Thank you. I kind of love her a little bit," she joked as the flush on her cheeks deepened. "Do you want to have coffee with me?"

Yes! "I would love to. How is Dylan?" I followed her to the counter, watching sexy sway of her hips as she walked.

"He was asleep when I left, but my mother will bring him and Calla over here for breakfast after they wake up. Today is Calla's half birthday. She's going to have her first bite of solid food." She paused for half a second before continuing. "If you want, I'll text you, and you can join us."

My heart soared. "I would love that. Dylan said something to me when you were at my house, and I wanted to talk to you about it. He asked if I could get to know Calla too. And I want to. I want all of us to spend time together."

Her eyes closed and her shoulders sagged. Had I pushed too far? "Luke, you are moving too fast. I can't think about this yet. I, um . . ." She opened her eyes. "Yes, you can get to know Calla. Dylan would love that." Then, more softly, she said, "And so would I, for that matter."

She jumped as her phone pinged with an incoming text message. Surreptitiously, I looked at the screen as she opened and read the text. It was from someone named Trevor. Frowning, she clutched her phone to her chest. The tension on her face was back.

"Everything okay?" I was hesitant to push for an answer. I had to hope she would just give it to me.

"Uh, I'm not sure. I think so. Trevor, Will's partner, just texted and asked me if anything weird has happened and told me to keep my eyes open. He's coming down to check on me. I had a hang-up call the other day, and thought I saw a flashlight in the yard the night before last. Dad checked it out and didn't find anyone out there. That's it. It's probably nothing, right?"

Alarm bells rang in my head. That's why her lights were on that night—she had been scared, and not only by the dark. "I don't know. I could stop by and check on you tonight."

"Thanks, but my dad has it covered. I'll tell him about Trevor's texts later."

"Good idea. Tell your dad. It's better to be safe. But let me know if you change your mind. I'd be happy to stop by tonight," I offered again.

She shook her head. "I'm sure it's nothing."

I threw out my empty coffee cup. Cade would know what was going on. There was no way I would let her be in that house alone and afraid. I'd sleep in my truck in the driveway if I had to. And if someone was trying to hurt her, that would be the last thing they would ever do. "Baby, I have to get to work. Text me when Dahlia gets here with the kids and I'll come over."

Baby. Her eyes widened and her hand went to her throat when she heard that word. Her blush deepened as her tongue darted out to wet her gorgeous full lips. She was not completely immune to me; she remembered what we had just as much as I did.

"Okay, Luke. Have a good morning. I'll text you," she murmured.

I grinned and ran a fingertip down her forearm before turning to head out the door.

Once I got back to my office, I sent a text to Cade. He assured me they were keeping an eye on Lily. But I decided I would add my eyes to the situation as well. Nobody would know if I drove by her house a few times a night, and it would give me peace of mind until I could keep them safe myself. My hackles were up. My years as a Ranger had trained me to trust my gut and I would let nothing slide when it came to Lily and the kids.

Work was slow and boring. Truthfully, I didn't belong in this office. I was better off chopping down trees and carving logs to add custom art to our builds. Working with my hands was what I had always loved. The only things I ever wanted to do in life were marry Lily and start a family, join the Army like Pops, and get into wood carving and selling my art when I retired. My father had never approved of any of it. The company had kind of floated along after my father passed away, relying on deals he had made before he died. His attorney, Jake Moretti, a friend of Violet's, had hired a firm to manage it until I got back and decided what to do.

I sat back in my chair and put my feet up while I waited for Lily's text.

* * *

"And here he is," Dahlia called out as I walked into Violet's, followed by Liam. "Over here, Luke, Liam."

Dylan spotted us and rushed over for high-fives.

"Hey, Dylan, ready for breakfast?" I asked.

"Yeah," he answered, then looked up at Liam. "Are you eating with us, Liam? You should. We have enough chairs. Come on!"

"I was just going to pick something up and take it back to the office, little dude," he answered.

Dahlia pointed to a chair. "Sit with us, Liam." We sat. People tended to do whatever she said. I recalled being with her as a kid. She was no-nonsense but kind, and had loved me like I was one of her own. I loved her right back—always had.

"Where is Rocky? I miss him," Dylan asked from his seat between me and Lily.

"Rocky goes to Jed's ranch sometimes when I'm at the office, but you are invited to visit him at my house whenever you want. My house is your house. Here's a secret about Rocky . . ." I leaned in. "He wasn't the best in his ESD training. In fact, he kind of failed most of it. But he's perfect for me. We bonded right away when I was staying on the ranch, so I kept him."

He nodded and grabbed my arm, turning it back and forth, examining my tattoos. "I like the forest on this arm better. Why do you have flowers on the other arm? Flowers are for girls."

"They remind me of a girl." I caught Lily's eye. "They are called lily of the valley." The tiny bell-shaped flowers twined around my entire arm, black ink with white highlights connecting the riot of shaded stems.

"Hey, that's my mom's name. Lily," Dylan said. His eyes got wide as he realized who I was talking about. "You missed my mom." He turned to Lily. "He missed you."

"She was my best friend," I told him. "I never should have left." Lily's eyes widened as she sipped her coffee. As she swallowed, the delicate line of her throat moved, catching my eye. I remembered how much she used to like it when I kissed her there, trailing my lips up and down her neck until she begged me for more.

"Is Liam your best friend too?" Dylan asked, breaking into my memory. "Does he live at your huge house with you? Do you play Xbox together? Were you kids together too?"

"We were in the Army together. He was the squad leader. My sergeant, in fact." I leaned in close and stage-whispered, "Now he's just my friend and can't order me around anymore."

Dylan looked at Liam with big eyes, impressed. "Are you sure you don't have gigantism? How tall are you?" he asked.

Liam laughed. "I'm six feet, six inches tall."

Dylan gave him a disappointed look. "You're not a giant,

then. You have to be seven feet tall to be a giant. Did you get hurt too? Is that why you aren't in the Army anymore?"

"Dylan, maybe they don't want to talk about that right now," Dahlia said softly.

"It's okay," I said. "We both got hurt." I exchanged a look with Liam, unsure of how to explain what happened and make it palatable to a child.

"A vehicle we were in drove over something that exploded, called an IED," Liam told him. He had been knocked unconscious by the blast, while I had been thrown clear of the vehicle, injuring my back.

"Liam and I got hurt, but we were still lucky. Our other friends were not. We were the only ones who survived." I choked on the lump that formed in my throat as I remembered the men we had lost that day.

Dylan got up and hugged each of us. "I'm glad you both are okay. I'm sorry about your friends. You must miss them a lot. I miss my best friend, Mikey, and he's just in Tacoma with Uncle Trevor." He thought for a minute. "You can't see your friends anymore, but they still love you. Just like my dad Will still loves me from heaven."

Liam discreetly scrubbed his hand under his eyes, then said, "I'm going to get a coffee. I'll get yours too, Luke. Lily, Dahlia?" he asked.

Mom gestured to her coffee on the table. "I have one already, darling." She smiled softly at him.

"I had my caffeine for the day, thanks, Liam," Lily answered, eyes full of compassion.

Mom sighed. "I love you boys and I'm glad you're finally home where you belong. Bring Liam with you to my house for dinner Sunday, Luke. And every other Sunday too for that matter," she demanded. "Six o'clock, like usual."

"Dinner at your house is something I'll never turn down. Thank you, Dahlia," I answered, thankful to her for changing the subject.

"Yay! Can we have hot dogs, Grandma? Oh, oh, oh, bring Rocky!" Dylan said.

"Will do." I chuckled. My laugh must have alerted Calla to my presence because she chose this moment to wake up and fuss.

Lily took her from Dahlia and cuddled her close. "It's time. Are you ready to eat some big girl food?" She placed Calla into the little highchair at the side of our table and strapped her in. "Do you want to do the honors, big brother?" She grinned at Dylan and offered him a tiny spoon.

"This food looks gross and mushy. What is it?" he asked as Lily fastened Calla's bib around her neck.

"Baby cereal. Put a little bit on the spoon and be gentle," she instructed. "Wait for me to get my camera ready."

Dylan scooped up a tiny bite and brought it to her lips. Calla stuck her tongue out, and it dripped onto her bib. We all laughed at the cute face she made. But she seemed to like the taste because she licked her lips and smacked them. He shrugged and handed the spoon to me, clearly more interested in his chocolate milk than feeding his baby sister.

"Can I try?" My hand trembled as I scooted closer to Calla's highchair. I'd never fed a baby before, or even held one. I inhaled a huge breath, thinking of all I'd missed out on with Dylan.

Lily's eyes met mine and she nodded while blinking furiously. I knew she was about to cry; that had always been her tell. I wanted to hold her. I wished we had shared this moment alone years ago, when Dylan was a baby. But we had this moment, right now. It was just as important, and I was grateful for it.

I dipped into the bowl and brought a small spoonful to Calla's lips. She opened and I marveled as her little mouth moved to lap up the food. She managed to swallow about half of it, and the rest dribbled down her chin. I scooped it back up and she opened her mouth again. "She likes it." I dipped into the bowl again to give her another bite.

I looked up with a start when Nick stopped in front of Lily bearing a plate filled with tiny scones.

"Thank you, Nick," she said with a bemused smile.

"You're welcome. These are chocolate." He placed it in front of her with a sage nod. He exchanged a look with a smiling Dahlia before he walked off. Clearly, he knew about Lily and her propensity toward stress eating.

"Come on, Dylan. Let's go check out the pastry case. I want a muffin." Dahlia took Dylan's hand and led him to the counter. She winked at me behind Lily's back. I would not throw away this moment alone with Lily.

Lily picked up a scone and took a huge bite. Calla sputtered and giggled as she dribbled the cereal down her chin and onto her bib. I smiled at her sweet face and wiped her mouth with a napkin.

"Ba. Da. Ma," babbled Calla. She pounded her tiny fists on the tray of her chair before reaching her arms up to me.

"Can I?" I asked Lily. I was nervous but determined.

"Sure." She unbuckled the straps and scooped Calla out of her seat and handed her to me.

"Ga. Da. Ba." Calla smiled at me, smacking my face with her tiny hands before grabbing two handfuls of my beard and pulling.

"Be soft," Lily whispered, reaching over to loosen the baby's grip. "Soft hands, Calla." She patted my cheeks again. Her big blue eyes met mine and her little lips pursed as she studied my face. Then she cuddled her cheek into the side of my neck and collapsed against my chest while her little arms spread out, giving me a baby hug. I inhaled a deep breath as I lost my heart completely. It just flew right out of my chest, rendering me helpless against this tiny baby girl in my arms.

I murmured softly to her, "You're a little angel. Aren't you?

Sweet little Calla . . ." I kissed the top of her sweet-smelling head before lifting my eyes to Lily. "She's precious, Lily."

"Thank you." Tears pooled in her eyes, hovering but not falling as she watched me with her daughter.

"You're welcome, Lily. Thank you for letting me hold her." I laughed as Calla leaned back and gave me a drooly baby kiss on the nose. Lily took her and passed me a napkin for my face.

"You're in for it now," she teased. "Calla kisses come with a little something extra."

"Yeah, spit," Dylan said as he ran up and jumped on my lap.

"I don't mind." I ruffled Dylan's hair as he hugged me around the neck.

"Ready to go, Luke?" Liam called from the door.

I helped Dylan down. "Dylan, I'll call you before bed. Bye sweet Calla. Lily, until tonight." Her eyes burned into mine before I turned and headed to the door.

Chapter 10
Lily

It was nine thirty in the morning a week after our breakfast and I hadn't seen Luke at all. If he had been drinking coffee, it wasn't from Violet's. He had called every night to say goodnight and chat with Dylan, and we had been talking and texting every day as well. But I missed seeing him. I had the feeling he was giving me space. I had told him I wanted to go slow, but it still bothered me. As the hours passed by with no Luke for yet another day, the looks Violet gave me while we worked grew more and more concerned.

"It's going to be fine, Lily," Violet finally said during a break between customers. "He's probably just busy at work."

Rose popped her head out of the kitchen. "What's going on?"

"Nothing." I banged the portafilter against the counter to clean it out.

"Lily, don't break it!" Violet cried as she rushed over. "You have to be gentle." Stroking the side of her espresso maker, she said sagely, "Men let you down, but coffee is always there to pick you back up." She took a sip of her—third?—coffee. I'd lost count of how many cups she'd had today. Violet ran on caffeine, and today, an added splash of cranky cynicism.

Rose finished up in the kitchen and joined us behind the counter. The morning rush was over. We had successfully caffeinated most of Sweetbriar and could now have a small break. Finn and Nick were already relaxing at the tables outside.

Violet turned to me. "I want you back with Luke—you two are like, fated mates out of a romance novel, or whatever—but I love what you said before about being independent. I don't think you should let a small thing like him not showing up this week shake you. Make him fit into *your* life, don't make him your entire world like before. No man is perfect, not even Luke. They all fuck up sometimes." She finished her tirade and stomped into the kitchen.

Rose and I exchanged a look. Was that little speech even about me?

"She must be fighting with Tom again. They haven't been spending a lot of time together. It's almost like they're separated," Rose whispered.

"Well, he wasn't at dinner on Sunday. I wondered why." I'd never really warmed up to Violet's husband. Tom was kind of standoffish. I had hoped it was just with me because I didn't live near them and only saw him on holidays, but now I wasn't so sure.

She checked the kitchen door, presumably to make sure Violet couldn't hear us. "He's a dick. I can't stand to be around him anymore."

I leaned a hip against the counter with a grin. I was ready to sink into this gossip session and forget about my troubles. Maybe being there for Violet in some way or cheering her up would help me get out of my own funk.

Rose continued, "Holly hates him too, and Jude. Levi wants to punch him, but Cade talked him out of it. Ash said we should mind our own business." She glanced at the door again. "I think he's having a midlife crisis. He bought a Porsche and hired a hot blonde secretary. I think she's in her twenties—like, over a decade younger than him."

Living out of town meant I'd missed the gossip that spread amongst my siblings. I guessed I was in for it now. It made me wonder what they'd said about me. Probably not much. I was pretty boring.

She suddenly grabbed my arm. "Look out the front windows. Look," she hissed.

I looked around frantically. "What? What am I looking for?" I hissed back.

"It's Jake," she said reverently.

"Jake? Oh, Jake." Jake was Tom's best friend from college, but Rose and I were sure he only stayed friends with Tom to be close to Violet. She was blind to it though.

"He is so hot. He reminds me of Alcide from *True Blood.* Don't you miss that show?" She kept rambling as the door *bing-bonged* Jake's presence in the store.

He smiled when he saw us. "Lily, darlin', I heard you were back in town. Good to see you. Hey, Rose. Is Violet around?" I sighed and blushed as I smiled at him like a simpleton. Rose and I had been drooling over Jake since we were tweens.

"Hey, Jake. She's in the kitchen. You can go on back," she answered sweetly. Rose was hardly ever sweet, and hearing her use that tone made me laugh. After he was out of earshot, she smacked my arm. "He saw you first. You got the 'darlin'. Ugh, not fair." Jake had been our ideal man for a long time. And it seemed as if he was still the barometer for Rose. Being around my twin made me feel like a teenager again.

She grabbed my arm again. "Look across the parking lot. It's Luke." He was headed into his office, his cell phone glued to his ear. "You should go over there and say hi."

"No, I don't think so. I don't want to bother him."

She rolled her eyes. "Don't be a wimp. You know you want to go over there. The kids are with Mom. If you go over there now, you can be alone with him." She waggled her eyebrows at me.

"I don't want to be alone with him. It's hard enough not to swoon like a fool when there are people around." I poured myself a cup of Violet's mediocre decaf. It was the best decaf coffee I had ever tasted, but it still sucked. I added a liberal amount of Violet's vanilla bean syrup and some cream and iced it. Yum-ish. I wanted a real coffee. I pouted comically at Rose, and she laughed.

"So, swoon, then. Faint and fall over. Luke will catch you. Have you talked everything out yet?" Rose grabbed a sponge and the purple bottle of spray cleaner and started wiping down the counters. I should probably help, but I didn't want to.

I shook my head and sipped my drink. "No, we haven't really talked. He said he wants to be friends again. I didn't want to make him talk about painful things and upset him."

"You mean you didn't want him to upset *you*." She scoffed and shook her head. "You sure do like to bury your head in the sand. If you knew how hard it was for him to stay away from you and why he did it, you'd take him back in a hot second."

"He hurt me, Rose." I had to try to defend myself, even though I knew I was being a coward.

"I know he did. *He* knows he did. Let him explain. Even if you don't want him back, you should at least talk about it." She shrugged. "For Dylan's sake."

I took another sponge and spray bottle and moved from behind the counter to help her clean up. "I will. Eventually."

"You'll never get over it if you don't hear him out. You only have one life, and you're putting it in park."

I looked out the window at Luke's office building. I just couldn't bring myself to go over there. Maybe tomorrow.

* * *

I ended up not seeing Luke all day—again. Now it was early evening, and I was getting ready to leave for Violet's book club.

I carefully lowered Calla into her crib, then headed downstairs.

Dylan was on the couch with my dad, eating popcorn and watching *Finding Dory.* "Are you sure you'll be okay with them?" I asked him again.

Dad sighed. "Lily, I have eight kids. You're all still alive, aren't you? I think I can manage to take care of yours while you go to Violet's."

"You're right. I'm sorry. Give me a kiss goodbye, Dylan." He stood up on the couch, and I hugged him and kissed his soft cheek. "I'll be back when you're asleep. Have sweet dreams."

"Bye, Mommy," he said and sat back down and cuddled up to my dad.

"Bye, Dyl. Later, Dad."

I stepped onto the porch just as Cade pulled up in his old Ford Bronco. He beeped the horn, and I rushed to get in. "Jeez, you saw me on the porch. No need to honk at me, butthead." Sometimes our kid-speak came out. It was unavoidable.

"You were walking too slow," he shouted out his window. "Mom made her buffalo chicken dip, and I want to get some before Rose eats it all. And now you're here, so I have to get to it before you do too. I should have made you walk," he teased.

My mouth started to water at the thought of buffalo chicken dip. I hurriedly climbed inside and buckled up. "So, what's the book?" I asked him. I wasn't worried; I read everything. I mean, there was a reason I'd become a librarian. Cade and I geeked out over books all the time.

"*Storm of Swords.* I can't wait." He turned down the street to Violet's shop and pulled in.

I got excited and smacked his arm. "That's my favorite one of the series! So, um, does Luke ever go to book club?" I was trying to be nonchalant. But I'd failed. Miserably. I was totally chalant.

Cade chuckled. "He came once. It was supposed to be Stephen King night. We were supposed to discuss *It*. Remember when we all read it together when we were kids? You slept on my bedroom floor for weeks. Then you got sick of sleeping on the floor and paid me five dollars a week to have me sleep on your floor." He had stopped chuckling and was just outright laughing at me. "Anyway, they ended up talking about *Outlander,* which is a good fucking book. But all they were doing was drooling all over the actor that plays Jamie on the show. I don't need to hear that shit. I have zero desire to hear my mother and sisters talking about what's under some guy's kilt. Luke and I left. We went to Holloway's and had a few beers. So, I guess he hasn't really been to a book club meeting."

My Auntie Delphine, Mom's only sibling, owned Holloway's, a pub up the street from Violet's shop. My late Uncle Pat had opened it years ago when they first got married, and keeping it up and running was now a family affair. After Cade's explanation, I had no idea whether to expect to see Luke tonight. I was thinking not.

"We're here. Race you to the dip," I hollered, hopping out before Cade shut the engine off. I sniffed and followed my nose to the coffee table. After taking a seat next to Rose on Violet's purple sofa, I grabbed a tortilla chip and dipped into the dip.

Rose nodded at me. Her mouth was too full to say hi. I nodded back and we preceded to stuff our faces.

"Where's Cade? Didn't you come together?" Violet asked.

I looked up. *Wow.* There were a lot of people here. I waved to the room. I felt a little embarrassed by my race to the dip, but decided it was worth it and let it go.

"He's parking the car." I didn't feel bad for ditching him.

I'd been gone a long time. I had years of buffalo chicken dip to make up for.

He stormed through the door and pointed at me. I waved, then stuffed some more dip in my mouth. *Gah!* So worth it. He sat next to me and loaded up a chip.

"Good, you're here, Cade. Now we can start." Violet turned to me. "We're going to discuss *Beautiful Bastard.*"

"You said *Storm of Swords* was this week," Cade interjected, mouth full.

Violet raised her eyebrows. Uh oh. "Pretty sure I didn't, Cade. We've been reading *Beautiful Bastard* all week."

Cade stood up. "Nope. No way. I've been waiting to talk about *Storm of Swords.* I am not about to discuss the merits of hate-fucking one's way to a successful relationship with my mother and my sisters. Hell no. Fuck this, I'm out of here." He strode angrily to the door. "Lily, I'm heading to Holloway's. Text me when you're finished here, and I'll pick you up."

I was not surprised that Cade had read *Beautiful Bastard.* He was not a sexist reader. He'd read anything, including romance novels. I nodded and waved goodbye. More dip for me.

Mom perked up at this. "Cade, if you're going over there, then get behind the bar and help Oliver out so you can send Delphine over here."

Oh, I hadn't seen Aunt Delphine yet. Yay!

Chapter 11
Luke

I was glad to see Cade behind the bar when I walked into Holloway's. I'd had a terrible day. I was worried about Liam, and I hadn't seen Lily in over a week. I had wanted to give her space, but not this much of it. "Hey, Cade." I took a seat at the bar and he slid me a beer. Holloway's looked like an old Irish pub: small black-and-white tiles covered the floor and dark wood paneling lined the walls. The walls were peppered with framed family pictures and neon beer signs hung here and there. A long, shiny, maple wood bar dominated the space, but there were several sets of tables and chairs and a few booths along the perimeter. They served great food, and I was about to partake.

"How's it going, Luke?"

I took a huge swallow of beer and shook my head. "Shit day, man. Liam's grandmother had a heart attack this morning. I went with him to the hospital. He was beside himself. She raised him since he was twelve. She's all the family he has left. The doctor says she'll be fine though. How is Lily? I didn't get to see her today. I haven't seen her all week. Work has been brutal."

"She's at Violet's. I got suckered into helping here so Delphine could go to book club. I think they all planned it."

I chuckled. I'd spent about ten minutes at one of those things, and I would never do it again.

"Did you eat yet? Oliver is in back making burgers. Want one?" Oliver was Lily's cousin. He was our age and a good friend. I nodded because hell yeah, I wanted one. That's why I'd come here. "Savannah is headed over to relieve me. You can join me if you want."

I nodded. Savannah was another one of Lily's cousins. There were so many that Lily and I had always joked about not being able to remember exactly how many cousins she had on this side of the family.

Cade turned to the kitchen entrance behind him at the bar. "Yo, Oliver! Throw another burger on. Luke's here!" He popped the cap off a beer for another customer and handed it over.

"Will do! Hey, Luke!" Oliver shouted back. Lily's family was huge and they were all close. I used to be close to all of them too. When I first got back, they'd all welcomed me unreservedly. Each one of them had come to visit me when I was laid up at Jed's. It meant a lot that they all forgave me. If I could get Lily to talk to me, hopefully she would too. Savannah arrived with smiles for the both of us and took over behind the bar. Cade grabbed a beer for himself, then we headed for a booth in the back.

"I'm pretty sure I already know the answer to this, but I'll ask anyway. Has Lily heard you out yet? And what are you doing about it?" Cade had always been like a big brother to me, but whenever the subject of Lily came up, he stopped being my brother and was all about her. I respected that. I respected *him*, and valued his opinion immensely.

"I can barely get her to even look at me."

Cade laughed. "You know her, lost in her own world." He

stopped laughing. "You left that world. Got to find a way back in."

"Yeah, but how?"

Cade thought for a minute. "I would never, ever give this kind of advice to anyone about any of my sisters." His eyes bored into mine. "But you're different. You two . . ." He sighed and took a sip of his beer. "If you don't get back together, it'll be a tragedy. I trust you. I get where you were coming from, so I'm going to help you."

"I'm all ears, Cade."

"You need to be alone and talk everything out. And when the kids are around, it's hard for her to focus on anything else. They're with Dad tonight so, for once, she has no worries. I'm supposed to pick her up. I think you should pick her up instead. I'll text Vi and tell her to give Lily the keys so Lily can lock up. You two can stay in the shop and talk it out."

"Thanks, Cade. And just so you know, I won't hurt her again. I didn't mean to before—"

"I know you didn't. We all get it. Hell, I might have even done the same thing in your place. I just wish you would have come to us, any of us. You're family, Luke. You shouldn't have been alone all that time. None of that shit again. Right?"

"Right. Thanks for the advice."

"It'll work. Plus, once she's settled in Sweetbriar again, comfortable and back in a routine, that will help, too. She's finding her footing, but she'll come around."

"She's been through a lot," I mused. "Should I back off?"

Cade shook his head. "No, you need each other, at least as friends. Don't give up on her again. You should know better by now, right?"

"You're right, I guess." This conversation took me back to the first time I saw her after she moved back, when Liam had said similar things. I nodded decisively at Cade. "You're absolutely right. I won't give up on her. Never again." But I wouldn't push her. There was a difference between not giving up on someone and being a pushy bastard. I had to be careful not to cross that line.

"That's more like it."

We ate our burgers and talked about innocuous things until his phone pinged with a text from Lily. "Showtime," he said with a grin. "Go get your girl."

Chapter 12
Lily

"Thanks for helping me clean up, Lily."

I placed the broom back into Violet's utility closet with a humph. Who knew a bunch of book-clubbing people could be so sloppy? My idea of a classy, intellectual group of readers gathering to discuss literature was forever tainted by Violet's book club. Sure, they'd discussed books for about half of the meeting, which was somewhat enriching, but the rest of the time was spent on gossiping and arguing. Basically, I loved it, and I was never going to miss a meeting.

"No problem, Vi."

Violet's phone pinged with a text message. She looked up at me, then back at her phone. "Any chance you could lock up? Finn needs me. Cade is picking you up, right? Just set the alarm when you leave, okay? Thanks, Lily, you're a doll." She tossed me the keys and rushed out the back.

What the heck? "Uh, okay, bye," I said to the empty store. I took out my phone, sent Cade a text, then I sat at a table by the window to wait. As I stared out at the darkness, a shudder ran through my body. Looking out a window into the dark night was a bad idea. I was not just afraid of the dark; I was afraid I would see someone peeking back at me. Which was why when I saw someone walk to the door out of the corner of my eye, I jumped out of my chair and knocked it over as I stood up. I choked back a scream when I saw the knob turn.

Get a grip. It's just Cade.

I shook it off and peeked through the blinds. It was Luke. I quickly unlocked the door and opened it. Fear of a different kind crawled over me. The determined look on his face told me that we were about to get serious. He smiled at me and stepped past me to enter the shop. I guess we weren't leaving. "Hey, Luke."

"I saw Cade at Holloway's. He has to work early, so he asked me to pick you up so he could go home and crash."

I nodded, but I knew it was more than that. My family was fully aware of my tendency to avoid upsetting anyone, especially myself. It was only a matter of time before they all started interfering. "Okay, should we go? I have to set the alarm." I started to head for the door.

He caught my hand and tugged gently. I felt that touch, the small pressure from my hand in his and I felt it *everywhere*. Removing my hand from his grasp, I faced him.

"Let's talk first. Please?" He tried to catch my eyes.

I managed to avoid his gaze. Every time I caught his eyes, I could see things I wasn't willing to face yet, even though I knew I should. "We can talk. For a bit." I moved across the store and chose a table away from the windows, near the couch in the back.

He sat across from me in a chair. "Why is this so hard?" A sad smile crossed his face, and I immediately felt guilty for making this so difficult for him.

"Because it means so much? I guess I haven't made this easy for you. I'm sorry, Luke."

"Don't apologize to me, Lily. I don't deserve it. This should be hard." His jaw clenched as his eyes burned into mine.

I looked down at the table. Snatching up a napkin, I

twisted it into a nervous spiral. *Gah!* Wasn't I supposed to be fearless? "I'll start." I looked up to find his eyes on me. "The Luke I grew up with, the one I fell in love with, would have talked to me and explained his reasoning. He wouldn't have abandoned me without a word. Make me understand it, Luke, so I can move on." There, I'd said it.

"Move on? From me?"

I cringed at the look of sorrow in his eyes. Crap, that didn't come out right. I grabbed his hand and held it. "No, from the hurt in my heart when I see you. I can't completely forgive you when it still hurts, if there is even anything to forgive . . . I don't even know anymore. Just make me understand, so I can let the pain go."

He closed his eyes against the memories that I could tell were painful. "I could have killed you. I still see my hands wrapped around your throat, and I can't wrap my head around how I could have not known it was you." He opened his eyes to study his hands on the table. I slid my hands over his to encourage him to hold on to me. He turned them palms up and linked his fingers with mine. "I still can't fathom how I could have hurt you, Lily. I was horrified. I still am." He closed his eyes again and let go of my hands, running them through his hair. "At that time, and for a long time afterward, I didn't understand what was happening to me. I love you more than anything in the world. I had to protect you." He opened his eyes and looked directly into mine. "But I loved you so much that I knew if I saw you again, I would not have had the strength to end it. I knew you would've wanted to help me, and I couldn't take that chance. I would have given in to anything you wanted if I saw you. So, I was a coward, and I didn't explain. Please believe that I thought I was protecting you, that I would die to protect you. I died inside every day I spent without you," he finished.

"I shouldn't have climbed into the hospital bed with you. You didn't expect to find anyone there." I refused to let him take all the responsibility for what had happened. While on patrol, his unit fell under heavy fire. Luke took a lot of shrapnel and almost bled out. After Jed got the call, he, my mother, and I flew to Germany to be with Luke in the hospital. He hadn't expected to find me next to him when he woke up and he attacked me in his sleep.

"That's no excuse. I had to make sure you were safe," he insisted.

"So you just left? How was that better than talking to me? I was alone and scared and in love with you. You broke my heart."

"I hurt you. Who knows what else I might have been capable of?" he argued.

He had it all wrong. I had forgiven him for attacking me the moment it happened. Yes, he had hurt me physically. But by leaving, he'd destroyed me. This huge misunderstanding of what really hurt me left me feeling incredulous. Did he even have a clue what he did to me by leaving was a million times worse?

"I tried to get to you when you were still in the hospital, and you had me escorted out—crying and humiliated—every single time. So, yeah, you *hurt* me. We had always been there for each other. Then, suddenly, you weren't there anymore." I looked away from him. I couldn't sit there and see the anguish in his eyes anymore. I stood up to pace.

"I *was* protecting you. *From me.* Lily, will you look at me?"

I stopped pacing and turned to him.

"I woke up in the hospital, and my hands were wrapped around your throat. Your mom was screaming at me to let go, your face was turning purple, and Jed was pulling me off you. I had no idea where I was, or how you even got there. I went to sleep in a desert and woke up in a hospital, and I was killing you. *You.* You are what I love most in this entire world, and I almost killed you. I wanted to be with you more than anything I have ever wanted in my whole life, and I kept myself away from you to protect you. That is how much I love you."

I began to see where he was coming from. I'd understood it on a rational level before, but the pain he'd caused me had clouded my judgment, preventing me from fully appreciating his perspective. My heart broke a little bit more when the pain started to fade away and I got a glimpse of how he must have felt when he'd thought he had no choice but to keep himself from me.

"But you were having a nightmare. It wasn't your fault," I whispered.

"I thought I was losing my mind. I couldn't trust myself around you. It was too much of a risk. I didn't know I had PTSD. I didn't know about flashback nightmares or any of that. I hurt you. I almost strangled you to death. *That's* what I knew. That was all I could think about. How could I have done that? I thought about the future, us married, me killing you in my sleep, killing our kids in a dream. Blood and death. I couldn't get away . . ." Tears filled his eyes, and he wiped them away.

I stood in front of him and grabbed his hands again. "Stop it, please, Luke." I couldn't stop the tears streaming down my face. "There is nothing to forgive. But if you need to hear me say the words, I forgive you. I forgive you."

"You forgive me for that morning. Do you forgive me for leaving you?" he asked softly.

"I understand it better now. But I still wish you had let me help you."

"Help me? How? I was terrified of hurting you again. You are so small, Lily. We're lucky that your mom and Jed were there, that they heard what was going on and stopped it. If we had been alone back then, you would be dead. I would have killed you. And, God, I would have killed Dylan too. You were pregnant."

We both paused as the horror of that possibility dawned on us.

I wiped away my tears. "I'm still not ready to—"

"You're not ready to trust me," he interrupted.

I shook my head. "That's not it. I trust you with my life. With Dylan's life. Calla, too. But I'm not ready to trust you with my heart yet. Can you understand that?"

"Can I have a chance to earn that back, Lily? Can I take you out to dinner? Next Friday?"

A startled laugh burst out of me. "Like a date? You're asking me out?" It seemed funny for him to ask me out. We had been through so much, and a date was such a simple thing.

"Yeah. Maybe we could start over." He smiled.

"Like, start over in the middle." I smiled back.

"Something like that." He cupped my cheek and wiped away a stray tear with his thumb. "Everything I've ever done is for you," he murmured.

"Oh, Luke," I breathed, and without even thinking about it, my body swayed toward his, my arms reached up for him, and like he always used to do, he swept me up and held me close, wrapping me up in his warmth.

He whispered into my neck, his beard tickling my skin. "I've missed you so much. I thought about you every day."

I pulled my head back to see his face. "I missed you too. I tried not to think about you, but I couldn't stop. I could never stop wondering what you were doing. I want you to read the letters. For a while, I wrote to you whenever I thought about you, so there are a lot."

Tears sparkled in his eyes as he looked at me. "I want to read them. I want to know about everything I missed."

I pulled his face closer, pressed my body closer. I felt a peace I hadn't felt since the last time I was in his arms. His lips brushed my forehead, then each of my cheeks. Once, twice, so soft, so sweet. But I wanted more. I wanted to keep this feeling. In this moment, I wanted it all back.

"I'm not going to kiss you yet, Lily. Because when I do, it will change everything, and you're not ready yet. And I'm not sure I am either." He put me down. "Let's get you home."

He held my hand for the entire drive. Relief and a sense that I was finally, truly *home* filled my heart. He pulled into the driveway and turned to me with a smile. We might not be where we were when he left me. But we had started as friends, and I knew for certain we got that back tonight.

"Thank you for taking me home, Luke."

He grinned. "Stay there. I'll walk you in." He got out and opened my door. Old Luke was back. Maybe he had been back, and I was just now allowing myself to notice him. He took my hand and led me to the door.

My dad woke with a start when I opened the front door. "Lily. And Luke." He seemed surprised but pleased to see Luke. "Both kids are out. Calla has been asleep the whole time. That would be a record, right?" I nodded. "Well, then, it looks like my work here is done. Night, Lily-girl. Good night, Luke." He kissed my cheek, then patted Luke on the shoulder as he walked out.

"Can I check on the kids? Maybe tuck Dylan in?" he asked.

I nodded and my heart melted a little bit. But a gooey heart led to a gooey mind, and I reminded myself to be careful.

He took off up the stairs after unleashing another grin on me.

After kicking off my shoes, I headed to the kitchen for a drink. Calla's cries from the baby monitor cemented into my mind my internal warning to be careful and not rush back into love with Luke. But I found myself wavering again when his voice came through the monitor to join the sounds of her fussing.

"Hey, little princess, can't sleep anymore?"

Tears filled my eyes, and I gulped down some of my water to stop them from falling. My imagination filled with images of him using that voice on Dylan as a baby and the tears fell freely despite my efforts to make them stop.

"You're a pretty little thing, aren't you? Beautiful, just like your mama. Are you hungry?" Calla let out a dainty burp and Luke chuckled. "You burp like her, all cute and quiet, like you're trying to keep it a secret."

I laughed through my tears as I headed upstairs to feed her, wiping my cheeks on the way. My heart was so warm it was almost on fire. I peeked in the room before I entered because I had to steal a glimpse of what it would have looked like for Luke to be holding our baby like this. I'd imagined so many times after I had Dylan what it would have been like if we'd been a real family. This was as close as I would get to being able to see it. I stood in the doorway unable to process the emotions that ran through me, burning a path straight to my heart like wildfire. Luke cradled Calla against his broad chest, gently rubbing her back.

I wanted to freeze this moment so I could remember it forever. I also wanted to escape it. My two lives had collided in such a way that I was euphoric at the sight of Luke holding Calla and stricken with guilt that Will had died for me to have it. Accepting there was nothing I could do about it even if I'd wanted to, I stopped trying to reconcile my conflicting feelings and entered the room.

"I think she needs to eat," I whispered. When I met Luke's eyes I froze at the anguish in his expression.

"God, Lily, I'm so sorry."

Overwhelmed, I couldn't hold back the sob that escaped. Luke passed Calla to me as I sat in the rocking chair in the corner. I pulled down my shirt, unhooked my nursing bra, and brought her to my breast.

Luke watched me intently. Not in a sexual way, but in a way that let me know that he was seeing everything he'd missed out on. Little moments, things that lucky people took for granted that really meant everything. Sorrow suffused his expression. "Will this always be between us?" he asked as he stood in the doorway, half in and half out of the room. Why did I feel like he wanted to get away?

"I don't think so. It's all new, and we're moving fast. There will always be new memories to make, Luke." I was struck by how similar this was to the conversation I'd had with Dylan the other day. I wished I believed it. Maybe I could—if this cloud of sorrow ever went away.

As if he could sense my doubts, he said, "Lily, I'm going home. Sweet dreams. I'll let myself out."

Chapter 13
Luke

I rushed down the stairs and out of the front door, locking it behind me. I had to get out of there before Lily saw me break down. I had no right to be this upset. I'd chosen this. I'd missed her pregnancy and Dylan's birth. I had never seen Dylan as a baby. I'd been there for none of it, all because of my stupid choices. As I turned from the door, I saw Ben leaning against the side of his truck still parked in the driveway.

"I thought I'd wait for you and make sure you're okay." He studied my face. "I knew it would hit you."

I blinked a few times, not wanting to cry in front of him. I didn't want to cry at all, but grief for the past I'd lost burned a hole in my heart. I pressed my palms into my eyes and nodded. I got a grip on myself and met his eyes. "How do I fix this, Ben?"

"Do what you've been doing. Be there for them and don't leave. There will be times like this that will burn, but you power through them because better things await. There is no way to go back in this life, Luke. You can only go forward. And maybe next time, you talk to Lily about this instead of me." He gave me a look. "Not that it's wrong to talk to me, but you two need to communicate. Honesty is the key. I always say it. Occasionally, it sinks in." He grinned and slapped me on the shoulder before pulling me in for a quick hug. "I'm glad you're back, Luke. I've told you that and I meant it. Go home and get some rest. Back at it tomorrow, okay?"

I nodded, and he got into his truck and took off.

I crossed the driveway to my own truck and got inside. I looked up at the lights in the windows and wished with my whole heart that I was in there, participating in it, living it. Instead of sitting outside in the dark. I started the truck and pulled away.

* * *

"It should have been you, Luke."

I woke up to words I hadn't heard since I was eighteen ringing in my ears, left over from my dream. I hadn't heard my father's shit for years, but ever since I'd come back here, I would remember from time to time. I inhaled a sharp breath, waiting for the words to leave their burn so I could force myself to forget them again. He hadn't wanted me; my mom had. And after she died, he quit pretending.

I rolled over in bed and blinked at Rocky's face hovering above mine. His hot breath tickled my cheeks as he barked gently and nudged my face with his cold nose. I hugged him around his neck and he settled down along my side to rest his head on my chest. He watched me closely as I scratched behind his ears.

"Ready for breakfast?" He shot up and started hopping around and wagging his tail. I laughed as I stood up and stretched, being careful of my stiff back and shoulders. I might never regain one hundred percent mobility, and that was still hard to accept. Even so, I was one of the lucky ones. I opened the door and headed downstairs to the kitchen with Rocky hot on my heels. I let him outside and placed his food dish next to the open sliding door.

I headed back upstairs to start the day. After I showered, I caught my reflection in the mirror. I looked rough with crazy hair and an out-of-control beard. After my injury I had stopped caring about a lot of things. For a while, I didn't even care if I got better or not. I dug around in the cabinet under the counter and found a bunch of clippers and razors and fancy beard maintenance crap my dad had always used. He had always been very vain and fastidious about his appearance. I was not vain, and I was a long way from fastidious, but I figured I should stop being a total slob. *Just a trim*, I decided.

If Lily could see my face, she might miss it more. It was weird to think about her again with any sort of hope. I had spent so many years trying not to think about her at all. Too many years spent trying not to die, without really living.

After I got out of the shower, I checked my phone. I had a text from Rose:

Rose: *FYI. Whatever progress you made with Lily has been undone. You "have to talk" to her when you get here.*

I shoved my phone into my pocket, marched into my room, and began to dig around in my closet. When I was deployed for the first time, Lily hugged me tight and slipped something to remember us by into my pocket. The locket and its delicate gold chain glinted in the light. I examined the lily of the valley embossed on the front before carefully popping it open. I smiled at Lily's toothless grin in the picture. We were both five and beaming at my mother as she told us to say "cheese." The other side held a picture of us at prom. Rose had gagged and threatened to toss the camera at my head if we didn't stop kissing in front of her.

I tucked it into my pocket. It was time to prove that I was not going to give up on her, and maybe remind her of a few things while I was at it.

It was barely seven in the morning when I pulled into my spot in front of my building. McCabe Contracting was now the largest contracting company in the area. As a kid, I had rejected all my father's attempts to get me interested in his work. He hadn't really wanted me to take over his business; he just wanted people to think he did. Dad had been all about appearances.

At first, I was surprised that he'd left everything to me, but then I remembered his obsession with his reputation and it made perfect sense. What would people think if I inherited nothing?

Truth was, he'd hated me and blamed me for my mother's death. She died in a car crash on the way to pick up my eighth birthday cake in town. If I hadn't been born, there would have been no need for a cake.

I keyed the code into the door and went inside. I crossed through the small lobby area to my office suite. I stuck my head into Liam's office. "How's your grandma?" Liam's grandmother was like family to me. I used to join Liam whenever he visited her.

"She'll be fine. She's scheduled for an angioplasty later this morning. I'm about to finish up here, then head out to be with her."

"Glad to hear it. Give her my love, and I'll swing by later to visit. I'm going to get a coffee. Want anything?"

"No thanks, I've already had two this morning. Violet is a coffee master. Not hard to look at either," he added. "She's married, right?"

I nodded.

"Too bad. Does Lily have any other sisters besides Violet and Rose?" he asked.

I laughed. "You don't like Rose? She's single."

"She's hot but kind of—" He glanced up at me, then stopped talking with a guilty look.

I laughed. "You won't offend me, man. Rose is a tough one. She's a tiny, evil ginger ninja. I grew up with her, and sometimes she scares me. There's also Holly, the youngest sister."

Liam looked intrigued, and I shook my head. "Nope, don't even think about it." I trusted Liam, but Holly had always been like a baby sister to me. I was compelled to warn him off.

He laughed at me. "Look at you going all big brother. Don't worry. I was just curious."

"I'm out. Later, Liam."

"Good luck."

Chapter 14
Lily

I had been a wreck all night, and it was hard to hide my mood this morning.

Part of me wanted to listen to my heart and dive right in. I wanted to know how he had changed. Every time I got the courage to look in his eyes, I could see the difference in him. There was a new depth there, one full of sorrow and loss. He had been places, seen things that I hadn't experienced with him. I was afraid of the differences as much as I was intrigued by them.

Lately, I had been letting my fears dictate my life, and I needed to stop. But weren't some fears valid?

"Lily, I know that look on your face. You overthink, then you freak out." I was in the kitchen with Rose. We were scrambling eggs and assembling various breakfast sandwiches. Violet, Nick, and Finn were up front handling customers. I looked up at Rose, who was brandishing a dripping whisk at me and accusing me of the truth. I did overthink. I was doing it just now.

"I'm just worried. This is happening too fast. This is crazy, right? Tell me it's crazy, Rose. Tell me we're moving too fast.

That's how I feel, and no one seems to understand. I don't even understand."

"It is fast." She put the whisk back in the bowl of eggs, then smiled softly at me. "But it's fate, Lily. I remember you two together. Don't you? You could have it all back. You and Luke light each other up. I believe in soul mates and true love and destiny and all that stupid crap because of you. I had a front row seat to your love story. Sure, you two were sometimes so sappy I thought I was going to puke, but it was beautiful too. Get out of your head. Listen to your heart a little bit."

Tears filled my eyes. I was so tired of crying. "I'm scared to trust him. Why do you trust him so much, Rose? Why can't I?"

"Well, duh, you have the most to lose. We would lose a childhood friend, a sort-of brother. You would lose everything —again. But think of it this way, if you don't try, you've already lost."

When did she get so much better at this emotional stuff than me? Rose was the least sentimental person I knew. She started whisking eggs again. "Suck it up, Lily. Don't be such a wuss."

Okay, that sounded more like Rose. I'd been worried for a second. "I'll talk to him today. We need to sort some things out."

Rose looked up at me and shook her head slightly. "Don't jerk him around, Lily. Be in or be out, okay?"

I wasn't trying to jerk him around. Was I doing that? I sighed and pulled out my phone to check my texts, and it reminded me that I'd had two hang-up calls last night on the landline at Gram's. I needed to make time to talk to my dad about that.

"I won't jerk him around." I looked up from the sandwich I was wrapping. "Was Luke planning to come by? Did he talk to you?"

Rose avoided my eyes and shrugged.

At that exact moment I heard Luke ask from out front, "Is Lily here today?"

"Yeah, she's in back. Lily!" Finn shouted my name, and I jumped.

"You'll be okay, Lily. I got it back here. Go talk to him. I wouldn't keep pushing you toward him if I didn't believe in this from the bottom of my heart. I love you. I love him too. He's the extra brother I never wanted but I'm glad I have. Remember what I told you before."

She'd told me a lot before. "Remember what?"

"Get out of your head and don't be a wuss. Go get your man back."

"He's not my man. Right now, he's my friend. And I always want to be his friend."

"Good. That's how you started anyway. But you know there will always be more than that between you."

I rolled my eyes and crossed to the kitchen door. Peeking through the window I could see Luke leaning on the end of the counter, waiting for me. I stepped back quickly. He looked different—again. I sighed and tried not to stare. His face was visible, the angle of his strong square jaw, his cheekbones high, and his lips luscious.

Opening the door, I stepped out. His hair was still long but swept back neatly, giving me the desire to sink my fingers into it. He was looking hot in a white button-down shirt tucked into his dark-wash jeans. The way it stretched across his broad chest when he turned and waved to me made my jaw drop a little bit as my eyes moved up and down his body, blatantly checking him out and liking what I saw. *Friends. Yeah, right.*

I took a step toward him, then one more. I managed to smile. "Hi, Luke." I looked past him, out the window, trying to get up the courage to break our date. We should talk more first. Or have coffee, or go for a walk, or do something with less pressure. Starting with a date was stupid. Or maybe it was just the word "date" that was tripping me up. I let out a sigh as I closed the distance between us.

"Lily, we need to talk," he said.

Huh? That was my line. "We do?" Of course we did. That was my plan. I felt thwarted. Foiled. And a little confused. Did he come over here looking all hot and handsome to throw me off?

"Come to my office with me." He took my hand and led me quickly through the shop and out the door.

I followed at his side, clutching his hand. I had to jog to keep up. "Slow down, Luke. I have short legs, dang it," I managed to say.

He slowed as we approached the door to his building. He held it open, and I crossed through. The log cabin mountain theme was in full effect in the lobby. It was all about wood paneling and dark green accents, leather furniture and heavy wooden tables. We headed to a set of double doors with McCabe Contracting engraved on a large plaque next to them. We passed through a small reception area with a dark brown leather couch, some wooden chairs around a low table, and a desk set up for a secretary or receptionist. But no one was here. He unlocked a door that had a small sign with his name on it, and I followed him into the spacious office.

"I like your desk. Oh, and your couch. Did you decorate your office?" I asked inanely, trying to keep things casual so I didn't freak out.

"What? No. It was like this. I guess Dad did, or he hired a decorator."

He closed the door behind us and turned to face me. He looked me up and down with a smile on his face. Kind of like I had done to him a few minutes ago.

I blushed. Yes, I'd dressed up. I had on my best skinny jeans. They sucked in the little pooch that wouldn't go away no matter how many walks I went on with my kids or how many crunches I did not do. I was wearing Rose's heels and my best bra. I had borrowed a cute blouse from Rose; it was red, Luke's favorite color, and flowy with spaghetti straps. I had hoped that if I gave good boob, it would distract him from getting upset when I postponed our date. I knew now that was foolish. Luke wasn't a simple guy.

I felt a little silly. I had planned to distract him, but his very fine-looking presence was distracting me from what I needed to do. "Luke—"

He looked at me expectantly and started to roll up his shirtsleeves. I stopped talking and watched him. Wow, he had nice forearms. All tattooed and strong, with a few delicious-looking veins running up and down and—*Gah!* Did he have the same plan I did? To distract me? Well, it was working. Apparently, he was a better person than me. He hadn't looked at my boobs once, save for the single up-and-down perusal from before. But nothing lingering.

Have I lost it?

I shook my head.

Focus.

"We need to postpone our date. We have to slow down so we can be sure. I don't want to hurt Dylan." There. It was out. I'd said it.

"Stop worrying. I'm sure." His voice was firm and unwavering, and his face was like stone. I knew that look. Even though I hadn't seen it for years, I knew it. It was his stubborn look. He was going to push me and not give in. That look was how we'd ended up skydiving on our twentieth birthday. Yeah, so it was exhilarating and sort of fun, but Lily liked to keep her feet on the ground.

He took a step in my direction, and I stepped away as I gazed up at him with big eyes. I was in trouble. He knew how he was affecting me. "How can you be so sure?" I asked. I found myself up against the back of his desk, so I leaned on it to appear casual. "We're different, Luke. It's been a long time. You don't really know me anymore. What if you get to know me again, and I annoy you? I'm a worrier and I can be a pain." I crossed my arms under my breasts, hugging myself. The air conditioning was ridiculous in here. But the action made him look! He licked his lips and stared at my chest. Ha! I still got it. But why did I want it? I was supposed to be trying to break our date so we could get our friendship solidified first.

He rolled his eyes. "Lily, you always did worry a lot. That's not new. As for anything else that may come up, I don't care. You're worth it." He took another step in my direction, then crossed his arms over his chest, mirroring my pose. His biceps bulged, and I quickly looked away.

Were we playing a game? I rejected that idea. Luke was too good for games. But he wasn't too good to push me beyond the border of my comfort zone, a limit we were rapidly approaching.

I cleared my throat. "I'm not trying to end things or like, break up. I don't know what we're doing. I just want to be friends first. Why can't we do that?"

"It's just a date, Lily. I'm not asking you to marry me." His irresistible half-grin was back, only this time I could see it better because of his trimmed beard.

My head snapped back to him. I held on to the edge of the desk. It wasn't *just* a date. Nothing would ever be that simple with him. There were too many feelings and expectations involved. And that was just between the two of us. Throw in my family and Dylan, not to mention Calla, and the complication level went up exponentially.

"I'm not trying to hurt your feelings and I'm really not trying to jerk you around. I'm just . . . I can't . . ." Why couldn't I explain how I felt?

Maybe because I don't know how I feel.

I finally said what I'd been worrying over. "Luke, what if we try to be together, and it doesn't work out?"

"What if we try, and we are happier than we were before?"

I closed my eyes. I couldn't stand to see the hope in his, not when I felt so hopelessly confused.

"Lily, you can't live in what-ifs. I did that. What if I hurt you in my sleep? What if you were afraid of me? And look where it got us. But what if I had fought for you back then? We could have been happy this whole time. I wouldn't have missed out on years with my son. Do you want to dwell on something that might never even happen?" His eyes bored into mine. I couldn't look away from him, even if I'd wanted to. His voice gentled. "When you are with me, I forget about everything except you, me, and the kids. I stop obsessing about the past and the struggles, and I'm just Luke again. I don't want to lose that."

"I don't want to keep Dylan from you. That isn't what this is about, it's—"

He cut me off. "Do you ever miss me, Lily?" I was floored by this question. Floored, then angry.

"How can you ask me that? You know what I went through trying to get to you. We talked about it yesterday." I was getting emotional again. I had been on a roller coaster since I got home, and it had to stop. I stood straight.

He flinched. "I'm sorry, that's not what I meant. I mean, since we've both been back, and you have an understanding about why I did what I did. Do you ever think about us? How it was when we were together?"

I turned away. I didn't want him to see the tears welling up in my eyes.

"Lily, please talk to me. Look at me."

I faced him. "Yes," I hissed. "I can't stop thinking about it. But I don't want to do this now. It shouldn't be this way, Luke."

He had never turned away from me. "What way?" he asked gently.

"It was never supposed to be this complicated!"

He looked stricken for a second, then controlled his expression. I kept getting the feeling that he was hiding how he really felt, that he held something back. It had always been one of our problems. He always wanted to protect me against things he thought would hurt me.

"I spent years being angry with you, Luke—and so hurt. I know now that you didn't deliberately abandon Dylan. But for a long time, it was like an open wound that wouldn't heal. I'm not ready for this. I don't want to need you. I don't want to want you like I do. I didn't want to feel this way ever again. Now I'm wondering if I can do this at all." The tears I'd been holding back spilled from my eyes as I turned to gaze out of the window behind his desk.

His footsteps sounded behind me as he approached. With a gentle hand, he turned me. "What are you afraid of?"

"Pain!" I cried. "I'm afraid of how much it will hurt when I lose you again. I couldn't take it. I can't stand the thought of it. My anger is gone, Luke. That anger is what kept the pain of losing you from overwhelming me." I wanted to look away, but his eyes held mine captive, and I couldn't.

"If you're not angry anymore, then talk to me," he pleaded. We can get through this—"

I cut him off. I felt like I was losing hold of myself, of the things that kept me safe and secure—and lonely. "God, Luke! What do you want from me?" I shouted.

His face changed from pleading to determined. "I want you to listen to me. I want you to forgive me. Then I want you to love me again. I want to kiss you when I feel like it, to touch you because you're mine. I want you in my house, in my bed, back in my life the way we always intended. The way we were meant to be." He paused, and I stared at him transfixed as his voice gentled. "I want you back, and I will do everything you need, anything it takes, to make you believe that I can't live without you anymore. But first, and foremost, I just want you to be okay." The look in his eyes changed from frustration to tenderness—and unraveled the fear that held me back. "Don't shut me out, Lily. Don't make the mistakes I made. I promise I won't push you away ever again, I won't leave—"

"Luke, stop." I covered my ears with my hands and turned back to the window. I couldn't look at his pleading eyes for one more second, or I would give in. Deep down, I wanted him as much as he wanted me. But I was terrified of going down that path again.

"I won't stop. I am in love with you. I have loved you since we were kids. I've loved you every second of the time I was gone. I was wrong to stay away. Let me spend every day of the rest of our lives making it up to you. Let me love you again."

I felt him standing behind me, so close. If I turned around, I could have it all back.

"Please, stop pressuring me."

"I came back once."

I whirled from the window. "What? When?" I demanded. My fear was immediately replaced by anger as I glared at him.

His eyes burned into mine. "It was a few months after what happened in the hospital. I wasn't planning to talk to you. I just wanted to check, to see that you were okay."

"It was right after Christmas, wasn't it?" I remembered that day. All day long, I'd felt that I would see him, that he was close. I'd anticipated it, waited for it, hoped and prayed for it, but it never happened. I never saw him. It was bitterly disappointing, and I'd cried myself to sleep that night. It was a setback that shook me.

"Yes. You were with Jane, walking up the path to your apartment. Will ran up to you and hugged you. He was in love with you. I always knew that . . ." He looked past me to the window. "I figured, eventually, you would let him take care of you."

I felt the pain of losing Luke again. The sorrow I'd felt back then came at me like a slap in the face. It hadn't needed to be that way. He'd been there.

"Damn it, Luke, you stubborn ass." His eyes darted to

mine. "You should have talked to me. Why didn't you just come to me? All these years . . ." Tears filled my eyes again, but this time I didn't fight them. I couldn't; there were too many to stop the flow. The drops hit my chest at the vee of my shirt, and I let out a harsh laugh as I brushed them away.

He reached a hand out to me and I stepped away to avoid it. My anger snaked through my body, leaving a cold numbness in its place.

"Let it out, Lily. I ran away from you all those years ago. I thought you would be better without me. I didn't want to hurt you ever again."

"I was not better without you!" I shouted, my voice harsh and broken. "And if you thought I was with Will— I wasn't with him then, but he took care of me. I was so—" I flinched at the terrible memories invading my thoughts. "I couldn't get out of bed. I wouldn't listen to anyone, not Jane, not even Rose. My family stayed away because I demanded it, and I was in such a state that they were afraid of not doing what I asked. But Will would not stay away. He brought me food, made me eat it. He dragged me out on walks. 'Fresh air will do you good,' he told me. Later, I started to get sick—nauseated for no reason, dizzy spells, insomnia. I stopped getting my period." I laughed, shaky and bitter. "Will was the one who figured out I was pregnant. He brought a bunch of tests home. Every single one was positive." My voice broke and I took a deep shuddering breath to regain control.

Tears ran openly down Luke's face. "I'm so sorry, Lily." He reached out his hand to touch me, then pulled it back.

My knees felt weak as I stood there with my head spinning. I'd never spoken about this with anyone, but I took a deep breath and continued anyway. "Will proposed to me right then, surrounded by all the used pregnancy tests in the bathroom. He told me he loved me and would raise my baby with me and treat it like his own child. I believed him, but I told him no. I loved *you*. I wanted *you*, Luke. I told him that, and he said he didn't care. He said he had loved me for years and—" A strangled sob escaped my throat, and I couldn't say any more.

"He was a good man." Luke sighed, defeat coloring his features.

"Luke, he was my best friend. I loved him. We didn't get together until Dylan was almost two. But before then, he— even though I was still writing all those letters to you, trying to get you to come back, making endless calls to try to find where you were—he refused to give up on me. He was there for Dylan like a father would be. He was there for me like a husband would be. And all that time I leaned on him, feeling so much guilt. I told him that he should find someone else to love him like he deserved, but he always said no. Then I got a box in the mail." I paused and studied his face. This would hurt, but keeping it from him would be like telling a lie. "It was full of every letter I had ever sent to you. All were unopened." I grabbed on to Luke's hands and held them tight. "I gave up then. I buried you in my heart and mourned you like you died."

His hands convulsed in mine as he pulled me closer. I was half a step away from being in his arms. His eyes stared into mine but this time I didn't want to look away.

Defeat settled across the features of his face. "I should have listened to my heart, not my fears. I should have listened to my soul screaming at me that it belonged with yours, not my fucked-up mind telling me I would hurt you again. I should have listened to *you*, Lily, and read your letters. Am I asking the impossible?"

I stood there holding Luke's hands and for the first time since I had been back home, I got out of my head. My heart demanded that I listen to it, listen to *him*. His words had shattered my doubts.

"I love you, Luke," I blurted, and his jaw dropped. "I never stopped loving you, not ever. I loved Will with all my heart. But you—Luke, you are part of my soul. I just wish—"

"I know, I wish it too. And I love you. I'll always love you." He choked the words out. His body was stiff, like he was holding himself back. "Lily, I can't stop myself anymore."

His grip on my hands tightened as he yanked me forward to band an arm around my hips and lift me closer to his mouth for a kiss. Winding a hand into my hair, he held on as I wrapped my arms around his neck. Electricity shot through me at the touch of his lips, the taste of him, the feel of his body finally against mine, the way we used to be. I threaded my fingers into that beautiful hair I'd been dying to touch and pulled him even closer. A low growl rumbled from his chest. I wanted to crawl inside of him. I couldn't get close enough. Stumbling backward, we crashed to the couch and I straddled him as he wrapped me tightly in his arms. All those lost years were no longer between us. Nothing was. Our tears had burned it all away—the fear, the doubt, the pain. Nothing had ever felt more right than this.

I pulled back, taking his face in my hands. The need I saw in his eyes reflected the need in my heart. I kissed him again, tasting the salt from his tears. He gripped my waist as his mouth moved down to my neck, tickling my skin and making me tremble. He caressed up my back and into my hair again to grip it lightly as he pulled my face to his. He kissed me deeply, exploring my mouth. Soon, I grew restless and hungry for more.

"Luke," I whispered on a moan. "Oh, God." I felt the hard planes of his body against my soft curves. I moved my hands over his shoulders, down his strong arms, up his chest, then back to his face again. My fingers trembled as I unbuttoned his shirt. All I wanted was his skin on mine. "I can't get close enough," I breathed.

He groaned, pushing the straps of my top down to pool around my waist as he trailed his lips down my neck to the lace of my bra. He reached behind me to unfastened it, then buried his face between my breasts as I squeezed his hips with my legs and arched against his mouth. He moaned as his hands dug into my hip bones, pulling me closer.

The small part of me that doubted—the part that made me afraid of succumbing to him again—whispered in my ear demanding that I stop before I got hurt. I ignored my doubts and ground down against him, relishing his labored breath against my fevered skin. He grabbed my hips even tighter and pulled me down as he pushed his pelvis up into mine. I gasped as we rocked together.

"Luke . . ." The intensity of this moment hit me in my soul, filling me with so much need that it burned me from the inside out. I grasped his shoulders and moved against him as he held me tight and gazed into my eyes.

"Yes." He gasped. In his eyes was everything—everything I had ever wanted, everything I thought I would always have but had lost . . . and everything in the future we could build together. All we had ever felt for each other boiled over as we moved, winding each other tighter with every stroke of our bodies until we exploded. He shuddered beneath me as his head fell back against the couch, and I collapsed onto his chest, tucking my head under his chin. He stroked my back and kissed the top of my head.

"I swear I'll never leave you," he whispered.

"I believe you." I felt him relax beneath me as I wrapped myself around him.

"I only want two things in this world. I want you, and I want those kids."

I laughed softly. "That's everything."

"I know it is. I want everything with you because you mean everything to me. I'll never let you go again."

"I'll fight you if you try," I promised.

He laughed softly. "Good."

I sighed and rested against his chest once more before popping back up with a start. "What now?" I exclaimed.

"What do you mean?" He grinned like he knew what was coming.

"Well, we can't go slow anymore, not after what we just did. *Ahh*, what have we done?" I started to scurry off his lap but two warm palms on my thighs held me still.

His smile broadened. "Shh. Quit worrying and calm down." He followed that dangerous order with a chuckle.

Had we just traveled through a time machine? This felt very familiar. "I will *not* calm down. I didn't like it when you said that back then, and I still don't." I looked at the ceiling, then at the wall behind him and tried to forget I was shirtless in his lap.

"Baby, everything will be fine." He stroked up my back and tilted my head down so he could look at my face. "I know what you're like, and I love every bit of it. Please never doubt it. It will take time to prove it to you, but I'll never leave again."

I whispered my doubts. "I'm scared. Of everything." Still, I didn't move from his lap. I needed more reassurances, but I was afraid I wouldn't believe him even if he gave them. I kissed him softly, on his lips, his cheeks. I looked into his eyes. "I don't want to go slow, but maybe we should." I pressed myself against him, loving the feel of our bare bodies pressed together.

"Slow is off the table." He sighed and nibbled sweet kisses up my neck. I tipped my head back so he could have better access. He groaned, gripped my waist, and nipped his way to my mouth.

As good as this felt, we couldn't stay here forever. I was supposed to be at Violet's. Plus, didn't he have a secretary? Coworkers? "Do you have a secretary? Anyone else coming in today? Is the door locked?" I whispered against his lips.

He pulled back. "Liam has the other office but he's not here. I need to hire another secretary. I fired the one I had because she wouldn't stop coming on to me even after I told her to knock it off."

My eyes got big as jealousy shot through me. The thought of Luke with another woman upset me, and then I felt guilty because I had been married and had a baby with someone else. I didn't like to think of what—or who—Luke might have done when we were apart. I sighed and started to climb off his lap, but he held my hips and stopped me.

"What's wrong? What thought put that look on your face?" His eyes searched mine, trying to glean the answer.

"What look?" I tried to evade the question, but he just raised his eyebrows and squeezed my hips. I sighed. "Oh, all right. I just felt a touch of jealousy when you said your secretary flirted with you. Then I thought of you with other women, dating or whatever . . ." I looked away. "I have no right to feel that way. I'm so sorry."

"You have every right to feel whatever you want. But I haven't been with any other women. I didn't date or do anything with anyone."

"What do you mean? You haven't been with anyone? You haven't even slept with anyone?" He nodded at me. My jaw dropped. "Have you seen you?"

He laughed, then his expression turned serious. "Lily, I love you. I never stopped. Didn't even try. I knew I would always belong to you and only you."

My heart nearly burst at his words, but he continued to give me more. "How could I be with someone else when all I could think about was you? I didn't want to taint the memories of us together by being with another woman. I couldn't put my hands on someone else when all I wanted was you. You own my heart. You own every part of me, Lily. I'm yours."

The tears were back, but these felt different. My heart had lightened and filled with hope. "Good, because I'm yours too, Luke."

He sat up and kissed me. His hands slid up and down my

thighs on either side of his lap, then up my back. He kissed my neck and warned with a grin. "I can kiss you whenever I feel like it now." The pain was gone from his eyes. The hesitation that had crept into all our interactions had been obliterated.

He leaned back against the couch and reached into his pocket. "I have something for you."

I gasped. "My locket . . ." He reached around my neck to fasten it. It fell against my skin to sit right between my breasts.

His eyes blazed into mine as he leaned into me and kissed it. "I have your engagement ring too, but it feels wrong to use that one. Like bad luck."

I inhaled a shaky breath. "Well, it's too soon for engagement rings. We haven't even been on our first date yet. You owe me dinner, mister." I smiled through my happy tears.

His eyes crinkled as he laughed. "It's like that, is it?"

"Oh yeah. I had a dress all picked out." My face fell. "I am so messed up over you. I was planning what to wear and at the same time trying to find a way to break the date without hurting your feelings. I'm so sorry."

"I understand. Don't forget that I've known you your whole life." His smile got bigger as he tickled my sides.

I squirmed in his lap. "Hey now." I poked him in the stomach, then started feeling him up. Ooh, nice abs. Feeling was so much better than seeing. He didn't have a six-pack anymore but he had a lot of definition down the sides and at the top. He yanked me forward and kissed me again with a groan. "We should stop," he whispered between kisses. "Asher is supposed to meet me here before we go to lunch."

I sat up fast, startled. I yanked up my shirt and started looking around for my bra.

Luke reached down to my side and snagged it from under my knee. He handed it to me with a smirk. "Lily and lace." He caressed my cheek, rawness in his eyes and a sad smile on his face. "You're so beautiful." His smile turned sweet, and he gave me a quick kiss before he shifted me off his lap and onto the couch at his side. He muttered, "I'm glad I keep clothes here," as he stood up, and I giggled.

Our eyes met, and we smiled at each other.

"I love you," he whispered, then entered the bathroom to change. I put my bra on, thankful that I'd pumped for Calla before I got here. How embarrassing would it have been to have a milk incident all over Luke? Yikes, that was something to consider for next time.

"Luke, are you here? Liam?" It was Asher's voice. Wow, that was too close. I stood up and opened the door.

"Hey, Asher," I called.

He turned to me with a grin. "All made up with Luke? I told everyone to just leave you alone and let you figure it out yourselves." That was Asher. He was quiet and serious and always there when I needed him. He was a good brother and a good dad to Mark and Mara. It was too bad he'd picked a crap wife. She took off years ago, leaving him with the kids. I walked over and gave him a hug. He kissed the top of my head.

"I think so. At least we're headed that way." I grinned up at him. Asher was tall, and solid as a rock. His body matched his personality—strong, steady, immovable. He was the only sibling who shared the redhead gene with me and Rose.

"I'm happy for you. It was meant to be."

Luke walked out of the bathroom, and I blew him a kiss goodbye. He shook his head and strode toward me. He bent low and kissed my lips. "That's how we say goodbye." He smiled at me, and I tried to keep my knees from buckling.

How could I have forgotten how sweet and romantic Luke could be?

"Bye," I whispered in response. Then I turned to head back to Violet's.

Chapter 15
Lily

I walked across the parking lot to Violet's with my head firmly in the clouds. My smile was goofy and my mood was a strange mixture of euphoric and nervous. My heart pounded a fast, terrified staccato while my brain swirled with giddy thoughts. A strange voice calling my name knocked me out of my deliriously muddled, confusingly ecstatic stupor.

"Lily Sullivan?"

I stopped with my hand on the doorknob and wrinkled my nose. "I'm sorry. Do I know you?"

"I used to work with Will. I am here to pick up his remaining files."

Fighting the urge to dart inside the shop, I answered. "I don't have any of Will's work things. It's been over a year since he died. Why are you here?" I studied his face. I didn't know him, but he looked vaguely familiar. If he knew Will, then he knew that Will did not break the rules and would never have stored evidence at home.

"I'm looking for a missing flash drive. Are you sure you haven't seen anything like that?" A phony smile crossed his face as he stood up.

I gripped the door handle tighter. "I'm sure. I'm supposed

to be at work. I don't know anything about Will's cases." I looked at him pointedly, studying his face so I would remember it. I was getting more suspicious by the second, and I wanted my dad. I hurried inside the shop and shut the door firmly behind me. I quickly sent texts to my father and Cade, then to Trevor. I watched from the window as he threw his cup away and left. I should have asked his name, damnit.

"Lily!" I jumped a foot after Rose yelled excitedly and hurried out of the kitchen door to bombard me with questions. "What happened over there? Tell me!" I pushed down my bad feelings about the weirdo outside. I didn't want to worry Rose or involve her in it.

"We're going to take it slowish. Sort of. Probably? Tell everyone for me, so I don't have to answer a million questions." I was only halfway joking.

Rose could keep a secret if I asked, but she had a huge mouth if something was free to share. I was glad I'd told her first. Well, second. Asher was first, but he wouldn't tell anybody anything unless you pried it out of him. Telling Asher didn't count. He was a vault.

She hugged me and kissed my cheek, then ran off with her phone. "I'm so happy for you. I'll text everyone!" She promptly shut herself in Violet's office and I would have sworn I could hear the sounds of her thumbs flying across her phone keyboard from here.

I finished tying my apron and stood in front of the counter. I couldn't help but wonder why Violet wanted me to work here. Finn and Nick always had everything under control. I watched as they hustled and bustled behind the counter while Violet directed it all with military precision. She winked at me when she caught me staring with my mouth open.

Between customers, Finn asked me, "Want a coffee, Aunt Lily?" He passed me a scone. I took a bite. Ooh, peach.

"Sure, but I can make it." I started to go behind the counter, but Nick passed me an iced coffee.

"Iced vanilla decaf, right? Take a break, Aunt Lily, we got it," he said. Wow. I had the best nephews.

"Thanks." I took a sip. "I feel like all I do here is drink coffee and take breaks," I muttered.

They looked at each other and laughed.

At the end of my shift—during which I did very little actual work—Luke walked in. "Lily, can we pick up the kids together? I'm done for the day." He lifted me by the waist and kissed me. My brain turned to mush the second he touched me. All thoughts of "slow" darted out of my head as I enjoyed the rush his touch gave me.

"Yes, Dylan will love that." I beamed up at him and wrapped my arms around his neck. He reached into my hair and undid the clip that was holding my bun up. My crazy curls came tumbling down. "Hey, my hair is too wild to have down while I work," I said.

"You have beautiful hair," he said as he put me down, then tugged softly on a curl. "I want to see it. And you're off now anyway."

I had been in mommy mode for so long that I'd forgotten what it felt like to be wanted for something other than snacks and stories and kid cuddles. Luke wanted *me*. This felt different from how my kids loved me. Luke made me feel feminine and desired. I felt turned on, electric, *alive*. I hardly remembered this Lily—the Lily who wore high heels so she could reach up for kisses, the Lily who wore her hair down and wild, and who loved with her whole heart because she was unafraid of having it break. I loved my kids with my whole heart, always. But with everyone else in my life, I was only half present. I had been walking through heavy clouds for too many years. Luke was like sunshine—he burned the clouds away, and I was finally allowing the light to shine on me.

"Luke," I whispered as I stared at him. I was lucky I caught myself before I jumped him. We used to be so tactile and affectionate. It had always been so easy, effortless, and natural between us that I had taken it for granted. When he left, I shut a lot of myself down. But bit by bit, Luke was ensuring I was no longer that version of me.

He gave me the half-grin, and I almost swooned. I took his hand and started for the door. We needed to get out of here before I gave Finn, Nick, Violet, and all her customers a show.

In my life as a mother, I had never *not* wanted to go get my kids. I always wanted to be around them. But right now, I was greedy for Luke. I wanted him to myself, wanted to explore all the changes in him, and I wanted to do it naked and for a long time. I sighed. We had time. And I was the idiot who wanted to take things slow.

"We should take your car. I don't have car seats for the kids yet." He winked as I handed him my keys.

Dylan was playing in the grass and Mom, Gram, and Calla were sitting on one of Gram's old quilts spread out on the sprawling front lawn when Luke and I pulled up to my parents' house. My mother did a double take when she noticed me get out of the passenger side. She gasped and covered her mouth with her hands when Luke exited on the driver's side.

Gram hollered at Luke, "Oh, thank God. I need a strong arm to hold on to so I can get up off this dang grass. Lily, I told your mama I needed a chair. My legs don't work the way they used to. Come over here and give me hugs and help me up. I have to piddle. Pretty soon, Calla won't be the only one around here wearing diapers," she muttered the last part. Luke leaned over and helped her up. Once she was on her feet, she gave us both a hug. "I keep missing you, Lily. You have to stop coming over here when I'm asleep."

"Or watching *Jeopardy*," I teased, and she smiled sheepishly.

Gram was about an inch taller than Rose and me. She'd always told us we got our height from her, then she would say, "You're welcome." She was tiny, with short, curly white hair that used to be red—we got that from her too. Gram was larger than life, with a big attitude to match. Rose got the attitude. I did not.

"I'll be right back. Don't leave yet." She rushed off toward the garage apartment.

Luke and Dylan had run off together. I laughed as he swept Dylan up to sit on his shoulders. Dylan held a bottle of bubbles that dripped all over Luke's head every time he put the wand in for a reload. I shook my head and sat down next to my mother and Calla. I cuddled Calla into my lap and looked at my mother out of the corner of my eye.

"Please don't freak out and make a big deal of this. We're taking it slow."

She sighed and wiped away a tear. "Lily, I'm so happy. And Diana would be beside herself. I wish she were here to see this. Though, if she were here, he never would have stayed away for so long . . ."

We shared a sad smile. Luke had been so close to his mom. She had been an angel on earth, and we all missed her.

"Yeah. We wouldn't have lost all this time."

Calla put her hands into my hair and tugged it. She wasn't used to seeing it down. She pulled my face to hers and kissed my nose. Well, more like put my nose in her mouth. I pulled back and kissed her forehead.

"Things have a way of working out." Mom stroked Calla's hair. "We wouldn't have this little darling if you hadn't been with Will."

She was right. There was no point in dwelling on what could have been. "I hope Jane will be okay with all of this," I said.

"She loves you. She'll understand. She'll always be a part of this family."

I nodded. "I think she's coming up on Sunday."

"Good, we'll have a barbecue. I already invited Luke and that adorable Liam. Too bad Asher won't be here. He's taking the kids camping."

"Don't try to matchmake Jane and Asher again, please. She was humiliated last time."

Mom scrunched up her face and shook her head. "I feel so bad about that. She's had a crush on him for so long. I just love her so much, and Asher needs a sweet woman like her. I mean, she's a doctor, for goodness' sake. Why wouldn't he want a sweet, beautiful doctor to be a stepmother to his kids? Plus, his kids already love her. *Everybody* loves her. That boy is stubborn. He should listen to his mother." She raised her eyebrows at me.

I shrugged. I wasn't getting into their business, at least not with my mother. She was about as subtle as a sledgehammer.

"Mommy, Mommy! Look at me!" I looked up over to the trees on the other side of the driveway. Dylan was on Luke's shoulders, touching the high branches and picking leaves. "I can touch the trees. When she's big enough, Calla can too," he shouted, and Luke smiled over at us. My two lives had intersected again. What might have been was now real, and it eclipsed what used to be. It blazed a trail of beautiful pain, and I shut my eyes as a tear fell.

"Oh, honey . . ." Mom put her arm around me. We both remembered a few years ago when Will had done the same thing with Dylan. "There will always be moments like this one, when we will remember him. Sometimes, the happy memories are what hurt the most."

I leaned my head against her shoulder, and we watched Luke and Dylan together. Calla broke our bittersweet reverie by saying "Mama" for the first time. We looked at each other, and Mom squeezed me tighter.

"New memories are being made every second, sweetheart. Don't miss them. Don't be afraid."

"I won't be afraid," I promised.

When it was time to go, we stopped by the garage apartment and said goodbye to Gram, then loaded up my car and headed home. The drive was uneventful until we pulled into the driveway. The second the car was in park, we noticed a foul stench originating from the back seat—specifically from Calla's side of the back seat. Dylan's exclamation of "*Ew*, Calla pooped, and her onesie is brown now" confirmed the source of the smell: blowout diaper. Shit just got real, and Luke was about to get a lesson in parenting that he'd missed with Dylan. It seemed like Calla's scheduled bath time got bumped up before dinner prep time.

"I have to give Calla a bath, Dylan. Judging by the smell, it will take a while. I'll make fried chicken tomorrow, and we can have something fast tonight, okay?"

Dylan grumbled from the backseat, "Aw, man. She needs to poop in the toilet. When's that gonna be?"

I felt bad. I'd promised his favorite dinner tonight. "Well, first she has to finish learning to crawl, then walk, then start talking. I'm thinking at least two more years. Sorry, bud."

"It's okay. I hope I never pooped like that. Yuck."

I turned around to peek at him in the back and informed him, "You totally pooped like that."

He scrunched up his face, then laughed. "Sorry, Mommy."

"It's all part of being a baby. We've all done it."

He laughed harder at that thought. Why did kids find poop so funny? And butts. What was funny about butts?

There was nothing funny about Luke's butt. *Luke's butt is fiiiine.* I found it bizarre how my mind could wander from blowout diapers to how hot Luke's ass was. I shrugged and decided to just go with it.

"I can make fried chicken," Luke volunteered with a smile.

I grinned back at him over the console, and he tugged one of my curls.

"Yay! Can I help you?" Dylan asked.

Dylan never wanted to help me in the kitchen unless it was tasting cookie dough or putting sprinkles on top of cupcakes. "Thank you, Luke." I hopped out of the car to get the kids out. Luke beat me to Dylan's side and helped him out of his booster seat, and I grabbed Calla's bucket car seat out of its base. "My gosh, little girl. You sure are stinky."

"How can something so foul come out of something so tiny and cute?" Luke asked as he looked over my shoulder at Calla. "Don't worry about dinner, Lily. I'll take care of it. I'll take care of Dylan too. You just rid us of that stench." He pushed my hair aside and bent down to kiss the side of my neck before heading to the front door to let us all inside.

I shivered. *I could get used to this.*

"Grandma fed her more of that gross baby cereal today. Calla gobbled it up like crazy. I wonder what she'd poo out if you gave her regular food?" Dylan asked.

I turned away from the car and shut the door. As I faced Dylan with Calla in my arms, he recoiled at the smell. So, I did what any responsible parent would do. I chased him up the driveway, brandishing his stinky little sister as a weapon.

Luke cracked up at our antics, then stepped aside, holding the door open for us to pass.

Later, after Calla was clean and we'd stuffed our faces with fried chicken and mashed potatoes, I went upstairs and filled the tub for Dylan to take a bath. Upon reentering the kitchen, I found Luke washing pots and pans at the sink. Calla sat in her highchair next to him, banging toys on the tray and giggling as Luke narrated what he was doing in a silly pirate voice to entertain her.

This was a fantasy come to life. I ate a dinner I did not have to cook, someone else was cleaning my kitchen, and the cherry on top was the smoking-hot man who I loved so much entertaining my daughter and making her laugh. I watched his fine behind in his jeans and the roll of the muscles bunching and un-bunching across his back as he scrubbed the pots and wondered if it could get any better. *If I had the guts to invite him into my bed tonight, that might make it better.* Were we in that place yet? As I stood there watching, my hope started blossoming out of control. Even if we weren't there yet, we would be in that place soon. Every minute spent with him made me more certain. I leaned against the frame of the entrance to the kitchen and closed my eyes. My heart burst with fierce longing.

He heard me sigh and turned around with a grin. "I'm all done. I'm going to go pick up Rocky from Jed and come back. Is that okay? I want to help tuck the kids into bed."

I nodded at him. I was in another Luke love haze. This one was worse than when we'd turned twelve and I'd realized that boys were not yucky, especially Luke. He was the least yucky boy in all the land, and I'd wanted to kiss him. I wanted to kiss him now. I wanted to do a lot of things to him now. I sighed again as he gently lifted Calla from her highchair.

"Who's a little princess?" he asked her. She slapped his cheeks and gave him a slobbery kiss on his chin. He laughed and crossed the four steps to me and handed her off. "Baby, I'll be right back. Don't start bedtime without me. I'll have to take your car though. Mine is still at the office." I nodded again. He smiled and leaned down to kiss my lips, then grabbed my keys from the counter and took off. Calla sighed and watched him leave.

"Oh, Calla. We're in big trouble, aren't we?" She blew out a raspberry, then put her hands on my cheeks and said, "Mama."

"Let's go check on Dylan."

When Luke returned, I was curled up under Gram's quilt on the couch nursing Calla and Dylan was sitting on the floor playing Minecraft on the new Xbox One that Jude and Levi had bought and installed. Rocky made a beeline for Dylan and curled up next to his side.

"Dad, check out my village." Luke smiled at me, then sat next to Dylan on the floor. Gram's phone rang, and I jumped in my seat. Luckily, Calla didn't wake up.

"Hello?" No one answered—again. I was sick of this. It freaked me out, and I was tired of all the weirdness going on. I hung it up with a slam. Well, a soft slam. I did have a sleeping baby on me, thus it was very unsatisfying. Not as unsatisfying as trying to end a call on a smartphone when you're pissed though. "No one there." Luke looked back at me with concern and stood. I held up a finger hoping he wouldn't voice his worry in front of Dylan. "Thirty more minutes, then it's bedtime, Dylan," I reminded. He grumbled.

"But Luke is here, and Rocky." He turned to Luke. "You should spend the night. Can Luke spend the night?" He shut down the Xbox and sat next to me. Luke sat in a wing chair by the fireplace. Rocky sat at my feet and stared up at me with the same puppy dog eyes Dylan was giving me.

Luke laughed and said, "I'm staying. I'll sleep on the couch. I'll get donuts in the morning."

Dylan was doing his fist-pumping happy dance, shaking his butt and wiggling his hips as he danced around the coffee table with Rocky bopping around at his side. Luke reached over and ruffled Dylan's hair with a grin.

"Text Violet. Tell her you'll be late tomorrow." He looked at me with that stony face, the one that said he was going to push and I was going to let him. I fully intended to let him push, especially tonight. I didn't want to be alone. Too many things were freaking me out, and Gram's baseball bat was not enough to make me feel safe. I nodded. Luke raised an eyebrow in surprise. I guess he'd expected an argument, but I wasn't stupid. I wanted safety for my kids. If he hadn't offered to stay here, I would have called one of my brothers to stay with me. Or Rose. She could get hostile sometimes. I wouldn't cross her.

Luke relaxed and smiled. "So, what do we do around here for bedtime? Read stories? Check the basement for zombies? Meditate?"

Dylan laughed. I rolled my eyes and smiled.

"Stories! I have all my favorites by my bed. Mommy, can Luke read to me tonight?"

I nodded. I used to dream of having nights like this with Luke, and now that it was real, I could hardly believe it.

Dylan raced for the stairs with Rocky right behind him.

"He already had a bath. He just needs to brush his teeth, then you can read to him." Luke looked at me. It was the same look as the night when he'd watched me nurse Calla. But this time, there was hope mixed in with the anguish. He caressed my cheek as he passed me to follow Dylan up the stairs.

Chapter 16
Luke

I finished tucking Calla into her pink blanket sleeper, turned on the baby monitor, and left her room, leaving the door open a crack like Lily told me to do. Next, I peered in at Dylan. Rocky slept curled up at his feet. I walked quietly to the bed and leaned over to kiss Dylan's cheek and tuck the covers around him, then patted Rocky's head and told him to stay here. He looked up at me, then settled back down, looking quite content to stay right where he was for the night.

The kids were asleep and Lily was waiting me downstairs. This was a fantasy come to life on so many different levels. I sped down the hall and quickly descended the stairs because I was dying to spend some time alone with her. I was heading into the life I should have fought for, the one I hoped I now deserved.

She was in the kitchen putting away the pots and pans I had washed earlier. I snuck up behind her to hug her around her tiny waist, twirling her around and grabbing onto the dream I wanted to finally come true.

She laughed and turned in my arms as I set her down. "Kids asleep?"

"Yep." I stared into her eyes, then down at her mouth. I wasn't in the mood to be subtle. "Can I kiss you?"

"Yes." She grinned and lifted her face to mine. "Wait." She turned sideways to hop onto the counter then grabbed me by my shirt to pull me close, threading her fingers into my hair while she wrapped her legs around my waist.

She was all in, so I took the kisses I wanted, the kisses I had longed for, the kisses I had missed from her over all these years. I dug my fingers into her hips, pulling her forward to grind myself against her center.

After a moment, I wasn't doing the kissing anymore—she was. I was now the one along for the ride, kissing her back, letting her in. Her lips moved over mine, soft, hard, licking, biting, all of it. Her tongue traced my lips and demanded entrance. I opened for her, more than willing to give her everything I had been holding back.

This kiss . . . it was more than a kiss. We responded to each other using a language only we knew. It said, *I missed you. I love you. I'm home.*

I wrapped one arm around her waist, letting my fingers trail up the hem of her shirt while gliding my other hand up her back and over her shoulder to caress her cheek. Tilting her head back, I positioned her where I liked, slanting my mouth over hers to deepen our kiss.

She unbuttoned my shirt and spread it apart, her hands on my skin sending electricity through my body until I was mindless with want.

This was nostalgia wrapped in lust. Love wrapped in rediscovery. I pulled her shirt over her head and tossed it to the side, kissing her breast over the lace of her bra before tugging the cup down to get a taste of her bare skin. I groaned as her nipple pebbled against my tongue.

She touched me all the way to my soul, filling my heart so full it was about to beat out of my chest straight into hers. This kiss was mind-melting, urgent, claiming, but I had to stop.

I stepped back and steadied her before moving to lean against the opposite corner of the counter. I was lost in a moment I didn't want to leave. Pressing my hand to my mouth, I exhaled sharply as I searched her eyes. "God, Lily," I whispered. "I'm sorry. One second more, and I wouldn't have been able to stop."

"Why did you?" she asked softly, hesitantly.

I stared out at the darkness beyond the kitchen window and sighed. "I was pushing, and you told me you don't want to move too fast—"

I saw it the same instant she did. The faint light from a flashlight, there then gone. In the trees at the rear of the yard. She nearly jumped out of her skin when there was a knock at the door.

"Holy crap," she exclaimed and hopped off the counter. I caught her as she stumbled against me. I quickly found her shirt and gave it to her. She slipped it on and started to head for the stairs, but I caught her hand and tugged her behind myself.

Stopping when we reached the staircase, I pushed her gently toward it. "Call your dad." She took her phone from her pocket and went up a few steps watching as I strode to the door. I was ready to stomp whoever was there into the ground if they proved to be a threat in any way.

"Who's there?" I all but growled at the door as I quickly buttoned my shirt.

"It's Cade. Everything okay in there?"

I swung the door open. "Backyard, flashlight, two minutes ago."

Cade rushed through the house and out the back like a shot.

"Upstairs. Check the kids," I told Lily.

She turned and ran up the stairs.

I stood at the bottom of the staircase, eyes to the kitchen door, waiting for Cade. I glanced up to find Lily behind me.

"They're fine. Rocky is in the middle of the hall, standing guard like a good dog. I'm glad Cade is here. He has a gun," she whispered.

She'd obviously forgotten the training I'd had. "I don't need a gun to catch whoever is out there fucking with you."

"Oh god." Her eyes were big. "Luke, I have to tell you something—"

"When Cade comes back in."

She nodded. Then we waited for Cade. It was a long five minutes.

"Someone was back there, no doubt about it. But they got away." The backyard was huge, and it backed up to an alleyway. A copse of trees and evergreen shrubbery lined the back of the yard, and there was no fence. It would be easy to hide within the trees and watch the house. Though it was stupid of whoever had been out there to use a flashlight, as it wasn't so far away that a light wouldn't be visible from the kitchen window or one of the bedroom windows upstairs. "There are footprints and trash in the trees, and tire tracks. They must have driven off when you were opening the door for me," he reasoned.

I nodded. "You aren't going to stay alone here, Lily."

Cade nodded his agreement. "Yeah, one of us will be with you. I don't want you going anywhere by yourself until we figure out what the hell is going on." He placed his gun in his shoulder holster under his jacket.

"Um, something happened today, and I kind of forgot about it until right now. After I left Luke's office this morning I ran into a man at Violet's. He was asking about some evidence Will had collected—a flash drive—and insinuating that they'd worked together. Which was obviously a bunch of crap."

Cade looked annoyed. Lily turned and tucked herself into my side. I wrapped an arm around her and gave her a squeeze. "I'm sorry. I should have mentioned it right away. So much is going on." She glanced at Cade. "I did text you to tell you to stop by so I could talk to you."

"That's why I'm here now, Lily. That, and I'll be crashing here again. Dad and I don't want you and the kids to be alone at night. He wants you to pack some bags and stay at the house for a while." He could see my preparing to protest and cut me off. "Chill out, Lily. I'm not going to lecture you."

"No need, Cade. I've already got the couch tonight," I informed him.

"Gotcha. Rose sent out a group text earlier. I'm glad you're working it out. I'll call Dad and brief him." After Lily gave Cade a description of the man she'd seen at Violet's earlier, he took off.

She relaxed against me as I pulled her closer. I cradled her head against my chest and rubbed her back. "You're tense, Lily. Relax. I won't let anything happen to you or the kids. We're safe. Cade is out looking for whoever was back there and I'm here now." I whispered.

I swept her up, walked to the couch, and sat, settling her in my lap. She tucked her knees into my chest and her feet next to my thigh on the couch. "I always loved holding you like this." I kissed the top of her head. "You're so small I can hug your whole body at once."

She laughed softly and wrapped her arms around my neck, tilting her head back to gaze up at me. I leaned forward and kissed her gently. "You're still tense," I whispered as I stroked her back. "What can we do to settle you down?"

"You could put your hand down my pants. That always used to work," she said without thinking. I chuckled as her body grew tighter in my arms. Her eyes slammed shut and her face turned red.

"I was going to suggest that I rub your shoulders. But I like your idea so much better." I almost thought I had heard her wrong. If she hadn't reacted to her own words the way she did, I would have questioned it.

Her lips parted, she took a deep breath, and let her leg drop to the side. My eyes flared as I ran one hand up her thigh and across the graceful curve of her hip. The way she looked up at me was almost too much; she was so trusting, like no time had passed between us.

My eyes locked to hers as my fingers lingered at her waistband, feeling the warmth of her skin and not quite believing I was lucky enough to be with her like this again. I was in heaven with her sweet little body curled up in my lap. She'd broken me back open again, my heart was hers. "Are you sure?" *Please be sure.*

"Yes. Touch me like you used to." I'd spent so many nights imagining being with her, wherever she was. Tasting her, touching her, pleasuring her until we were both crazy from it. I had to slow down or I would lose my mind.

I shifted our bodies until she reclined on my chest. She spread her legs over mine, feet to the cushions. My fingers ran across the skin at her waist, loosening the drawstring and lowering her pants until they rested low around her hips. I kissed her and she gasped against my mouth. Taking advantage, I plunged my tongue in her mouth as I slid my fingers down, parting her, groaning as her slick skin wet my fingertips. Her head dropped back to rest against my shoulder and her lips fell from mine. Burying my face in her neck, I entered her silky heat with my fingers and pressed my palm tight against her clit.

She gave herself over, arching her back against my chest as I stroked my fingers inside her. My cock grew impossibly harder as I pressed it against her.

"I want to touch you," she moaned, sliding her hand between us along my stomach. She lifted her face to mine, eyes glazed with pleasure.

I whispered against her lips, "Later. This is for you." I couldn't let her touch me now. I was already overwhelmed; anything else would shoot me over the edge embarrassingly fast and I needed to stay aware. Now was not the time for me.

She gazed into my eyes as her hips moved in time with my fingers. "Luke . . . Oh . . ." Her eyes drifted closed as I worked her closer to release.

"Look at me, please. Tell me you're mine again, Lily. Say it," I demanded.

"I'm yours." She opened her eyes. "I'm yours, I'm yours . . ." she repeated as her orgasm washed over her. I cupped her softly between her legs, caressing gently as she came down.

"It's my turn now." She sat up, then slid to her knees on the floor. She was about to reach for my zipper but froze as Calla cried in the baby monitor. She cringed. "I'm so sorry, Luke."

I leaned forward to kiss her lips. "We have time. We have forever."

"I'll be right back. Hopefully fast."

While she was upstairs, I made up the couch to sleep on. I was desperate to feel her curled up against me all night the way she used to sleep but I didn't want to be presumptuous. I had been alone for so long and was desperate for contact. I ached just to hold her.

I grabbed a book from the shelf in the corner to distract myself from the fantasies that were rapidly unfolding in my thoughts as I stretched out on the couch to wait.

"Hey." Her voice was a whisper as she climbed over me. I tucked her along my side with her back to the couch. Tossing the book to the floor, I kissed her until we were both stupid from lust.

"Come to bed with me," she whispered in my ear, then licked the lobe.

"I want to be alone with you the first time," I whispered back.

"Well, it's not our first time. Exhibit A is asleep upstairs."

Her giggle was adorable—and went straight to my cock. This was going to be difficult.

"Aren't you worried they'll wake up?" I asked and nuzzled her neck, gripping her ass and tugging her closer.

"Dylan won't, unless he gets sick or something. Calla might wake up one more time . . ." I lifted her shirt and buried my face between her breasts. She pulled back. "You're a tease. Stop it."

"I'm not trying to tease you. I'll take care of you again," I whispered. My breath ruffled her hair, which tickled my face.

"I'm so sorry, Luke," she whispered. "I don't want to pressure you into something you're not ready for."

I pulled back, bursting into loud laughter. "Oh, Lily. I'd almost forgotten about the crazy shit that would come out of your mouth. You're not pressuring me. I just—" My eyes darkened. "I haven't been with you in almost seven years. I haven't been with *anyone* in all that time. When I finally get between your legs again, I do not want to be interrupted. I also have to keep some kind of awareness. There was someone in your back yard tonight. Understand?"

Her body melted back into mine. "I understand, and I'm sorry for acting like such a dude."

Smiling against the flushed skin of her neck, I said, "What am I going to do with you?"

"I'll get started on a list. And with all this build-up, the list will be long. Do you really want to sleep down here? We could just leave the couch made up, and you could wake up before Dylan, so he won't see us in bed together. He doesn't need to see that until we've at least gone on our first date," she teased.

I laughed softly. "I would love to sleep in your bed." Her eyes were hot on mine as she took my hand and led me upstairs.

Chapter 17
Luke

My eyes opened to sunlight from Lily's window shining on my face. Red hair fanned out across my shoulder, tickling its way down my arm. I blinked a few times to make sure this was real. *Please be real . . .*

I'd dreamed of moments like this for so long. Even when she'd been mine, I'd had dreams like this. I'd been gone more often than I was home, so I was always missing her. I was tired of being alone, tired of being without. I groaned when I looked down and saw the tent I was making out of the quilt. Tonight would be the night. I reached for her phone and turned her alarm off. She needed rest, and I needed her to know that I was here to take care of her. Carefully, I shifted her head to the pillow and disentangled myself from her arms. I tucked the quilt around her shoulders and smiled as she sighed and snuggled under it.

I got ready for the day, grabbed the baby monitor, and headed for the kitchen, checking on the kids as I passed their rooms. Both were still asleep. Rocky perked up when I passed to follow me downstairs. After starting a pot of coffee, I sent a text to Jed asking him to stop by here to pick up Rocky and bring donuts. I poured myself a cup and headed out to the covered front porch to sit on the swing. Rocky sniffed around the front yard, hunting for a good spot.

I rocked and sipped my coffee. The peaceful street arched over with green trees and glinting with early morning sunlight was a hard contrast to the desert where I'd spent most of my adult life. I was not used to hearing the rustle of trees blowing in the breeze or the chatter of squirrels and birds bustling about. As I took a deep breath and the smell of flowers and fresh-cut grass filled my nostrils, I found that I couldn't relax.

I stopped the swing so Rocky could hop up and put his head on my shoulder. He licked my cheek and I put my free arm around him. Rocky always knew when I needed him. I settled into the swing and allowed the gentle rocking and calm surroundings to ease my mind.

Jed pulled into the driveway. I shielded my face against the sun as he walked toward me. He limped a bit from his knee replacement earlier this year, but he still stood tall, military straight. His hair had turned white while I was gone. He carried a donut box, waving as he approached.

"Morning, Pop. How's the knee?" I called out.

He made it to the porch and grinned. "Oh, just fine. I'm collecting scars this year. I made it through four tours with only some shrapnel and an itty-bitty bullet hole. This year, I got four new scars, just from old age." He chuckled. "I'm glad to see you here, boy. Finally taking my advice. Getting your family back. Good for you." He placed the box of donuts on a side table before patting my shoulder and kissing the top of my head and sitting across from me.

"There's coffee in the kitchen. Want a cup?" I offered.

He waved it off. "Nah, already had some."

Rocky trotted over to greet him, then lay down on his feet. Jed leaned over and patted his head. "This is a good dog. Failed all my certification tests, but still a good boy, aren't you?" Rocky licked his hand, and Jed laughed. "He was meant to stay in the family—meant to be with you, Luke." He was a big believer in fate and destiny and all that kind of crap.

I believed life was what you made it to be. I had seen too much, watched too many good men die, to believe in fate. Life was random and unfair. I hoped to someday understand Jed's optimism. We both turned to look through the screen door when we heard Dylan bounding down the stairs.

He made it to the doorway, then rushed through to jump onto Jed's lap. "Papa, you're here! Yay! I smell donuts." He scrambled down from Jed's lap and opened the box. "Oooh, sprinkle ones." Jed laughed as Dylan snatched one, then sat by me on the swing to snuggle into my side. I put my arm around him and grinned down at his upturned smiling face as donut sprinkles rained down on my leg.

"There's my little sunshine," Jed said, holding his arms out for Calla as Lily walked onto the porch. I held the baby monitor up with a confused smile for Lily.

"I turned it off when I got up. Thank you for letting me sleep." She rummaged through the donut box with a smile, then took a bite of an apple fritter.

I reached for the box and got my own apple fritter.

Jed chuckled. "You two and the apple fritters. Some things never change. Not as good as my Diana's, but they'll do." My mom used to make the best apple fritters. A collective hush fell over us as we remembered her.

"Who's Diana?" Dylan asked.

"My daughter. Luke's mom," Jed answered.

"Oh yeah. My other grandma."

"She sure would have loved you, Dylan. And you too, little princess," Jed said.

"Mommy said she was an angel in heaven. I wonder if she knows my dad Will," he mused as he ate his donut.

I leaned back into the swing. It was impossible to escape the memories. Even happy ones were bittersweet.

Thankfully Jed broke the mood. "That reminds me, Luke,

I have something for you. I'll give it to you when you pick up Rocky tomorrow morning." I raised my eyebrows, and he shook his head. "I've got to head out." He stood up and handed Calla off to me.

She gave me big eyes, patted my cheeks, and said, "Ba."

Jed called Rocky to him, said goodbye to everyone, and took off in his truck.

I wiped Calla's chin with her bib. Her mouth was like a leaky faucet.

"She's cutting a tooth," Lily said. "That's why she's always drooling."

I pulled her lip down and saw the tiny white spot poking through her lower gums. Calla put her mouth around my finger and bit down, making me laugh.

"Sure, it's funny when it's your finger. Not so funny when I was nursing her earlier," Lily said, and I grimaced.

I leaned in and rubbed my nose against Calla's. "Naughty baby. Biting is only good when fish do it."

Dylan and Lily laughed. I tugged my finger out of Calla's mouth and sat her on my lap facing out. She waved at Lily and said, "Mama, mama."

Lily waved back, then covered her eyes to play peek-a-boo.

Calla giggled and clapped her hands.

"Hey, do you like to fish?" Dylan asked. "My dad Will took me fishing a lot with Uncle Trevor on his fishing boat."

"I like to go fishing. The Sweetbriar River runs through the back of my property. I usually fish there. I'll take you."

"Yes! I have a Lightning McQueen fishing pole. But I can't fish today. I'm spending the night at Mark and Mara's and we're going to play miniature golf and eat pizza. Uncle Ash has the day off tomorrow."

A bird landed on the railing, behind Lily's shoulder. Calla squealed and reached for it. I had the strange urge to catch it for her, but it flew away before I could even move to try. I turned her and held her to stand on my legs. I grinned at her smiling baby face as she reached up and tried to grab ahold of my beard.

I looked up to see Lily smiling with an expression I had never seen before. This must be her "mom" look. Her eyes were soft as her gaze settled on my face, moving to Dylan tucked tight to my side, eating his donut, then to Calla dancing on my legs as I held her up.

Suddenly I recalled the same look on my mother's face and realized this was a part of Lily I didn't know anything about: her life as a mother. The fact that she made me remember my own mother with just her smile told me she was a good one. I took a deep breath as my heart filled. There were so many things I loved about her, and I had just discovered a new one. Familiar regret burned through me, blazing a path right alongside the joy that had been sparking up all morning.

Jed said that regret takes the place of action. He told me to set aside the things I could not change so I could concentrate on what was possible. So I smiled at Lily and watched her eyes warm. We'd always talked about having a big family; I decided right then I would give her more babies. As many as she wanted.

Shutting my eyes, I felt the sun warm my skin. The scent of the roses in the yard, the fresh donuts, and the soft floral of Lily's perfume washed over me, grounding me against the bad memories threatening to steal this moment from me.

I wished the soft breeze on the air could blow them away. But they were rooted so deeply that a simple breeze was not enough to budge them. I could only do what Jed had said— take the good with the bad. He told me I deserved good things, and I was finally starting to believe him. But right now, as I sat here in the sunlight with my arms full of my family, it was easy to fight the bad. I locked this moment up tight, to use when I needed it.

Chapter 18
Lily

I was buzzing. I still hadn't come down from earlier this morning. My head was spinning, from Luke, to the kids, to what to wear tonight, to what we would do when we were alone together.

"Lily! What are you doing here?" Violet shouted as I entered her shop.

"Sorry I'm late. Did you think I wasn't coming?" I yelled back as I headed to her office to grab an apron and put my purse away.

"No. Don't you have a date with Luke tonight?"

"Yeah, in like, nine hours. How much time do you think I need to get ready? And watch what you say. I'm about to get offended."

Nick and Finn laughed as I headed toward the cash register.

"Well, we weren't going to say anything . . ." Rose snickered, making Finn and Nick laugh harder.

"We're going on break, Mom. This is the kind of sister fight we don't want to see," Nick said. Finn nodded his agreement as they took off for the patio out front, leaving the customers and the fighting to me and the sister squad.

Rose hugged me and said, "Lily, I was planning to pick you up and take you for a pedicure." She pulled back and looked down at my hands and added, "Yeesh, and a manicure. We're finally together in the same town and can hang out just like real sisters. No more FaceTime, no more emails. We'll do lunch at least once a week, drink wine, get our nails done, pick out date clothes, talk about boys . . ."

I laughed and hugged her back. "That sounds wonderful, Rose." I looked over at Violet, who was grinning at us and shaking her head.

"Get out of here. Go get beautified with Rose and have fun tonight, Lily. Tomorrow, I'm going to be all big sisterly and demand details. And since I'm letting you both out of here early, you're gonna spill it *all*."

Rose tossed my purse to me, and I tossed my apron to Violet.

"Send the boys back in," she called out.

"Are you nervous?" Rose whispered after I shut the door of her blue Beetle and fastened the seat belt. She started the car and turned out of the parking lot.

"A little bit. We almost had sex last night. What if he's disappointed? I've had two kids. I'm different."

"Pshhh, shut up. You're not different. And even if you were, one of those kids is his, so if anything happened to your hootenanny, it's half his fault anyway."

"Hootenanny? You're a nut. I didn't mean physically, but now that I'm thinking about it . . ." I shook my head. *Focus, Lily. You don't need more to worry about.* "I meant it's been years. What if we don't have chemistry anymore?"

"Didn't you text me to tell me you dry humped each other in his office? Dry humping means you have chemistry. If you can get off with your pants on, you've still got it."

I laughed instead of answering. Dry humping was such a ridiculous phrase.

"Want to go to Becca's salon to get our nails done, or do it at my place?" Rose asked.

"Your place," I answered.

Rose stopped at the red light, lost in thought.

"It's green, Rose," I said, and she stuck her tongue out at me before she moved through the quiet intersection. "It's deserted in town today. Where is everyone?"

"Work. Not everyone is lucky enough to get summers off like us. Becoming a teacher was the best idea I've ever had. Deep inside, I'm just a big kindergartener anyway. Plus, I've always wanted to be Ms. Frizzle."

I laughed, then I noticed a small yellow car speed through the newly turned green light and switch lanes to head right for us.

"Shit!" Rose yelled. "Hold on." Rose hit the gas and swerved to the side of the road, narrowly avoiding a head-on impact. I turned around in my seat to look, sure I'd seen that car before. Racking my brain, I tried to remember where I had seen the lemon-yellow old model car. The driver slowed down, then made a clumsy U-turn in the road.

I yelled at Rose, "He's turning around! Go, go, go!"

Rose floored it but the driver still managed to bump us from behind. Rose and I both screamed as her Beetle jolted forward from the impact. She sped up and switched lanes to avoid another collision. The yellow car sped up as well and tried to sideswipe us, but Rose was faster and pulled ahead before he could hit us again. I looked nervously behind us as we sped crazily down the road.

"Oh, hell no. I just bought this car!" Rose shouted as she punched the gas, shooting us forward.

I gripped the handle tighter and tried not to panic. Dad said a clear head in a crisis would prevent—oh my gosh—I didn't remember what it would prevent, but panicking was bad anyway. I took a deep, shaky breath and looked at Rose. She looked pissed.

"I'm headed for the police station. Call Dad. Or Cade. Or nine-one-one. Shit, just get your phone out, Lily, and call for help."

I forced my fingers to let go of the handle and unzip my purse. My phone wasn't there. I jumped in my seat as Rose's phone rang in the console. A quick glance showed my picture on the screen with "Wonder Twin" spelled out above it. *Huh?* I picked it up and answered.

"Missing something?" a deep voice asked. I spun in my seat and saw the driver of the truck had a phone to his ear. He was so close behind us that I could see that it was in a bright pink case just like mine. How did he get my phone? When did I misplace it? I felt a chill run through my body. Had he been near my kids?

"Who are you? What do you want?" I managed to squeak out.

"I need the files. It's probably on a thumb drive. You're not helping. Look through your stuff *and find Will's files,*" he growled. "Consider this a warning." He threw my phone out the window, slowed down, and made another U-turn, then careened off in the opposite direction, disappearing from our view.

I let out a trembling breath. Just what in the heck was going on? "Pull over, Rose. Whoever that was just threw my phone out his window. Let's go get it."

She pulled to the side of the road. We were just lucky we weren't on the highway. Someone could have gotten hurt. I ran over and picked up my phone. Rose jogged to my side as I swiped the screen. It still worked. Not a scratch on it.

"Holy shit, it still works," she said.

I shrugged. "Dylan likes to use my phone. I got a really good case."

Rose took my hand and led me back to her Beetle. "I called Dad. He'll be here in a minute."

"We should have taken my Expedition. He would have just bounced off my back tires when he hit us. Your car is too small, Rose. You need to get a bigger one. He had my phone. How did he get my phone? Why didn't I notice?" I rambled. I tended to lose both my filter and my focus when I was nervous.

"Chill, Lily. We're fine for now. Dad's coming." She squeezed my hand and patted my head. I was pretty sure nothing scared Rose.

"My kids . . . What if he tries to get near them, or hurt them? Rose—"

She put her hands on my shoulders. "They are at Mom's house. First, you know all about the alarm Dad installed and the fences and motion detectors and all that. And if that doesn't make you feel better, Levi and Jude are there, and Ash and his kids. Plus, Dad said Cade just got there for lunch. Don't worry, your kids are fine. Promise. And Dad will be here any minute."

He pulled up in his police SUV followed by another officer in a squad car before Rose could even finish her sentence, looking around as he got out. I stupidly held out my phone to him, belatedly realizing that I probably shouldn't have picked it up. Hopefully, I didn't screw up any fingerprints or evidence. Dad sidestepped my outstretched arm holding the phone and pulled me close with one arm. His other arm wrapped around Rose, and just like that, I felt a little bit better.

"You girls okay?" he asked. Rose nodded and pulled away to check out the damage to the back of her car.

"We are now," I said. "Someone called us from my phone. I don't know how or exactly when they got it, but it had to have been when I was at Violet's because I had it this morning. He wants some file of Will's, and you know that's crazy, right? Will never brought evidence home. Plus, it's been over a year since he died. Why now? I don't know anything about what he investigated or his cases, and I never did. And Trevor hasn't called me back yet."

Dad carefully took the phone and put it in a bag. "You're moving into the house. Today. No more staying at Gram's. You can move back there after I figure out what is going on."

I nodded. I was no fool. I was also a great big scaredy-cat. Plus, Dad had guns and an epic alarm system and the town's entire police force at his disposal. I needed all hands on deck. I needed bodyguards. But what I really needed was someone to talk me down from this edge of panic I was teetering on.

Rose turned back to Dad, and I felt myself start to slip into a panic mode, where everything was in sharp focus but also strangely muted by fear.

"Snap out of it, Lily. You've got that panicky, crazed look in your eyes. Nothing will happen to you or the kids. Focus on me, on Dad. It's going to be okay." Rose hugged me quickly, then headed back to her car.

"Rose is right, honey. Everything will be fine." Dad gave me a reassuring smile. "I talked to Trevor. He's on his way down with the kids. I told him he can stay at your Gram's house. I don't like this. There is too much weirdness going on. This just caps it all off and tells me I made the right decision about you moving in with your mom and me."

"Trevor? Why didn't he tell me himself?"

"We'll talk about that later," Dad said.

"I should cancel my date with Luke. I can't leave the kids at a time like this."

"No, I don't think that's necessary. You'll be safe with Luke and the kids will be safe with us. You're all covered. Go with Luke, try to get your mind off all this. We have a reason to worry, but I don't want you to—" He looked away from me for a second, then added, "I'm taking care of it. So is Trevor." He didn't want me to lose my mind and freak out is what he didn't say. He was hoping that spending time with Luke would distract me.

I wished I was a stronger person, like Rose. I wished I didn't overthink and overreact and make everything seem worse than it was. "Thanks, Dad." I hugged him quickly.

"You girls go straight to the house."

Chapter 19
Luke

I stood on Lily's parents' front porch and stared at the doorbell with memories of ringing it at age sixteen blasting through my head. I took a deep breath to try to calm my out-of-control nerves. I'd been nervous back then too, but with happy anticipation rather than the fear that one misstep could cause me to lose everything. I blew out a breath and pressed the doorbell.

Rose answered. "We had an incident today." I shook off the memories and focused on Rose as she explained. "Your job is to distract Lily and keep her mind off all this crap going on. Don't let her freak out."

I had assumed I was picking her up here because the kids were here. "Is she okay? Is it safe to go out?" I asked.

"I don't have to tell you to keep your guard up. From what I've seen, it's always up now." Rose smiled softly. "A car followed us today, bumped the back of us, and he had her phone. Dad is taking care of it. Asher was supposed to take the kids out, but we're all going to hang here tonight instead." She stepped aside to let me in. "Everyone is out back, grilling and swimming. I'm going to head out there." On her way out she yelled for Lily to come downstairs.

I stood at the foot of the stairs to wait. When I glanced up, I saw her foot—clad in a sexy, strappy, black high heel—hit the top of the staircase, followed by a beautiful leg that went up, up, up to reach the bottom of a tight silvery black dress. My eyes trailed up and down her beautiful body, over her tiny waist, along her curvy hips. Then she bent to adjust the strap on her heel and treated me to a view of the locket I'd given her as it fell from her cleavage. I blinked and took a deep breath. I looked up again to see her beautiful face framed by soft red curls falling in a cascade over one bare shoulder. I grinned at her, and she returned it. She had always been beautiful to me, *always*. But now, she was breathtaking. I smoothed down my shirt and straightened my tie as she approached.

"God, you're so beautiful," I said as she stopped in front of me and stood on the bottom stair. She was in heels, so her eyes were level with mine. Her mouth was *right there*. I seized her face between my palms and kissed her. I knew that I just messed up her lipstick—that always used to make her mad— but I didn't care. She was right there, so beautiful and so *mine*. I slid my arms down and wrapped them around her, crossing them behind her back to grip her hips in my palms. I lifted her off her feet. Her little purse hit the staircase as she wound her arms around my neck, her fingers curling into my hair. This date would start with a kiss and end with a whole lot more. I growled into her mouth as I felt her tongue touch mine. God, how I wanted her. I had always wanted her.

"Luke, you're supposed to kiss me at the end of the date," she whispered against my lips.

I smiled against her mouth. "I'll kiss you at the end, don't worry about that," I whispered back. "And, baby, prepare. I'll probably kiss you during the date too."

She pulled back with a smile. "Noted. And just so you know, I approve of your plans."

"You don't even know where I'm taking you, and you already approve. This bodes well for me."

"I meant I approve of the kissing, silly. I'll let you know if I approve of the location later," she teased.

I winked at her and put her down. I picked up her purse and offered her my arm. "Shall we?" She took my arm with a laugh, we said goodbye to the kids, then I escorted her outside to my truck. I opened her door, and she frowned up at me.

"Your truck is too high. And I think my dress is too tight to climb up." She looked down at her body in that dress.

Her amazing body in that tight, sexy dress was slowly going to kill me until I could hopefully take it off her later tonight. I grinned down at her bemused expression and picked her up, placing her on the passenger seat before carefully closing the door.

After I got in and started the truck, I turned to her. "There is no such thing as a dress too tight when it comes to you. You are stunning. It's a bonus that I get to put my hands all over you when I help you in and out of my truck."

She blushed, and her eyes shifted down so she was looking at me through her lashes. It looked like Shy Lily was back. Shy Lily had made an appearance when we'd first started dating. I'd found her irresistible then and was glad to see that I still did. I winked at her again, just to watch her blush one more time.

"So, where are we going?" she finally asked.

"You have to wait and see." I turned down her parents' circular driveway and headed for the road. I was taking her to the restaurant where we'd had our first date. But this time, I didn't have to borrow money from Jed to pay for it.

"Oooh, I'm gonna guess," she announced, making me laugh.

"Go for it."

"Are we going up the mountain or into Portland?"

"No questions. Just guessing." I laughed. "Better hurry. Time is almost up."

"Hardass. Fine, hmmm . . ." She drew it out, probably

waiting to see which direction I would turn once we got onto Main Street. I turned toward the mountain and away from the city to merge onto the highway and the "hmmm" stopped. "Are we going to the Riverview Grille?"

I took my eyes off the road for a brief second to smile at her and saw tears briefly fill her eyes. She remembered. But then again, how could she forget?

"Oh, Luke." She reached over and placed her hand on my thigh. I gripped her hand and squeezed briefly. She interlaced her fingers with mine and held on. We held hands until we arrived thirty minutes later. The drive was quiet, both of us lost in memories. Every so often she would squeeze my hand, I would squeeze back, and she'd smile at me.

I pulled into the parking lot. She knew where we were going, but I still had a surprise in store. "Stay put. I'm coming around to get you." I quickly went around to open her door and help her down. She took my hand, and we headed inside.

The Riverview Grille was the premier event destination around here. If you had something to celebrate and money to spend, you came here. It stood alone, overlooking the Sweetbriar River. It was, like almost everything else around here, designed with the mountains in mind. Lots of dark wood inside and out, from the floors to the beams that lined the ceiling. Floor-to-ceiling double-paned windows opened the rear of the restaurant to a view of the river.

But we weren't going to be in the dining room tonight, or even out on the dock. I had reserved the private dining room. Up a spiral staircase in the corner and down a long hall was a small space that extended over the massive, covered dock that hosted outdoor dining. It had pocket doors that opened on all four sides so that it would feel like you were floating right over the water. Our first date, so many years ago, had been on the dock. Lily had talked about the private dining room and wondered what it would be like when we could finally go there together. Tonight, we would find out.

"I've always loved it here," she said as I slipped my arm around her waist and led her up the stairs to the heavy, intricately carved wooden doors. "Do you remember when we were here last? We had so many plans, so much hope," she whispered softly.

"I remember. We're here to get it all back, Lily." We paused at the door. Being with her made me forget, made the pain go away. All my senses filled with her, and I wanted to stay this way forever.

Chapter 20
Lily

We ascended the staircase and took our seats. The hostess asked if we would like a drink, and Luke and I grinned at each other. "This time, we can have a drink," I said. I would have to pump and dump later, but it would be worth it.

Luke chuckled and ordered a beer, while I ordered a lemon drop.

I smiled as I looked around the beautiful, dark wood-paneled room with its windows fully opened to the spectacular view of the river. The reflection of the lights from the restaurant began to twinkle along the water as the sun started to set. There were candles in sconces on the walls and one in the center of our table. It couldn't have been more romantic in here even if Cupid himself were sitting in the corner firing arrows at us.

"Thank you for bringing me here. This is perfect."

It *was* perfect. But I didn't know what to talk about. We were well beyond a first date. I didn't want to ruin the mood or break this spell we seemed to be under. Starting a serious conversation seemed wrong, yet I wanted to know more about him. Where had he gone when he was on leave? It wasn't here in town. I had questions—lots of them—but I was too afraid to start asking them. My worry was not a fear of the answers, but that he would shut me out. That had been a problem when we were together before. Luke would come home, and I could tell he was bothered by what he had seen and done, but he wouldn't talk to me. After he got injured, he refused to talk to me at all. Then everything ended.

I wanted to crawl onto his lap and make out with him and forget all that was troubling me. But I also wanted to crawl into his mind and find out what it was that had hurt him so much that it stole him away from me all those years ago. I wanted to trust him again, completely, without these doubts that kept me up at night.

I studied his beautiful face, lit only by the candles and the setting sun. The burnished orange glow of the remaining light brought out the auburn hues hidden in the dark brown of his hair. His golden skin and shining eyes had me in thrall. He was almost too beautiful to look at. His gaze was steady and sweet on me, and his hand held mine firm and safe in his grip.

I knew we both had expectations of something happening tonight. The anticipation was almost palpable in its intensity. I swayed toward him in my chair. He leaned forward, reaching out to cup my cheek in his big palm. I leaned into that soft touch, that touch I'd rejected once before, and immediately felt bad about it. Regret had burned through me that day, and I hated the thought that I'd hurt him. I turned my lips into his palm and kissed it. His eyes closed briefly as he sifted his fingers into my hair and pulled my face toward his. I was willing, already swaying even further, ever nearer until our lips touched. Once, softly. Twice, deeply. And a third time I wished would never end.

He let go of my hand and pulled my chair closer to his until my legs brushed his and we were side by side. His arm came around me, low across my back, so he could squeeze my hip and pull me even closer. I was about to end up in his lap. It was hard to resist just straddling him and going for it like we'd done in his office the other day. I sighed and looked up at him just as his face lowered to mine for another kiss. We sat there making out, with tongues and hands and everything everywhere, and I was already drunk on him.

Drunk on Luke without a sip of alcohol. I was about to climb into his lap when our waiter came in with our drinks. She cleared her throat and set our drinks down. "I can come back . . ." She was unsurprised at our clinch. I mean, really, it must happen a lot up here.

"That's okay. We'll order," Luke said, then winked at me. I felt my cheeks go up in flames. I looked at the table as he chuckled. He chose for me, ordering everything we couldn't afford when we'd come here almost fifteen years ago plus a fancy bottle of wine that I couldn't even pronounce the name of. I was going to get food wasted, wine wasted, and even drunker on Luke. And if he ordered dessert, I would likely lapse into a happy, sugary, love-induced coma.

In other words, I was in trouble. We had to talk. Not just about the obvious attraction still between us, not about Dylan, and not about the fact that we still loved each other. We needed to talk about the problems we'd had before—the problems that had driven him away from me. What happened in the hospital wasn't the issue; it was the distance between us that had made him leave me and not come back for years. We needed to address the pedestal he had put me on and the fact that for this to work, we both needed to have our feet on the ground. We had to get real and having dinner in this fantasy come to life made it hard for me to muster up the courage or the desire to address any of it.

"You have a good memory, Luke—" I started.

"I remember everything."

"Luke, can we . . . are we . . . um, do you remember right before you left the last time? Before you got hurt? We had a fight. Do you remember that?" I asked softly.

His eyes closed, and he let go of me to reach for his beer and take a sip. "I do remember that. You were upset because you said I wouldn't talk to you, right? I didn't know what to tell you, Lily. I didn't want you to know any of it. I still don't."

I inhaled sharply at the guard I sensed him putting up. "I didn't want details, Luke. I never expected to hear every little thing. I think I told you that. Didn't I?"

He nodded at me.

"I just wanted to be included in your life. You were friends with Liam when you were with me, right? But I never met him. You never even mentioned his name to me. He was a big part of your life and still is. You never told me anything at all. It couldn't have been all bad. Was it?"

"It wasn't all bad, but it was intense, always. When I was with you, you made me feel like myself again, and I wanted that separation. I didn't mean to create a distance between us, Lily, or make you feel left out of part of my life."

"I can't help but think that if you had let me in, even just a little bit, then you wouldn't have left me," I whispered.

"I wanted to shield you from all of that. A lot of it was too ugly to share. You were everything beautiful in my life. I wanted to keep you that way. I didn't want to tarnish you—"

"Tarnish me? I don't even know what to say, other than life is not always beautiful. Sometimes it's terrifying and sad and can break your heart. But you wouldn't let me see your broken heart. You were scared of—what? Driving me away or freaking me out? Like I couldn't handle being there when you needed me, really needed me, for something other than kisses and sex and happy things. Was that it?"

"No, that wasn't it," he bit out. "I didn't want to burden you with it, to drag you down into it. The kisses and the sex and the love you gave me were all I needed from you. God, Lily, it was everything. You were everything I needed, and I—"

We were both startled when our waitress entered with a

tray laden heavy with our dream dinner, and set it at the end of our long table.

"Let's talk about this later, please?" he asked with a soft but tense smile.

I nodded and reached for my drink. We could talk about this later. We had to. So, I did what I always used to do. I buried my worries and gave Luke what he said he wanted. Part of me wanted it too. I wanted to live in this moment and keep the past out of it.

We ate, we chatted about Dylan, about Luke's work, my family, and my career as a librarian. Luke finished his beer and had a small glass of the wine he'd ordered. I put the lemon drop aside and finished off the bottle of wine. It was delicious, and I was so keyed up that I let myself go. I let myself enjoy a fantasy dinner in a beautiful place with this beautiful man who I had loved forever and beyond all reason.

I had an odd sense of freedom, like everything that had been happening wasn't real and I could just float above the earth, over this beautiful river sparkling with moonlight and candles and have a moment of peace.

After dinner, I sat next to Luke, wrapped in his arms on the tiny couch in the corner of the dining room. We gazed out at the river and ate dessert. He turned me in his arms and kissed me. I let him back in my heart tonight, as I knew I always would. I only hoped he would return the favor.

Chapter 21
Luke

I pulled up to the curb at Lily's place and immediately I sensed something was wrong. The front of the house was pitch dark.

Blindly, she reached for me as she looked out the passenger window. "The porch light should be on. It's on a timer." Since the house was set far back from the curb, the trees kept it shaded from the streetlights. It was impossible to see anything from here.

"Stay here and call your dad," I commanded and exited the truck. I started up the dark front path to the door to see if maybe the light had burned out. Halfway there, I stopped and turned back. "The door is wide open. We'll stay out here and wait for your father." I climbed back into the truck and locked the doors. There was no way I would leave her alone. Something was definitely going on.

"He's on his way. He said to stay in the truck."

"I want you to stay with me at my house. Whoever is fucking with you doesn't know where I live. And even if they had my address, they'd never be able to find the place."

"I can't stay with you. We don't even know what happened. It could just be a random robbery, or the door could have blown open from the wind, or the light burned out, or something simple."

"We both know it's not random, Lily. You are in danger. I won't let anything or anyone hurt you or the kids. Trust me, I know how to protect you."

"I know you do. I don't doubt that. But we've just started dating again. I can't move in with you after one date. That's crazy! We're not completely back together yet."

"We are together." I grabbed her hand and kissed it before shoving my seat back and lifting her across the console to sit sideways in my lap, her back to the door, my arm around her waist. She tucked her legs in sideways, knees to the side of my chest, feet to the seat.

"It doesn't work that way, Luke. We're not back together just because you say we are. We have to get it right this time." Her gaze was cast out into the night, watching the house instead of on me.

"It does work that way. Because that's the way it's going to be, Lily. I'm yours, and I always have been. I won't wait for anything when it comes to keeping you all safe."

Her eyes blazed into mine as I declared my intentions. She started to argue. "Calla isn't yours. She's not your responsibility. You've been through enough, and you just got home. None of this is fair to you—"

"Fair? Nothing in my life has ever been fair. And Calla? She's not mine yet, but she will be." Her eyes widened. "Don't argue with me on this, please. You and the kids should stay with me. You can have your own room if you like, for now."

"I'm staying with my parents. The kids are already packed up and there."

"You'll end up with me anyway. It doesn't make sense to move your things twice," I insisted.

Her jaw dropped and a nervous laugh escaped. "Presumptuous, aren't you?"

"Lily, we are inevitable. You know it, but you're scared,

and I don't blame you." I caressed her cheek, turning her face back to mine. "You'll trust me again," I whispered as I leaned down to place a gentle kiss on her lips.

"This has nothing to do with trust, Luke. It's too soon to live together. It's too much pressure for us. We're not ready. Please," she begged.

"In the end, we'll be together like we should have been all along. Calla will be my daughter. If that's a worry for you, forget it. Of course she'll know about Will, just like Dylan knew about me. But she won't ever be without a father's love and protection. I'll adopt her if you let me."

Her eyes welled up as she took a sharp breath in. "Luke . .." she breathed, overcome with emotion. "Please slow down. I don't want to hurt you. I won't let us rush and ruin this. It's too precious to put at risk. We both just got back to Sweetbriar. We have time. We have forever."

"Okay. You'll stay with your parents." I conceded. I never could say no to her, and maybe she was right about moving too fast. My desire to protect her and my desire to have her back in my life had collided, taking my reason away.

She clung to me as she spoke. "Everything in my life has changed so fast. Don't give up on me. Please."

"I'll never give up on you. I will wait forever if I have to. In this life and into the next, I swear it."

She buried her face in my chest and held on to me.

My arms convulsed, squeezing her tighter before I pulled back to kiss her forehead. "I don't know what I would do without you now. When I was gone, I would remember things like this—holding you, being close to you. I lost my head. Someone is out there threatening you and I want to be the one to protect you."

"I get it, I do. I'll be fine with my dad. I promise."

The headlights of Ben's police SUV broke our moment as he headed toward the house, with Cade's cruiser following close behind. They parked, then headed for the front door, guns drawn. Ben put his hand up, indicating we should stay in the truck. He followed swiftly behind Cade, then disappeared up the dark walkway and into the house.

She shuddered in my arms. "I hate this," she whispered. "I hate everyone being in danger because of me."

"How is any of this because of you? And it isn't even because of Will. It's because some asshole he probably busted thinks he can mess with you now that he's dead. He can't, and everything will be okay. I'll make sure of it."

Another police cruiser pulled up behind us and two more officers exited and headed into the house. We held each other in the cab of my truck, eyes glued to the dark-as-pitch front porch.

The not knowing was driving me crazy. I gathered her close and whispered, "Whatever happens, we'll fix it." Ben came out through the front door and began walking down the steps. I shifted her back to her seat, asking her to stay inside as I exited the truck to talk to her father.

Ben clipped his gun back into his shoulder holster. "Whoever it was, they're gone."

"And they trashed Gram's house. She's going to have a fit. They were looking for something and did a thorough job of tearing the place up," Cade added, shaking his head.

Turning at the slam of her door, I pulled her into my side.

"Oh no." Lily gasped. "Can I go in? I need my stuff. I was going to pack."

"I'll take you. Don't touch anything unless I clear it first. Got it?" Ben told her. She nodded and took his hand.

I waited with Cade knowing she would be safe with her father while she packed a few things. "I wanted her to stay with me."

"Bit soon for that, don't you think?" An eyebrow went up as he pointed out the obvious.

"That's what she said, and you're both right. But I want to be there for her and the kids. I need to prove that I am not going anywhere this time. I'm trying not to scare her off by pushing her, but someone is out there threatening her safety and I can't look the other way—"

"Hey, it's going to be okay. You can be there for her even if you aren't living with them. She'll be safe at the house with my parents, you know that."

"I know. I hate everything about this."

"So do I. There is no doubt Will was a good cop. Nothing about this situation sits right with me."

It felt like only a minute or two had passed before Lily and Ben reappeared, walking toward us.

"You're not taking anything?" I asked. Ben shook his head behind Lily's back.

"No, I—maybe tomorrow. Right now, I don't want to touch any of it. I'll ride home with my dad. You don't have to drive all the way out to the house. Will I see you tomorrow?"

"Of course. I'll come by first thing in the morning." I kissed her goodbye and brushed her hair over her shoulder. "Call me if you need me. I mean it—I don't care what time it is." I glanced over at Ben. "Make her call me if she needs me."

He nodded. "Will do, Luke. See you in the morning. Bring Rocky. The kids miss him."

I lifted my chin, kissed her one more time, then took off to pick up Rocky and go home. There was nothing more I could do right now.

Chapter 22
Lily

My mother got up from the couch and rushed over to me the second I crossed through the doorway. It felt good to be engulfed by her the way I'd been as a child. Bumps, bruises, and hurt feelings could always be soothed away by my mother. I wished she could make this situation better too.

I hugged her back as she offered me some hot chocolate and banana bread. I was always willing to be distracted by sweets, so it was easy to say yes and follow her into the kitchen. Asher was sitting at a stool at the center island, sipping his own mug of hot chocolate. I saw the bottle of Bailey's next to his plate and smiled. Even better. Then I frowned when I remembered I couldn't drink it.

"Are you okay, Lily?" Asher asked as I sat next to him on a stool.

I nodded as Mom passed me a slice of banana bread and the Keurig bubbled and brewed out the hot chocolate.

"I laid out some pajamas for you, and you can use my bathroom. Just borrow whichever face wash and lotion you need, honey." Mom handed me my mug.

"Thanks. How were the kids?" It was past their bedtime,

and Dad had already told me on our drive home they were asleep.

"Perfect as usual. Calla has been asleep for about three hours, and Dylan is crashed out with Mark and Mara on the pullout couch upstairs in the living room. They all fell asleep during the movie."

"Good. That's good." I nodded blankly and watched as Asher and Mom exchanged a look. I didn't want to participate in their nonverbal conversation, so I ignored it and sipped my drink. I cupped my hands around the warm mug to take away my sudden chill. I took another sip and stared out the French doors into the darkness outside. I felt a wave of panic coming on as I thought about everything that had happened today.

"Want a bubble bath? I'll run one for you." Without waiting for my answer, she clapped her hands once. "Yes, come upstairs and have a soak in my tub. I have lavender bubbles. Lavender is very relaxing."

I blinked and turned my head toward her. I was frustrated by the concern in her voice, then felt bad for being frustrated. I just wanted to blank out this entire day.

"I just want a shower, then I'm going to bed. Where is the baby monitor?"

"I'll keep it, and you can get some sleep. You look tired."

"Mom, I can take care of Calla. I'm fine," I insisted as I reached for the monitor.

Mom and Asher exchanged another look.

I was officially annoyed. "Seriously, I'm fine."

"I'm crashing on the other couch upstairs, right across from the kids. You don't have to worry about Dylan," Asher said.

"Thanks." I rinsed out my mug and set it in the sink. I hugged my mom, took the baby monitor from her, and headed out of the kitchen. "Good night. Thanks for watching the kids," I called over my shoulder as I went upstairs.

I showered, went to bed, and fell into a restless sleep. I woke up to the sound of Calla crying in the monitor. Disoriented, I looked around the room, trying to figure out where I was. *Home,* I remembered as I got up. I dragged myself into the nursery and saw Mom had beat me there. She had just picked Calla up. She jumped when she turned around and saw me in the doorway.

"Hey, honey. I heard her wake up. You can go back to sleep if you like," she offered as she cuddled Calla.

I shook my head. "I need some water. And I have a headache. Do you have any Advil?" My head was pounding almost as hard as my heart was.

"In the kitchen." She cradled my cheek with her palm, then felt my forehead with the back of her hand like she used to do when I was a kid. "Come on, I'll get you both fixed up." I nodded and followed her to the kitchen. Bypassing the island, I decided to sit at the small table by the window. I watched in a daze as she meandered around the kitchen, warming a bottle of pumped milk for Calla and filling a glass with water for me.

I looked out the bay window behind me. It was so dark tonight. Anything could be happening right outside the window, and I wouldn't be able to see it. I turned around to refocus on Mom and Calla. But I could still feel the dark looming behind me. I was too close to it. I got up quickly, knocking over the chair behind me. "Oh, sorry," I mumbled as I bent to pick it up. My head spun as I stood, my headache making it pound from the quick change in direction.

"It's fine, honey. Just sit down." Mom's voice was soothing, but came at me like I was underwater.

I didn't answer as I stumbled clumsily back into my chair. My heart was pounding too hard to hear anything else. The rapid beat filled my head and echoed in my ears. I tried taking a deep breath, but it didn't help. My chest expanded and contracted, but no air went in or out. I started to pant. The shallow breaths made me feel light-headed.

What is wrong with me?

Every sound in the house rang in my ears. I jumped out of

my chair, knocking it over again as I heard someone at the front door. I ran into the living room to stop them from hurting Mom and Calla. I stopped fast, bumping into the couch when I saw it was just my dad coming home from work.

My heart thumped like a bass drum in my chest. Every beat jolted my body like a shock. My chest felt tight, constricted, crushed like an elephant was standing on it. I pressed my hands to my sternum, trying to slow it down, to ease the pressure.

Was my heart breaking?

My head spun. I could see my mom talking to me, see her mouth moving, but all I could hear was my heartbeat and all I could feel was the dark outside, getting in. I couldn't let it get in. I turned and ran back into the kitchen. I had to close the curtains. I had to keep the dark out. I ran faster when I heard someone running behind me.

My mom shouted, "Ben! Help her, Ben!"

I ran through the archway that led into the kitchen and crashed into someone, falling backward and landing on my ass. I got to my knees and started crawling toward the window. I tried to scream when hands gripped my upper arms and lifted me up, but no sound came out. I tried again. All I could hear was gasping. The hands at my arms turned me around, and I saw my dad in front of me.

Oh, thank God.

"I'm having a heart attack." I managed to tell him. "Am I going to die?" I felt hot tears leak out of my eyes, and I brushed them away.

"Honey, you're only thirty years old. This is no heart attack. But I'm pretty sure you're having a panic attack." Dad's hand was at my wrist. "Your heartbeat is fast but you're not going to die." He picked me up and carried me to the couch in the living room. He sat down with me sideways across his lap, like he'd done when I was a little girl.

"Dahlia, call an ambulance. Better to be safe," he said.

"I already did. They're on the way. It's okay, honey. The paramedics will be here in two minutes."

Calla started to cry. I tried to get up, but Dad held me firmly in his arms.

"Stay still, sweetheart. Rest." I struggled against his hold. I had to get to my baby.

"Calla. She needs me," I argued.

"Your mama has the baby. She's okay, she's okay, everything's going to be okay. I've got you, and you're safe. I won't let anything happen to my girls." he stroked my hair as he crooned and pressed my cheek back into his chest.

"Calla is fine, honey. She just needs her bottle. See?" Mom rushed back through the archway that divided the family room and kitchen and sat down on the chair across from the couch.

I could see that Calla was fine and slurping away at her bottle. I nodded and relaxed back into Dad's arms.

"Have I lost my mind?" I whispered.

"No, darlin', you've just had one hell of a day. In fact, you've had one hell of a last two years." He rocked me gently. "And I'm glad that you're here with me and your mom when it all finally hit you. This was bound to happen."

"You keep everything inside, Lily," Mom said. "It has to come out. If you don't let it out, it will force its way."

I nodded as tears crept down my cheeks to land on my chest. I had done this to myself, of course.

The front door burst open. Cade ran in, followed by Levi and a paramedic I didn't recognize. Great. Mom called nine-one-one, and of course my brothers were the ones to respond.

Cade rushed over to me and knelt in front of the couch. "Lily," he said, then he looked up at Dad. "What's wrong?"

"Cade, move," Levi ordered as he rushed over. He was wearing a paramedic uniform and carried a case full of supplies. He'd been a paramedic before becoming a firefighter. I didn't know he still did it.

"Panic attack," Dad said. I closed my eyes in embarrassment.

Levi nodded and put a blood pressure cuff on my arm. He smiled at me and patted my leg. I'd never had a panic attack before. I had been anxious before. I had freaked out a little bit here and there. But I had never lost my shit to the point that I didn't know what was going on. It scared me.

Trying to reassure myself as much as my family, I said, "I think I'm okay now."

Levi nodded his agreement. "Pressure is normal," he said as he removed the cuff. "How do you feel? Want to ride in the ambo?" He grinned at me. "I'll put on the lights and everything. You can sit up front."

I shook my head. "No thanks, Levi. I'm just embarrassed now."

"Nothing to be embarrassed about, Lil. Feel better, okay?"

I nodded as he packed up his bag and left with his partner.

I shifted off Dad's lap and tucked myself into the corner of the couch. Cade pulled a throw blanket from the chair he was sitting on and covered me. I burrowed under it and thought about my life and how I'd screwed it up. I'd lost my mind tonight. Now that I was thinking clearly, I was horrified that I'd let myself get so out of control. My mother was probably right; I kept too much inside. What I had been doing was no longer working.

In the spirit of change . . . "Mom, will you take care of Calla tonight? I think you were right, and I need to sleep."

She sat there and just blinked at me. I must have shocked her. "Yes. Yes, I will. And you can sleep in too. Lily, darling, you don't have to worry about a thing." Her smile was caring and genuine.

I needed to get it through my head that she *wanted* to help me. Accepting her help did not make me weak, or needy. It made me smart. No one could do it all, and what happened to me tonight was all the proof I needed. I thought about Calla and Dylan as adults. Would I still want to be there for them? Be a part of their lives? I absolutely would, and I would be hurt if they didn't let me. I needed help. I was drowning and exhausted, and I felt ridiculous.

"Thank you for taking care of me." I leaned over to hug my dad. He squeezed me back.

I got up and kissed my mom on the cheek. "I love you, Mom," I whispered. I took a step back and almost crashed into Cade. Wow, he was fast.

He wrapped me into a big bear hug and whispered into my ear, "You can talk to me, Lily. I expect you to. Please?"

I nodded against his chest. Best brother ever. To be fair, I could say that about any one of my brothers, but Cade was right here, so he got the honor for the moment.

"Promise," I whispered back after he let me go. "I'm going to crash," I announced. "Good night, guys."

After I crawled back into bed, I thought again about the day I'd had—the car chase, my stolen phone, the awesome date with Luke. But this time, I thought about how I *felt* about all of it. I never thought about how I felt. I mean, I had feelings, but I usually just ended up trying to bury them and get on with it. I stared up at the dark ceiling, trying to analyze my day.

Is this what people do?

If I didn't know how to process what I felt, then I couldn't process my confusion about how to process my feelings.

Gah, I'm an idiot.

My eyes shot to the door as it opened and light from the hallway shined in. My mom stood in the doorway. I could feel her eyes on me, probably checking on me.

"I'm awake," I announced. I saw her smile as she crossed the threshold and closed the door behind her.

She threw back the covers and crawled in the bed next to me. "Come here," she demanded, opening her arms.

I turned to face her and just stared at her.

"Come here," she repeated. I scooted over, and she wrapped her arms around me and pulled my face to her chest.

At first, I just lay there stiffly, unable to relax.

"*Shh*," she whispered in my ear.

I remembered that—that whispery hush in my ear when she used to hold me and comfort me as a child. Tears filled my eyes, and I melted into her arms, just like I had when I was a little girl.

"*Shh*, you're okay now."

I wrapped my arm around her waist and tucked my other hand under my cheek.

"You don't need to talk right now if you don't want to. But you do need to let me be here for you," she said.

I nodded against her, and she hugged me tighter.

"I don't know what I'm doing," I whispered.

"Oh, honey, none of us do," she whispered back.

I didn't believe that. She always seemed to have the answers. "You do," I insisted.

"Just yesterday, I was crying to Gram and Delphine because you wouldn't talk to me, and I was worried about you."

Surprised, I glanced up at her face, and she smiled at me. "Oh," I said.

She wiped the tears from my cheek and squeezed me tighter. "You used to talk to me, until you were about five or six." She laughed softly. "After that, you were all about Luke and Rose. I would see you three, whispering to each other, giggling together, and it made me happy and sad at the same time. Happy that you were all so close, but sad because you're my baby and I wanted you to confide in me too. Rose wasn't quiet like you. She let it all hang out. No secrets with that one. You were always my little mystery girl."

"I don't talk to Luke like that anymore. We went out tonight and—" I sighed. I don't even know what he did for all these years when he was home on leave. I have never met Liam before, and they were friends when we were still together. He has secrets, or just stuff he doesn't want to talk about. He thinks he has to protect me, but I don't like that. I don't expect to know every little detail about his life without me, but I don't like how it makes me feel. I feel like I can't talk freely. It feels like there are things that will push him away if I say them out loud." It felt good to talk to my mother, to confide in her. These thoughts were like thorns, poking me from the inside, and now they were out.

"He's been through a lot. It probably hurts to talk about some of it. He's in therapy. I can only assume he's getting it out that way," she said.

"That's good, but, well, I guess I feel left out. We used to talk about everything, and it was easy."

"He's always put you on a pedestal. But after you two fell in love, I could tell that he was sort of in awe of you, like he couldn't believe he'd gotten so lucky and didn't want to ruin it."

I nodded. When we first got together, I'd thought I was the luckiest girl in the world to have a boyfriend who was so romantic and giving. "That was becoming a problem between us. Sometimes I wanted to be the one to take care of him, to comfort him or just talk about what he was going through." I paused, remembering. "But then he got hurt, and it was too late because he was gone."

"Did you talk about it back then? The distance between the two of you?" she asked.

I didn't want to admit the truth, but I did it anyway. "No. I didn't. I just waited for him to tell me on his own. I would ask questions, and I wouldn't argue when he deflected them. I never told him it bothered me."

"Honey, you aren't exactly an open book, you know. You keep everything inside. If you want him to be open, you have to do it too."

"I could tell he was hurting and I didn't want to make it worse. Instead, I caused a problem."

"I don't think either one of you *caused* it. It just grew from each of you trying to protect the other. Luke was never any good at asking for what he needed, something I blame his dad for. After Diana died, Chuck closed himself off and Luke was pretty much alone in that house. Jed and I tried to get him to let Luke live here or move in with Jed. But Chuck wouldn't hear of it. 'What would people think?'"

I looked up at her, surprised. I never knew she'd tried to help Luke get away from his dad.

"I know!" she exclaimed. "You need to seduce him."

My head shot back at that odd change of topic. *What?*

"What?" I said, shocked.

"I'm not kidding myself. I know you guys have had sex before. Obviously. You have a child together. But just . . . jump him. Shock him." She shook her head and said matter-of-factly, "Get off that pedestal, Lily. You need to be on equal footing."

I was still agape. "What?" I repeated.

"Normally, I would never tell one of my daughters such a thing. But it's Luke. He loves you, and he always has. He needs to see you as an equal, not as a fragile angel he needs to protect. So, yeah, seduce him. Wear something red and sexy and jump his bones."

"Oh my God. So you're telling me to use sex to get what I want?" I laughed.

"Normally, that would be terrible advice. But in this case, I think it might work. I love you both. You belong together. Sex muddles men's brains. Get his mind good and muddled, then make your point."

She's nuts, but she might be right. "I'll think about it, but we're not talking about this ever again."

I felt her nod against the top of my head. "Okay, we won't. But one more thing—you must talk to him too. It won't work if you expect him to bare all his deepest feelings and you keep yours to yourself. Now I'm done, and I won't bring it up ever again."

"Thanks, Mom. For the insane advice, and for checking on me."

She laughed. "You're welcome, honey. Thanks for letting me be here with you. I've missed you." She kissed my cheek, then got up. "Sleep tight. Love you, baby."

"Love you too. Good night." She closed the door behind her. When the room was once again bathed in darkness, I shut my eyes and fell asleep.

Chapter 23
Luke

I stood with Calla in my arms in the doorway to Lily's old room at her parent's house surrounded by Dylan, Mark, and Mara. We were waiting for her to wake up, but the light snoring coming from her bed indicated that she was sound asleep, and I was glad she was finally getting the rest she needed.

When I arrived earlier this morning, Dahlia told me she'd had a panic attack. I wished I were here to help her last night, but I was grateful she wasn't alone when it hit.

Her voice called out from with the cocoon of covers she nestled in. "I'm up. You guys can come in."

Dylan, Mark, and Mara rushed through to go to her. They were just as worried as I was.

"Aunt Lily!"

"Mommy!"

But there was no tackling, no jumping. Just gentle hugs.

"Good morning. Did you have fun last night?" Her question was interrupted by Rocky bounding through the door and hopping up to join the kids.

She smiled at me. "Come on, Luke, don't be scared."

Chuckling, I made my way to the bed and sat on the edge.

She grabbed Calla and kissed her cheeks, cuddling her close.

"Are you better, Aunt Lily?" Mara asked, placing her hand to Lily's forehead. "Daddy said you were sick last night."

"I'm fine now, Mara. You don't have to worry about me anymore."

"Good. Let's go see if Grandma will make pancakes for breakfast," she said to the boys. Mark got up to follow, but Dylan stayed put.

"I'll come in a minute," he told Mara before sitting next to Lily. "Are you really better? I heard Uncle Levi talking about your pressure and your blood when I was on the stairs listening. Uncle Asher made me come back to bed. He said you were going to be okay, and I should go back to sleep so you wouldn't worry about me. So, are you okay? What was on your arm?" Her eyes closed, as if she were gathering strength before answering him.

"I had an anxiety attack." I tightened my arm around her but kept quiet so she could explain it to him in her own way.

"I got too tired and too worried about everything going on. I woke up to get Calla when she cried, and I wasn't thinking clearly. I scared Grandma and Grandpa, and they called an ambulance. Uncle Levi was the paramedic who came over. Uncle Cade came too."

"I saw Grandpa carry you. I saw you sitting on his lap," Dylan said, clearly still worried about her.

"I'm sorry you saw that and I'm sorry I scared you. But I'm okay now, I promise. I let them help me feel better, and I'll keep letting them help, so I don't get so tired or worried again. I promise you, I'm okay, Dylan."

He hugged her. "Okay, Mommy. I love you."

"I love you, bug," she whispered.

"Is Dad going to take care of you too?"

"Yes I am." I answered him. "I'm always going to take care of your mom. And you too, Dylan. I'm sorry I wasn't here last night." I turned my attention to Lily. "I would have been if I'd known you needed me."

She looked at me over the top of Dylan's head. "It happened fast. I had been asleep. Maybe I should have called you, but I went back to bed when it was over. The kids were okay. Asher and everyone was here with them."

"Lily, if you're about to apologize to me, don't. I understand, and I'm here now. Don't worry."

She nodded, then leaned forward and kissed me softly. On the lips.

"You kissed my mom."

"I love your mom," I said. It was simple, as it should be. As it would be.

"And I love Luke. And we both love you," she added.

"Do you love Calla?" he asked.

"How could I not? She might just be the cutest baby girl I've ever seen. Plus, she's yours and your mom's. She might not be my blood, but she has all of my love."

"I love you," he whispered.

"Love you too. And I always will. All of you, I promise," I whispered back. I heard a muffled sob and looked up in time to see Dahlia wipe her eyes and rush through the doorway.

After breakfast, Lily and I got in my truck to drop Rocky off with Jed, and then Lily at Violet's before I headed off to meet with Liam at the office. We were talking about nothing, listening to music, and enjoying the sunny summer morning when we were interrupted by my phone ringing over the Bluetooth connection. "Hey, Liam."

"Luke," he greeted. I snapped to attention. He didn't sound right. "I'll meet you tomorrow. I'm not feeling well." I did not like the way he sounded. It made me uneasy.

"Sure, man. Get some rest." I disconnected the call while contemplating if I should drive over and check on him.

"I don't like the way he sounded," Lily and I both said, almost in unison.

"I'm going to stop by and check on him."

She nodded and I was glad that she'd noticed it too.

I made a left off Main Street and headed up into the residential neighborhood on the bluff where Liam's rental house was. I was tense in my seat. Something in his voice had me seriously on edge.

After I pulled into Liam's driveway and the second I got my door open, Rocky launched himself from the back seat, over my shoulder to land on the floor of the truck by my feet. He jumped out of the truck and raced for the front porch. He immediately started scratching the door and barking.

"Liam, open up!" I pounded on the door. Rocky started whining, then howling.

"Kick it in, Luke," Lily said.

I didn't stop to think. I took a step back and kicked hard. The door flew open, and Rocky rushed through our legs, darting past us into the house.

"I don't want to do this," Liam said. He was on his couch with tears running down his face. He gestured to a gun sitting in the middle of the coffee table. Rocky hopped up onto Liam's lap while I carefully grabbed the gun, quickly unloaded, and took it apart, setting the pieces on the side table by the couch.

"I took a couple of these," Liam said and gestured to a mostly full prescription bottle sitting next to a half-empty bottle of whiskey on the coffee table.

Rocky barked softly and burrowed into Liam's side. Liam wrapped his arms around him and cried into his fur.

"Call nine-one-one," I told Lily.

"I already did. They'll be here any minute," she whispered.

I sat by Liam on the couch, unsure of how to help him.

"She died, Luke. She made me feel normal again, and now she's gone. I have no one left now. I wasn't even there when it happened. She was all alone." He sobbed as Rocky licked the tears from his cheek.

"Shit, Liam, she's gone?" Tears filled my eyes too, but I blinked them away and wrapped my arm around his shoulder. "Elsie's gone?" Liam wasn't the only one she had helped. Every leave I'd had, I'd spent with Liam and Elsie at her place. She'd taken care of both of us. She'd treated me like I was her grandson too. "I can't believe it. I just saw her yesterday. She was looking so much better. I'm so sorry."

"I didn't mean to do any of this. I drank too much." Liam looked me and Lily in turn before addressing me again. "I wasn't going to do it. I swear. I don't know what I was thinking —" He choked on the words before hiding his face in his hands.

I related all too well to the despair my friend was feeling. "You'll be okay, Liam. We're going to take care of you."

He looked at me with an almost imperceptible nod. "I'm sorry. I didn't want to be alone. I couldn't stand how it felt." He shut his eyes and sagged into me. Whether from grief or from the pills and alcohol, I couldn't tell.

Rocky whined, then licked and nudged Liam's face. He barked in his ear, forcing his eyes to open.

"You're not alone, Liam. Don't apologize. Not to me. You've pulled me back from the edge before, brother. Now it's my turn. Stay with me." I shook him. He was struggling to focus.

"I didn't know how to tell you she passed. I got drunk and—"

We jumped when we heard the sirens out front. Lily rushed to the door to let them in. But it was already open.

The paramedics made quick work of loading Liam up in the ambulance. I had to go with him; I couldn't let him face this alone. "I'm going with him," I told Lily. "Can you take care of Rocky and get someone to fix the door?" I gave her my wallet and the keys to the truck. "My credit card is in there. I'll pay for the door. Use my truck." I kissed her hard and short. "Love you. I'll call you."

The ride to the hospital was a blur. I followed alongside Liam's stretcher as far as they would let me go before I was directed to a waiting room.

Lily texted a few times, but I ignored it. I would text her back when I had an update on what was going on with Liam.

I got up to pace the waiting room. This reminded me of when we were laid up together after the IED attack. My back had been injured and I'd been shaken up, cut, bruised, and in need of stitches. Liam had been knocked unconscious after suffering a severe concussion. I'd had a mild head injury, but luckily, had remained alert enough to get us to safety.

Flashes from the past infiltrated my thoughts as I walked the waiting room. It was as though I wasn't in a brightly lit hospital but back on the ground, dust flying everywhere as I looked to the side, praying that Liam would be okay before I drifted off into the black.

I sat down hard, dragging my hands through my hair and pressing my palms into my eyes to get the images to go away, but they wouldn't. The sterile white walls and florescent lights pulsed as I looked around, trying to force myself back to reality. My heart beat a rapid tempo in my ears. I was out of control. I itched; the memories burned like sand, gritty and course against my skin. Panic overtook logic as I gasped for breath and slammed my eyes shut against the onslaught of sensation.

Breathe. Focus. Liam's voice saying those words floated through my mind. Goodness knows I'd heard them often enough over the years. I grabbed onto the mantra like it was a hand to hold. Taking a deep breath, I looked around the waiting room, forcing my eyes back to the present. Inhaling to a count of four, I chose a potted fig tree in the corner to focus on. There were no potted fig trees in Afghanistan, at least not where I had been. I counted backward and let out the breath.

"Luke McCabe?"

Startled, I stood. "Yes. I'm here," I wheezed.

"Liam is asking for you. Come with me." I followed behind the nurse. Her flowery pink scrubs and sweet, smiling face serving as a reminder that I was home. She gestured to an open door. "Go on in. He's going to be okay."

"Thank you." I went inside, shutting the door behind myself. "How are you feeling?" He looked fine, back to normal. His eyes were bright, and he smiled as I approached.

"I feel like an idiot. I'm so sorry, Luke."

"No apologies. Not between us. You look a lot better." I couldn't quite believe what I was seeing.

"I feel better, at least physically. I was pretty fucked up earlier, drunk as shit. Now I remember why I stopped drinking. Never again, man. Elsie would be pissed." His face twisted painfully as his eyes filled with tears. He inhaled a shuddering sigh and looked out the window.

"I think she would understand," I murmured. "I do."

"I wasn't going to do it, Luke." His jaw steeled as he lifted his chin.

I pulled the chair close to his bed and sat. "I'm glad to hear that—"

"But it scares me how close I got. Like a switch was flipping in my mind as I sat there. Stay or go. I was about to unload the gun when you got there. But that doesn't mean I don't need help."

"I'm here for you."

He met my eyes. "I know you are."

"I think you should stay at my place. It's fucking huge. It's ridiculous for me to have all that space to myself. Neither one of us needs to be alone now."

"I think I'll take you up on that. I should be out of here tomorrow." He yawned, rolling his shoulders then reclining the bed.

"Good. I'll go and let you get some rest. My phone is on. Call me whenever, any time. I'll pick you up tomorrow."

"Call Lily. Tell her I'm sorry when you see her. I'll tell her myself when I get out of here."

"I will. I'll see you soon. I'm going to find her and make sure she's okay."

The white walls blurred into an empty tunnel as I headed for the exit. All I wanted to do was go home and be alone to sort my feelings into something I could handle talking about.

Chapter 24
Lily

Hours had passed. I had called and texted Luke several times with no answer. I was getting frantic. It took some time to get someone to secure the door. Then, embarrassingly, I had to have Rose pick me up because I was too short to drive Luke's truck. I'd locked it up and left it in Liam's driveway. After Rose and I dropped Rocky off with Jed, I decided to make the drive to the hospital and check on them myself.

I finally made it to Liam's room and peeked in the doorway. He was lying in bed, his eyes opened and staring at the wall when I stepped through.

His head whipped toward me and his face fell. "Lily. I'm so sorry," he said softly.

"Liam, there is nothing to be sorry for. I'm just glad you're still here." I crossed to him and took his hand. "I don't know you that well yet, but I know enough to say I would miss you if you were gone."

He smiled at me. I squeezed his hand.

"Is Luke still around here somewhere? He hasn't been answering his phone."

Liam's eyes showed concern. "No. He didn't call you? He said he was going to."

I shook my head.

"Go to him, Lily. Don't let him push you away."

I stood straighter. "He won't push me away. I'm done with that. Any idea where he went?" Liam shook his head. "He said he was going to find you. Try his house."

I leaned over and kissed his cheek. "You're not alone, Liam. You're part of the family. You are Uncle Liam, okay? Don't forget it," I whispered.

His head jolted back with surprise, then a small smile lit his face. "I won't forget. Find our boy," he murmured.

I nodded, then headed out, driving as quickly as I dared to Luke's house.

I ran to the front door and pounded on it. No answer.

I tried the doorknob. Locked.

I stepped back to kick it in like Luke had done earlier, then reality struck me. There was no way could I kick in a door. I pounded again, then rang the bell.

"Damn it, Luke, let me in!" I shouted. Still, no answer. I knew he was in there. His truck was in the driveway. He had to have picked it up, then come home.

I stopped for a minute to plan my next move, then remembered that Luke had given me a set of his keys. With shaking hands, I pulled them out of my pocket, found the right one, and let myself in. I rushed through the doorway and frantically looked around. I found him on his couch.

He quickly wiped his cheeks with his hands and stood up when he saw me. "Lily, what are you doing here?"

"What am I doing here? Where else would I be, Luke?" I burst out. The adrenaline left me once I saw he was okay. Cold fear replaced it when I saw the blank expression in his eyes as I took a step toward him.

He stepped back. "I need to be alone right now. Can I call you later?" He was cold, distant. My Luke was gone.

I felt myself start to retreat. But I managed to gain some courage and stood my ground. "I don't think you should be alone right now. I can just sit with you, or I could fix you a snack, or a drink—"

"No, thank you. I want to—I just need to . . . Damn it, Lily, just go, and I'll call you later. I can't do this right now," he barked.

I flinched, but I wasn't about to give up. "Do *this*? Is nothing going to change? You can be there for me, even when I don't want you to, but I can't be there for you when you so obviously need me? I'm not going. You don't have to talk to me, but I won't let you be alone."

"I want to be alone, and it has nothing to do with you," he insisted.

"It has to do with both of us. Being with someone isn't always going to be good times, sunshine, and rainbows, Luke. You have to let me be with you in the bad times too."

"Lily, you don't understand this. There is no way you could."

"Maybe not, but you're beating yourself up, blaming yourself for things out of your control. You feel responsible for Liam, and for other things you won't talk about. I see the ghosts in your eyes, and I always have. I have seen the way you talk to Liam and to Jed. I know you talk about your past with them, and I don't know if I have the right to ask for details. Honestly, I don't even want details unless you want to give them to me. But I think I have the right to know you're hurting when it's affecting us, when it takes you away from me. You're here, but you're not with me. You promised no more running. If we can't be honest, then what do we have?"

"I don't know!" he cried. "We have each other, don't we?"

"Do we? If so, then tell me what you need, so I can give it to you," I implored. "But don't tell me to leave. I can't do that." *Please listen to me, Luke, please.*

"I've taken too much from you, Lily," he insisted again.

196

"You have not. I want to give my love to you. But if you can't let me in, then we have nothing."

He just stared at me with that cold, undecipherable look on his face. His blank eyes cut through me. God, it hurt.

"I don't understand why you even wanted me back if things are going to be the same. I'll just leave you alone then." Feeling stupid and hurt, I turned away from him and stumbled as I rushed toward the door, trying to get out before the tears started falling.

I heard his boots pounding over the floor behind me. I was almost to the door when I felt his arms band around my waist from behind. His lips touched my neck. "Don't leave, Lily, please. I don't want to be alone anymore."

I melted back into him. *He heard me.*

His arms split; one banded around my hips and the other across my chest with his palm under my chin, turning my face to his. He kissed me hard.

"I need you." He kissed me again, tongue pushing harshly into my mouth. He abruptly released me and stepped back.

"Then take what you need, Luke," I offered.

"I want you. I need *you*. I am tired of feeling like a dead man walking. I feel alive when I'm with you."

I reached up and pushed the straps of my sundress down, letting it fall to the floor, leaving me in my underwear and heels. I looked over my shoulder at him. "Then take me."

I felt his hard chest hit my back as he wrapped me up in his arms, moving us toward the couch in the living room. All the while his hands moved over my body, cupping my breasts, between my legs. He continued kissing me, my lips, my neck. Kissing and nibbling his way over my shoulders as he pushed the straps of my bra down. I felt him kneel behind me as he unhooked it and tossed it aside. Kisses rained down over my back as he pushed my panties down my hips. I stepped out of them and kicked them aside just in time for him to reach up and put a big warm palm between my shoulder blades before pushing me gently over the side of the couch. I felt his breath between my legs. He kissed the inside of my thigh. I felt him at my center, his tongue entering me, his hands spanning my hips, pulling me into his face, fingers reaching around to swirl right where I needed it.

"Oh, God, Luke," I gasped.

He groaned against my skin. "Can I be inside you?"

"Yes."

He abruptly stood. His shirt flew over my head to land in front of me on the couch. I heard his boots, then his belt buckle hitting the floor. I felt his warm skin and the hard muscles of his torso against my back. His chest hair tickled me in the most delicious way as he kissed my neck and his thick length rubbed between my folds. Then he shoved into my body, pushing into me with rough, delicious strokes.

His tears hit my back as he relentlessly pounded inside me, somehow breaking my heart and mending it back together at the same time. He traced the top of my spine with featherlight kisses as his hands dug into my hips to pull me back into his thrusts before he suddenly stopped and stepped away.

Confused, I turned my head to look at him.

He steadied me and moved around me to sit on the couch. "Jesus, Lily." His voice was broken when he asked, "Did I hurt you?"

"You didn't hurt me. Is that why you stopped?"

"Yes."

"Stop hiding how you feel. I want you, Luke. I want the real you, without the apologetic mask. Quit protecting me and just be with me."

"But I have to protect you," he insisted. He moved his hands to my waist, gently caressing me as he gazed up into my eyes.

"Rejecting me is not protecting me. Leaving me is not protecting me." I kicked off my heels, stepped closer, then climbed onto his lap, my knees on the cushions on either side of him.

"I never wanted you to see me out of control like this. I need to be by myself to get a handle on it," he said. It broke my heart that he still felt this way.

"No, you don't." I sank down, taking him back inside.

He inhaled sharply as his head dropped forward to my chest.

I cradled his face between my palms, lifting his face to mine. Wiping the tears from his cheeks, I kissed each one. "I love you, Luke. I don't want you to be alone anymore. Let me in," I whispered against his lips.

"Lily—don't stop." His eyes burned into mine as I rode him slowly, gently. His hands tightened on my hips, then caressed up my ribcage to glide softly over my breasts, over my face, then into my hair. With a light tug, he brought my lips to his and kissed me tenderly.

"I want all of you. The happy and sad, the angry and scared. Everything. It's all I ever wanted."

He gripped my hips in his big palms, and I gasped as he stood up, driving himself all the way inside me. "Wrap your legs around me," he ordered. "I'm taking you to my bed."

I did as he said, and he walked us to the staircase and up. We were still connected. Each step ground him into me in all the best places until I was almost mindless with the feelings coursing through my body. I wound my arms around his neck and held on. I loved how his big body felt against mine as he moved. But feeling him inside me, finally back where he belonged, was euphoric.

He was all I could see as he walked us through the huge upstairs hallway to his room.

He stopped at his doorway, pressing my back against his door as he thrust up into me.

"Yes, Luke." I gripped his big shoulders and writhed against him as we came together against the door. He buried his face into my neck with a soft groan, slid out of me, and shifted me up higher with his hands on my behind.

He looked at me with a grin and opened the door behind me, took a few more steps, then let go so I fell to my back on his bed. He knelt between my legs, lowering himself over me, bracing his arms on either side of my head. I tucked my legs against his sides as he kissed me deep, tangling my tongue with his own.

"I'm not done," he said between kisses. "That was too fast. I haven't had nearly enough. We can talk after."

"Are you with me now?" I whispered.

Something primal that I had only ever felt with him flowed between us as our eyes met. He whispered back, "I'm with you, Lily. I'll never leave you. On my life, I swear it." Then he kissed me again.

He took my hands in his and held them, interlacing our fingers as he entered me slowly. "You feel so good. You feel like home," he whispered.

"Luke . . ." My breath hitched because I felt it too.

Home.

I was finally where I was meant to be. Tears spilled down my cheeks. I couldn't stop them. One of his hands let go of mine and wiped them away. But the other hand held tight, and I knew—*I knew*—that he was never letting go again.

"I love you, Lily. I never stopped, and I never will. You have me back, you have me." I felt his labored breaths against my ear as he whispered those words. The hand at my cheek moved down, between our bodies.

"Come with me again." He gave me what I needed to push me closer to the edge. I wrapped my legs around his hips, and he thrust harder.

"Yes," I cried into his mouth. His tongue touched mine, and I felt myself come apart. But he wasn't done giving me more, faster, even harder. I jolted with each thrust, ran my fingers into his hair, and held on tight. My head flew back as it hit me. He buried his face into my neck and shoved his arm around my hips to lift them so he could get deeper. I had it all —his weight on me, his hand held in mine. I sighed while his beautiful body surrendered and he filled me.

When I was finally able to speak, I murmured, "I love you too."

He shifted to his back and pulled me on top of him. I nestled closer. He hugged me tighter.

"I had no intention of leaving you," he finally said. I nodded and moved to lie on my side next to him. He rolled over to face me. "I didn't intend to do a lot of things, Lily. But leaving you was the stupidest thing I've ever done. I let years slip through my fingers."

"That's over now," I insisted.

He shook his head. "Is it?"

"Where are we?" I kissed his chest, right next to a jagged little scar.

He grinned. "In my bed."

"Yep, all naked in your bed. You're not leaving this time. I won't let it happen. Plus, you're getting help, and that makes a huge difference."

"I just wanted to think today, to sort it all out in my head. I was about to call Jed. I didn't want to dump it all on you."

"Love is all about dumping on each other," I informed him as he laughed and grabbed my hip, pushing me to lie on my back.

"I want to see you. Naked Lily, finally in my bed where you belong."

I pushed my body back against his chest. "No, it's too bright in here. And I don't look the same."

He frowned. "You're beautiful. What are you talking about?" His hands on my skin made me feel beautiful, but my insecurities about my body had taken over.

"I've had two kids, Luke. Things aren't as tight and smooth as they used to be."

He grabbed my behind and squeezed, making me giggle. Then his hands started wandering, up over my breasts, back down over my waist. I shut my eyes. "Hmm, your tits are bigger." I gasped, before a startled giggle escaped. "Your hips are rounder but that only makes your waist feel smaller. And your ass . . ." He gave it another squeeze. "All I see is beauty and all I feel is *you.*"

"I have scars, from Calla," I whispered.

"I have scars too, and none of them are from something as beautiful as Calla." He sat up and grabbed my hands when I moved to cover myself.

"Uh-uh," he said. "Don't hide from me."

I relaxed, and he let my hands go. His eyes traveled over me, followed by his hands, softly moving over my skin. He stopped at the scar from my C-section. "Is this it?"

I nodded, and he bent down to kiss it, tickling my skin with his beard.

"And where is the one from Dylan?" His lips quirked up at the corner. He knew.

"Uh, you already kissed that one. Earlier, on the couch."

He smirked. "Should I kiss it again?" His smile now was pure flirty Luke. It transported me back to the past when our love had been simple and easy.

"You can kiss that one whenever you want. I recommend you do it often because it hurt worse." I laughed as my insecurities flew away. I suddenly felt silly for even having them in the first place. I sat up. "My turn. I want to see yours."

He smiled and held his arms wide. "Go for it."

I started with the one on his chest that I'd discovered a few minutes ago, right below his nipple. I kissed it and laughed when it made his muscle flex. "Ticklish?"

"Some things never change. Be careful," he warned on a grin.

I pushed his shoulders to make him lie on his back. He relaxed into the bed with a grin. "I have a lot of scars, baby.

This could take a while. And mine aren't pretty little pink and white ribbons like yours are."

"I'm going to kiss them all better, Luke. No matter how long it takes. I'm going to know you again, every inch."

His eyes grew serious. "Don't ever let me go, Lily," he said.

"Never, Luke. You're mine, and I'm yours, and it will stay that way. Forever."

He pulled me down on top of him and wrapped me in his arms.

Chapter 25
Luke

"We should get up." I opened my eyes at Lily's whisper, mentally rejecting her words because I liked it right where I was. Lily was draped across my chest and I could feel every inch of her warm, sweet body against mine. Her beautiful hair was spread out behind her as she traced meandering patterns across my skin.

I was in sensory overload. The dream I'd had since I'd left her had finally come true. I was in heaven, and I did not want to move. This was the moment I'd been hoping to have from the moment I laid eyes on her again. I hugged her tighter against me and shook my head.

"I have to get the kids from my mother. Rocky is there, and we should bring the kids to go see Liam," she murmured against my chest. Despite her words, she pulled me closer, tucking herself tighter against me.

I couldn't get close enough to her. Even being inside her wasn't close enough. My heart was bursting at the seams while tears pricked against the back of my eyes. I wanted her to need me. I was desperate for it, because I needed her so much. I trembled when she kissed me gently across my chest. I sifted my hand through the hair at her nape, and she leaned forward to give me better access. She'd always loved it when I played with her hair. Funny how this could feel so new yet so familiar at the same time.

I pulled her hair gently to tip her head back so I could look at her face. I got distracted by her expectant smile, so I kissed her before I answered her. "You're right. But first, I have to confess something. I understand where Liam's head was at."

Her smile turned soft with concern, and she nodded encouragement.

"I understand it because I have been there—without hope, feeling alone, and desperate for the pain to stop. It was after I got hurt, after I came home. I didn't go as far as he did, not nearly. The thoughts were enough to scare me. I called Jed, then later got help from my therapist. But I have felt that way before. I thought you should know. Toward the end, right before the explosion, I was starting to doubt everything I had done. It was getting harder to stay away from you. I had so many regrets and carried so much shame for abandoning you. Then the explosion happened, friends died, Liam came close, and I knew right then that I had been a fool for leaving. My life flashed in front of me, and every mistake I'd made was at the forefront. Then I got home, and Jed told me I had a son. The magnitude of my choices hit me, and at that moment, I felt I didn't deserve a second chance with you or any chance with Dylan. I thought maybe you would be better off if I had just died. I was lucky that I had Jed, so lucky that I had him to talk to . . ."

"Thank you for telling me, Luke," she murmured softly. I opened my eyes. I needed to see her to believe she was really here. "It means a lot that you would share that with me. I can't even begin to tell you how glad I am that you are still here. I have no words except I love you and I thought of you every day you were gone. Every time I looked into Dylan's eyes, I saw you. And I ached for what could have been. I knew you were suffering—there was no way you would have left me if you'd been in your right frame of mind." The love shining from her eyes warmed me straight to my soul. The way she understood me was a miracle.

"I want to kiss you," I blurted.

"So, do it," she said. Her eyes drifted shut as I kissed her hard. I turned with her held in my arms until she was beneath me again. Her thighs pressed high against my sides, and her arms wrapped around my back. I shifted my weight to my forearms so I wouldn't crush her.

"I think the lesson has finally sunk in," I whispered between kisses. "I won't keep things from you anymore. I want to be like we were before I enlisted." I couldn't help it; I was hard again, and she was right there, open and ready for me, wanting me, so I slipped inside.

She groaned into my mouth and pushed her hips up. I would never get enough of her. She was in my blood, under my skin. I had to have her.

"So, we're sharing all our secrets again?" She gasped against my mouth. I nodded and watched a smile light up her face. "I missed that. I missed you, so much, Luke. I'm glad you're back. I'm glad *we're* back." Her head pressed back into the pillow as I moved inside her. Her back arched, crushing her breasts up against my chest.

I wanted to see. I wanted to touch. I rose to my knees and watched her body react as I took her. She was so fucking beautiful.

"You never have to miss me again, Lily. I promise." I grabbed her under her arms and turned. I fell back to recline against the headboard so she was on top. She sank down, and we found another rhythm together.

I looked in her beautiful hazel eyes and saw everything I had ever wanted. How could I have stayed away for so long?

My eyes traveled down to where we were joined. She was

finally mine again. She arched back suddenly. Her hands shot out behind her to grip my thighs as she slammed down and came apart on top of me. I held her hips still, thrusting up until I went over the edge with her.

Her eyes were at half-mast, hair a wreck from my hands, lips swollen from my kisses, and she had never looked more beautiful. "Now that this is officially official, I have something for you." I sat up, gathering her in my arms. Her legs squeezed around my hips as I stretched to the side, reached into the drawer of my nightstand, and pulled out the little white box containing my mom's engagement ring.

Lily's eyes got big when she saw it.

"I want you to wear this. Will you marry me, Lily?" I opened the box and pulled the ring out. It was a huge square-shaped diamond surrounded by a bunch of little round diamonds. It would dwarf her tiny little hand just like it did my mom's, but it was beautiful despite its ostentatious nature. Beautiful and perfect, just like Lily. I watched tears fill her eyes as she recognized the ring.

"Diana's ring." She gazed at me with tears shimmering in her eyes. "I used to sit on her lap and twirl it around her finger when I was little. Oh, Luke." I slipped it on her finger, and she held her hand out. It fit perfectly. "I have always loved this ring. I wish she were here to see this."

"She knows. I believe that. Say yes."

Her head crashed into my chest, and she wrapped her arms around me whispering, "Yes. But I can't wear this yet. We need to talk to Dylan first, and I'm worried about how Jane will handle it. I should talk to her too. If everyone sees this ring on my finger, they'll know what it means, and Dylan and Jane should know first. I want us to tell him together and make it special, and I'll find some time tonight to call Jane."

"You're right. I didn't think about that. I only had one thing on my mind."

She blushed. After all we'd just done together, I found it adorable that I could still make her blush.

"But it's going back on your finger as soon as possible." She nodded against my chest, and I felt her smile against me.

"Soon, I promise. I can't wait to wear it forever."

Chapter 26
Lily

We were on the way to Gram's. Mom had called in a cleaning service to fix the mess after the police had been through it. I needed to pack more before we went to my parents' house. I felt like a freaking ping-pong ball, bouncing back and forth between homes. We pulled up to the curb because the driveway was full. Cade's truck and Dad's police SUV were parked in it and a big moving truck, fully loaded with the back open, blocked it.

What was going on now? I hopped out of the passenger seat and braced when I saw a tiny blonde blur headed my way. Madison? What were Trevor's kids doing here?

I caught her in my arms and picked her up as she screeched, "Aunt Lily! We're moving here, and this is our new house." I hefted her up and gave her a big hug. She hugged me back, winding her tiny arms and legs around me. I was thrilled to see her, but what the ever-loving heck?

"What? Where's your dad?" Then I felt Mikey hit my legs and wrap his arms around my hips.

"Where's Dylan?" he demanded. I was a bit flabbergasted, so I didn't answer, just reached down to stroke his soft brown hair.

"Um, what is going on?" I said as Luke reached my side and wrapped his arm around me. And by extension, Madison, who looked up at him with a smile.

Mikey pulled back and gave Luke an assessing look. "Who's this, Aunt Lily? You got a boyfriend?"

"This is Luke. Dylan's dad."

Mikey smiled huge and stuck his hand out like a grown-up would do. "Hi, Luke. I'm Michael Austin Hale, but everyone calls me Mikey. I'm Dylan's best friend in the entire known universe, and probably all the unknown parts too. We've been best friends since we met at age two and a half. We are both six years old and were in the same class for kindergarten. So, basically, we're exactly like brothers."

Luke shook Mikey's hand with a bemused smile. "Nice to meet you, Mikey."

Mikey pointed up at Madison. "This is my little sister, Madison Elizabeth Hale. She's four, but she'll be five next week. I'm going to be in first grade with Dylan, and Madison will be a kindergartener when school starts." We heard the front door open. Mikey turned around and pointed. "That's my dad. His name is Trevor Joseph Hale, but I call him Dad, and Dylan calls him Uncle Trev. Our dads used to be partners before Uncle Will died. I miss him a lot, but I'm glad Dylan has another dad. You seem nice, but if you weren't, Aunt Lily would kick your butt, so I'm not going to worry about it." Mikey smiled up at Luke, then looked at me. "Aunt Lily, can I play with that Xbox that's hooked up in the living room? Mine is in a box on the truck." Gosh, this kid. Precocious, to say the least.

"Go for it," I told him and watched him run off into the house.

Trevor smiled at me as he strode down the front walkway. Trevor was handsome and tall and sweet and a great dad. I guessed this was the reason why he had been incommunicado lately. He'd been too busy packing and moving to answer my texts.

"Hey, Trev. What's going on?"

He opened his mouth to answer, but my dad beat him to it as he popped out of the garage.

"Trev is the new detective on the force. Isn't that great? We needed another good man on board. He'll partner up with Cade eventually. And he's going to stay here until his house sells and he gets into another one in town." He turned to Trevor. "There's room in the garage now, son. Let's unload your stuff."

Trevor laughed. "Well, that's the story. I didn't intend to keep it from you. Everything just fell into place quickly. One minute, I'm on the phone with your dad, and the next day, I'm in a truck driving down. It's good." He smiled softly. "We'll be closer to my family, and Dylan and Mikey can be closer too." He stroked Madison's cheek. "And this one was really missing you." She looked at me with her huge blue eyes. I cuddled her closer as she tucked her head into my neck.

"I missed you too, honey," I whispered in her ear.

Trevor stuck his hand out to Luke. "I'm Trevor. You must be Luke. It's nice to meet you," he said.

"You too, man." They shook hands. This day had been a roller coaster, and it seemed we still weren't ready to get off.

Cade came out the front door with a huge smile. "We're all in luck. Mom heard you're here, Trev. She and Gram are cooking right now. Dinner tonight, all of us, at the house."

Dad poked his head out of the garage again. "Lily, I packed you up. It's all loaded in the back of Cade's truck, and when we finish unloading Trev, we'll take it to the house. You and the kids are all set."

I guess that was one less thing to worry about. Maybe I could get someone to unpack too. Then repack and unpack again when this whole weird mess was over. I groaned.

"Thanks, Dad. We'll head over, then." I turned to Trev.

"I'll take Madison and Mikey with me, if you like." My answer came when Mikey shot out of the front door like a bullet. It was impossible to keep anything from Mikey; he had the hearing of a bat and was nosy like you wouldn't believe.

"Dad, say yes. I can't wait to see Dylan. A man needs his best friend. Am I right?" I shifted Madison to my hip and stuck my hand out for a high-five. Mikey smacked my palm with a grin.

"You sure?" Trevor asked me, and I nodded. "Thanks, Lily. This will make unloading go by so much faster, and I'll help unload your stuff too." He hugged me and Madison goodbye, did his secret handshake with Mikey, and headed for the moving truck.

"Mikey, my boy, Dylan will be so happy to see you. Best surprise ever." I smiled down at him. "Let's go."

Luke helped me load the kids up. Then we were off. Again.

I spotted Jane's car in the driveway when we turned down the windy lane to my parents' house and did a happy dance in my head when I saw her. Jane was tall and full of curves I was jealous of. She had light brown hair the same shade as Will's hair cut into a wavy bob. And she shared the same beautiful green eyes as Will and Calla. She got out of her car just as Luke pulled to a stop. I hopped out with a squeal.

"Jane!" I called. The look on her face squelched my excitement.

Yeesh, the roller coaster was on a down slope again.

Jane took a step toward me as Luke moved around to the back to unload the kids. "I opened the family safe deposit box today to get my passport and I found an envelope with your dad's name on it in Will's handwriting."

"That is definitely weird. Did you open it?" I asked as I hugged her.

She hugged me back. "No, I figured I'd let your dad open

it." As we pulled apart, Luke came around the car with Trevor's kids. "Hi, Luke. Hey, kids," she said.

"Hey, Jane," Luke's voice was cautious as he returned Jane's hug. Hugging was a good sign, right?

I was worried about how she would take the news that I was back with Luke. I had been texting with her, so she knew it was a possibility, but seeing it in person made it seem so much more real. I looked at her, unsure of how to bring it up. I shouldn't have worried though. Jane always knew just what to say. "I'm glad you're back, Luke. You should have never left." She smiled sadly. She was my roommate and best friend, then later my sister-in-law. She knew how I'd always felt about Luke, and I hoped she knew that I would always love Will too.

This situation had awkward written all over it.

"We're not going to be awkward," she said, as if reading my mind. I didn't know what to say to that. Apparently, Luke didn't either because we both just looked at her with big eyes.

Madison held my hand, and Mikey, for once, didn't say a word.

Jane continued, "It's just—I love you, Lily."

Then she looked at Luke. "I missed you when you were gone, Luke. You were a good friend, and I hope we can be friends again." A determined look crossed her face. "My brother was no fool. Will knew the score when he went after you, Lily. But he's gone. He wouldn't want you to be alone. I don't want you to be alone, and I don't want you to feel weird around me. I'm happy for you. I believe, from the bottom of my heart, that Will would be happy for you too, so—no awkward, zero weirdness. We're moving forward. Onward and upward and all that jazz."

I hugged her again. "I love you, Jane."

She smiled and hugged me back. "I love you too. Always. Is your dad around? We should give him the envelope. What if it's important?"

"No, but he will be soon. Let's go in. Mom and Gram are cooking dinner, and you know them—the more, the merrier."

"Awesome. I love your mom's food. Um, is Asher here?" She looked nervous. Jane had a massive, hopelessly-devoted-to-him, heart-eyed-emoji-come-to-life crush on my big brother. Asher was deliberately unaware of it, and it was heartbreaking to witness.

"He's working," Luke answered gently. "I bribed him into taking a meeting for me so I could be here, and it doesn't start until six, so it will be a late night for him."

Luke knew about Jane's crush. Heck, everyone knew about it. She had been crushing on Asher for years, ever since the moment she first saw him when he was helping me unload boxes into our dorm room.

We all looked down at Mikey when he let out a huge, dramatic sigh. "You guys done talking yet? I'm ready to see Dylan now, and it's getting real hard to be polite and quiet and patient. I'm only six, you know. I'm pretty sure I've reached my limit."

At that point, he started jumping up and down, and Madison started giggling. I took both of their hands and ran them up to the front door, much to the amusement of Luke and Jane, who followed at a more sedate pace. Mikey rang the bell, I knocked, and it only took a moment for my mother to open the door with Calla in her arms. Dylan, Mark, and Mara were right behind her with Rocky bringing up the rear. Mikey immediately shouted for Dylan when the door opened, letting him know that he would be moving here for good.

"Mikey!" Dylan shouted back. "I'm so happy!" They hugged and jumped up and down amid shouts of "I missed you," the giggles of the other kids, and the barks from an excited Rocky. Dylan gestured to Mark. "This is Mark. He's going to be our best friend. And this is Rocky, the best dog ever." Rocky accepted a rubdown from Mikey, then licked his face. "Oh, and this is Mara." Mara rolled her eyes, but then she saw Madison.

"Hi," Mara said. Madison smiled, and I witnessed the birth of a new friendship as they ran off together up the stairs followed by the boys. Rocky looked plaintively up at Luke. Luke nodded, then Rocky bounded up the stairs after the kids.

The stairs led into a small living room that was open to the foyer and sitting room below. I watched the girls head into the playroom as the boys sat on the huge, overstuffed sectional with Jude. The sounds of a game coming from the television filtered down. I waved to Jude, who was sitting there, remote in hand. He waved back, then turned his attention to the television after high-fiving the boys and passing them a bag of chips. I focused on Calla in my mother's arms and kissed her chubby cheeks, making her giggle. She patted my face, then reached for Luke, who took her with a huge smile.

"Someone needs to have a baby for Calla to play with," my mom said with a wink directed at Luke. Then she turned to embrace Jane. "Jane, honey, I'm so glad to see you. You're just in time for dinner. What brings you over?"

"I have something for Ben. From Will. I opened the family safe deposit box and found it. It's in my bag." She patted her big purse.

"Well, put that bag down for now, darling. You can show Ben when he gets here. In the meantime, let's go have a glass of wine and catch up. Dinner is almost ready and nibbles are out, so it's time to relax." They headed into the kitchen arm in arm, leaving me with Luke. I watched him snuggle Calla. I saw her totally at ease in his arms as she patted his face and babbled at him. At that moment, everything that had been weighing on me floated away, and my heart smiled.

I beamed up at Luke. "That went well. I think Jane will be okay with all of this. Let's take Dylan to the park tomorrow and tell him. Then I can put the ring back on, and we can have a big ol' party and tell everyone else. Or just tell my mother and let her spread the word." I couldn't help it, I was bouncing on my feet just like Mikey had been earlier. I was excited. I was happy. I'd just had great sex—so much great sex. I was still tingly, I felt awesome, and the best part was it would happen again. Soon.

Luke smiled down at me as Calla tugged on his beard and giggled. "You got it, baby. But no to the park, too risky. We can go to my place instead."

"Perfect. I'm so happy, Luke. I almost can't stand it."

He leaned down and kissed me. That intense, on-a-mission look was back in his eyes. "I've been dreaming of you for so long, Lily, I'm not sure I'm awake. I love you."

"Love you back, Luke." Then I pinched his behind and grinned when he jumped. "See? We're awake, even though this feels like a dream come true." I watched his swift intake of breath and saw his shoulders relax as he nodded and grinned back at me.

Chapter 27
Lily

I watched Jane jump in her seat at the kitchen island as my dad's booming voice shouted hello from the living room. She turned to me with a nervous giggle.

"Want me to come with you to show him the safety deposit stuff?" I asked through a mouthful of cupcake. My mother hadn't been lying about the "nibbles." There was food everywhere.

She nodded and we got up to greet my dad at the door.

"Jane! Hey, darlin'," my dad said as he hugged Jane. He'd always treated her as if she were another daughter. She hugged him back.

"Jane opened her family's safe deposit box today and there was a package in there for you from Will," I blurted. Jane went to the foyer to get her purse, and Dad sat on the couch with an expectant look on his face. "What if it has to do with all this weird crap that keeps coming up lately?" I asked.

"Maybe. Hopefully there are clues in here." He took the large manila envelope from Jane and emptied it onto the coffee table. It contained a bunch of papers and a flash drive. Holy crap, a flash drive! That weird guy had been asking about a flash drive the other day in front of Violet's. Dad started sifting through the papers and shaking his head. He looked frustrated. "I wish he would have left a note or something instead of just my name on the envelope. This is a bunch of nothing—maps and lists of street names. Lily, grab my laptop, and we can check out this flash drive." I opened the drawer on the coffee table and pulled out the laptop, then snatched the flash drive and booted up the computer. I stared in confusion at what appeared to be rows of numbers, more street names, and even more maps. I scrolled through the information and stopped when I saw a picture. It was a man, good looking, with long blond hair tied back in a ponytail. I had no idea who he was, but at least it was something besides lists of seemingly random information.

"I have no idea who that is," Jane said from over my shoulder as she stood at the side of the couch.

"I'll run this picture and find out who this is, then go from there," Dad said.

"Maybe Trevor knows what this is about." I looked up as Dylan bounded down the stairs. Jane was standing, so he hugged her, then hopped onto my dad's lap and hugged him.

"I don't like that guy. He's mean," Dylan said. He was looking at the picture on the laptop. We all glanced at each other at Dylan's announcement.

"When did you meet this man?" I asked. I was trying to remain calm and not freak Dylan out.

"I was at the park with Daddy." I knew he meant Will. I had noticed he had started referring to Will as "Daddy" and Luke as "Dad."

He stopped to think. "We were at the swings. That guy yelled at Daddy to mind his own business. He had another guy with him—a big, tall, mean guy. That other guy didn't say anything. I was scared for a minute because they were all mad. But then the two guys left, and Daddy said I shouldn't worry. I remember him because he had a ponytail and a flowery shirt like in this picture."

"Did your dad say the man's name?" Dad asked. Dylan tilted his head and made the scrunchy face he always made when he was thinking hard.

After a moment, he looked at me and said, "The guy called Daddy a bad word. Can I say it?"

"Yes, go ahead and say everything you remember, Dylan," I answered quickly.

"He called Daddy a nosy asshole." Dylan's eyes were big. "And Daddy called him Rick. No, it was Derry Rick, I think. Daddy didn't say any bad words though."

"Derrick?" I asked

"Yes, that's it. Derrick," Dylan said, smiling.

Dad spoke up. "What about the other guy? Did anyone say his name?" Dylan just shook his head. "Do you remember anything else?" Dad encouraged.

"Not really," Dylan replied. "I want to go play again."

I nodded, and he took off back up the stairs.

I shook my head. "I don't like this at all. This freaks me out."

Jane sat down and side hugged me, and I leaned into her.

"What's going on?" Luke asked as he crossed the foyer and entered the living room.

"We're not exactly sure. But it's not good." Dad nodded as he removed the flash drive and shut the laptop. "I'm going to the station. I'll be back soon." He gathered all the papers and the envelope and headed out the front door.

"Well, that was clear as mud," Jane said with a grimace. "I vote for letting your dad handle it. I'm going to go back to drinking wine with your mom. As long as we're in this house we're all fine. I'm getting drunk." She got up, leaving me alone with Luke.

"Calla's down. I rocked her in the chair, and she went right out," he said as he sat next to me and pulled me close. "She's right. We're fine here, all together."

"You're right. We're okay for now. And you're a natural

when it comes to Calla." I could tell that he was excited about his nap time success. He smiled at me. The light in his eyes was mesmerizing.

I stared up at him and returned his smile. Even though something weird and possibly dangerous was hanging over me, I was happy. "Kiss me," I ordered, and he quickly obliged. When his lips touched mine, all thoughts left my head. I wrapped my arms around his neck and scooted onto his lap to sit sideways across his legs. We were so into each other that we didn't hear the front door open and break apart until I heard gagging sounds. I looked up to see Rose standing there.

"My God, you guys. Did I step into a time machine?" She grinned at us, and I felt the déjà vu as well. "This is like old times. This house. Me walking in on you guys and interrupting your make-out session. I'm sorry I gagged at you. Old habits die hard." She laughed and flopped down on the chair across from us. I tried to move off Luke's lap and back onto the couch, but he held me tight. I shrugged and smiled back at Rose.

"I'm happy for you guys. But I smell food, so later." She stood up as the front door opened and Trevor and my dad walked through.

"Rosalie," Trevor said.

My sister froze in her tracks. Her back stiffened, then she all but ran past them as she called out that she had to go. Trevor turned and watched her leave. It was obvious something was going on—or had gone on—between them. First, no one aside from my mother was allowed to call her Rosalie. Second, I knew she had met Trevor, but the look he gave her was more than friendly. It was stricken and hopeful. It appeared that I had another mystery to solve.

My dad, oblivious to the mini-drama that had just unfolded, announced, "I'm on my way to the station. I forgot my keys." Then he crossed the room and entered the kitchen.

Trevor looked at me and said, "Before you ask me what I

know you're about to ask—I don't want to talk about it." He followed my dad into the kitchen.

"Well. That was rude," I said, and Luke chuckled.

"Let's worry about that another time," he whispered in my ear, then kissed me again. I melted back into his arms so we could continue our make-out session.

The rest of the day passed without any news from my father regarding the flash drive or Hawaiian-shirted Derrick and the other bad guy. I couldn't understand why this was happening now, more than a year after Will's death.

It proved that whenever I got a little bit of happy something had to come along and threaten it.

Chapter 28
Lily

I rolled over and stared at the clock on my mom's guest bedroom nightstand. For once, the blaring, beeping, annoying alarm on my cell hadn't woken me up. I stretched and sighed. There was no crying baby, no Dylan standing at my bedside staring at me, nothing in this room but me and the sunshine streaming through the window.

I smiled to myself. Soon the ring would be back on my finger to stay, and I couldn't freaking wait. Luke and I had planned to take the kids to his place and tell Dylan we were engaged, but with my stalker still stalking about and one, maybe two more potential bad guys sniffing around, we'd decided I would just stay here and he would stop by with sprinkle donuts for breakfast, and we'd break the news first thing.

After breakfast, I was going to work at Violet's for the last time and Luke would pick Liam up from the hospital and help him get settled. Violet would make a big deal out of my last day, I just knew it. I didn't really like parties or being the center of attention, but I was hoping for cake. And maybe some good punch. If I got lucky, maybe even a few presents. I kicked off the quilt and got up to stick my head into the hallway to see what was going on in the house. I heard my mother cooing to Calla and Dylan talking to Asher and his kids, so I headed into the bathroom to shower and change. I knew this wouldn't last, and I felt a little bit spoiled as I stepped under the spray of the shower. I decided to think of this stay at my parents' house as a mini vacation. When all this craziness was over and I was back into my own place, then I could have my frantic, crazy, rushing-all-around mornings back. Until then, I would enjoy the help. And right now, I was about to take the longest, hottest shower of my life. I would blow-dry my hair, do up my makeup, and dress in something pretty. No mom-bun, half-assed mascara and lip balm today. I turned on the tap and stepped under the hot spray.

The bathroom door opened, and I jumped in surprise.

"Baby, it's just me. Don't slip and fall." Luke laughed as he rolled the shower door open and grabbed my waist to steady me.

"Be careful. I'm all wet." I gasped as his big, warm hands slid up my waist and around my back. He gripped my hair and gave me a quick kiss.

"I can feel that. I'm going to love waking up to this every day." He grinned at me, then released me. "I'll go find Dylan, but first . . ." He reached into his pocket, took my hand, and slipped his mother's ring on my finger. Before he left, he kissed the back of my hand and winked at me. My knees went weak. Luke winking at me was definitely my weakness. Well, one of them anyway. When it came to Luke, I had a lot.

I felt a chill, even though I was in a hot shower, when I realized that this would be my life. Luke and me, Dylan, and Calla—every day. It was happening already. Everything I'd ever wanted was within my reach. But no matter how hard I kept trying, I couldn't erase the fear that something would ruin it all.

Chapter 29
Luke

I couldn't wait to put the ring back on Lily's finger where it belonged. I had rushed straight upstairs to do that, leaving donuts in my truck to bring in after I saw her. As I walked back through the house, I passed Dahlia feeding Calla in the kitchen and Asher sipping coffee at the counter. I spied Jude and Levi through the kitchen windows sitting on the patio that surrounded the pool, also drinking coffee. But no Dylan yet. I crossed through the kitchen into the living room and saw Rose with a weird look on her face eating a donut.

"You left donuts in your truck," she said. "So many donuts."

"Yeah, I got enough for everybody. Is something wrong?" I prompted.

"The kids found them. I guess they saw you drive up through the window, and I'm assuming you rushed off to see Lily. Is she in the shower, Luke?" She smirked and looked down at my shirt. It was a little damp in front.

I pulled it off. It was a plaid button-up. I had a T-shirt on underneath. "Yeah, I saw Lily. We're going to have news later. Stick around, okay?"

"Good news, I hope? I almost feel bad about what you're

about to find in your truck." She laughed and darted past me to the kitchen. "I need coffee. You're gonna need it too."

I rushed outside to my truck. I heard giggling and saw tiny people sitting in the bed of the truck. Dylan sat in the back seat, passing donuts through the rear slide window to the kids in the truck bed. They were covered in chocolate and whatever the white kind of icing is. Oh damn, the sprinkles were everywhere. I had bought five boxes of donuts, a dozen in each. Icing smeared my seats, the steering wheel, the windows—it was everywhere.

"Donuts good?" I asked.

Maddie whirled with big eyes and Dylan turned from his knees to stare at me. The rest of them froze, all except for Mikey, the only one brave enough to answer.

"They're good. But you forgot the kind with the cream inside," he said.

I was thankful for small mercies by that point. What kind of mess would they have made with cream-filled donuts? We all looked up as Rose walked up to the truck armed with a package of baby wipes and a roll of paper towels with a bottle of cleaner hooked on the waistband of her jeans.

"Never leave donuts unattended in these parts." She grinned. "You'll learn." She passed me the baby wipes. "You're on sticky hand and face duty. We can't let them in the house like this." I took the wipes as Rose started giving orders. "All right, donuts down, and get your little behinds out of the truck and line up."

They all did what she said with no hesitation, all lining up in front of her like tiny soldiers. Maybe it was because she was a kindergarten teacher. "You're up, Luke," she ordered, then climbed into the truck.

I handed each kid a wipe for their hands, then went down the line wiping their silent, guilt-ridden faces before doubling back to check their hands.

Was I supposed to laugh at this? Or was I supposed to give

a time-out or something dad-like? Finally, I cracked and let out a laugh. I couldn't help it. They were all so cute with their hang-dog expressions. "I'm not mad," I announced.

Dylan hugged me. "I'm sorry. We came out to say hi, but you weren't here. Then we saw one million donuts and we wondered if they had sprinkles. We just meant to peek at them. I don't know what happened," he said.

Mikey picked this moment to offer his two cents. "Yeah, you really shouldn't leave that many donuts around without a grown-up to watch them. Kids can be unpredictable when it comes to sweets."

"We're sorry," Mike and Mara chimed in.

Little Madison was still just staring at me. I smiled at her, and she gave me a tiny grin. Rose hopped out of the back of the truck and tipped up Madison's chin. "How come the littlest kid always makes the biggest mess?" Rose brushed sprinkles out of Madison's pigtails. Madison shrugged in response. "Maybe you'll be in my class when school starts," Rose said. Then she looked at me.

"Bad news, Luke. Every box was opened, and every donut was tasted or licked." She grinned. "Luckily, all the truck needs now is a whisk broom and a vacuum. And we'll have to be on tummy ache watch for a few hours," she added.

"Thanks, Rose. I'm going to steal Dylan for a bit and find Lily."

He took my hand. "Okay, Dad." I was a dad. It was beginning to feel real. The more time I spent with Dylan and Calla, the more I felt myself getting comfortable with it. As soon as Lily was my wife, it would be irrevocable. Everyone would know they were mine. My heart burst with pride and love. I felt like he could fill my truck with a million sprinkles and get sticky handprints on everything I owned, and I wouldn't care because my heart melted every time he called me Dad. This boy and his baby sister owned my heart right along with their mom.

"Let's find your mom. We have something to tell you."

"Okay. She was asleep when I got up. Let's go upstairs. Are we going to go live with you? Can I have my own room? Can I bring my Xbox One? Can I have a Nintendo Switch? Mikey has Mario Kart and the new Zelda. We can play together. I'm sorry we messed up your truck. I kind of knew it was a bad idea. But seeing all the different donuts all lined up in all the boxes made it hard to make a good choice. We wanted to taste them all. I'm pretty sure we were all crazy for a few minutes."

When I was sure he was finished talking, I attempted an answer, something fatherly and adultish. My father had been a shit dad, so I thought of Ben. What would Ben say?

"I forgive you. I can understand being tempted by something you think you can't resist. But it could be dangerous to get into a vehicle without an adult. Did you think about that?"

He shook his head.

"Next time try to think before you do something. Can you promise me you'll try?" I asked.

"I pinky promise." He held out his hand. After locking pinkies, I swung him up into my arms. He was so innocent and cute and could ramble on and on when he spoke, but he was also astute and self-aware.

"Hey, guys!" Lily was at the top of the stairs with Calla in her arms. She wore a yellow-flowered sundress and high heels that did things to her legs that made me wish we were alone. She was like the sun. She brought the warmth back to my heart. The ring sparkled on her finger, shining like a little sunbeam, telling me she was mine. "Everyone is outside. Let's talk up here." We followed her the rest of the way to settle on the sectional couch.

"What's going on?" Dylan demanded. "Are we going to live with Luke now?"

"I have a very important question to ask you. Would it be okay if I marry your mom?" I asked.

"Yes!" he shouted, then hopped up to face Lily and me. "We can be a family together. You won't have to live in that huge house all by yourself. Oh, and can Rocky sleep in my room? I saw you guys kissing so many times when you thought I wasn't looking. I guessed this would happen, and I was right!"

Lily melted into my side with Calla in her arms, then Dylan stood up and threw himself at me, I caught him with a smile. We sat there, holding each other, when Dahlia suddenly appeared at the top of the stairs.

"What's going on? Is everything okay?" she asked. Lily stuck her hand out and waved it around as an answer.

Dahlia gasped. "You're wearing Diana's ring. Are you . . .? Does this mean . . .? Oh my goodness." She burst into tears, rushed over, sat on the coffee table, and joined our hug.

Dylan pulled away and patted her cheeks. "Don't cry, Grandma, we're all going to be a family together now."

"I know, honey. I'm just so happy." She shifted Dylan to her side and grabbed Lily's hand, examining the ring on her finger. "Diana used to call this her ice rink. We used to laugh at how huge and ostentatious this ring was, but it's never looked more beautiful than right now. She would be so happy for you both, and I'm overjoyed, and I am planning your wedding. Oh, and I'm throwing the engagement party too. Don't argue. I'll go call Ben." She got up and rushed down the hall to her room.

Lily laughed. "How long do you think it will be before everyone knows?"

I shrugged. I had what I needed. As far as I was concerned, the rest was just details.

Footsteps bounded up the stairs. "Lily, Luke, oh my God!" Rose shrieked when she reached us.

"I know!" Lily cried as they hugged. "I've got to get to Violet's for my last day. Let's all have dinner and celebrate tonight."

Chapter 30
Lily

I walked into Violet's to the sound of a lot of hooting and hollering, cheering, assorted whoops and one "You go, girl," which none of us were cool enough to pull off. I looked around the shop to see my mother had beaten me here, along with Rose. Violet was behind the counter, and Finn and Nick rushed over to me bearing my favorite vanilla iced coffee and a cupcake, bless them. Gram sat on the big couch in the corner, waving excitedly with Liam and Jed sitting by her side. And at the tables, interspersed with a few of Violet's customers, were many of my cousins and all my brothers except for Cade, who was on duty with my father and Trev. Everyone was smiling at me, and for once, I didn't mind being the center of attention. Aunt Delphine rushed over and gave me a big hug and an "I'm so happy for you."

I marveled at how fast this had come together. Purple and white streamers hung across the ceiling and silver and purple balloons floated on their strings tied to the chairs. The news of our engagement had only broken about an hour ago. Luke had stopped at his office with the kids and I'd walked over here for my last day of work to find this extravaganza instead. How in the holy heck was all this possible? I looked to my mother sitting on one of the chairs across from my grandma. She looked a little bit disgruntled—happy, but disgruntled all the same.

Violet came up behind me and gave me a hug. "I texted Luke. He's coming over with the kids," she whispered.

"Was this you? Did you plan this? How?" I asked.

"Of course it was me," Violet answered. "I've been planning a lot of things," she said with a smile.

"You're amazing, Violet. I had been feeling badly about this being my last day. Are you sure you don't need me for another week or two?" I asked.

She threw back her head and laughed. "Oh, Lily. Don't worry. I never needed you to work here," she announced. "My shop is like a well-oiled machine. I wanted you here because Luke's office is right across the parking lot." She gestured to the window. "He came in here almost every day. You two belong together. It's fate, and I am the hand of fate right now." She pointed over at Mom, who looked even more disgruntled. "I am the matchmaking queen. I will bask forevermore in the glory of being right, being determined, and"—she raised her fists in the air—"beating Mom to make the ultimate match."

I stared at her, agape. I hadn't had one single clue. She really was the master.

Violet was laughing, and Mom had finally broken a smile. She lost the smile when Violet called out, "Who's the master now, Dahlia?"

Violet turned to Finn and Nick. "Boys, what were the magic words?"

They laughed and said in unison, "Don't worry about it. We got it, Aunt Lily. Take a break."

"What else?" she prompted.

"Give her scones when it looks like she wants to run away," Nick shouted while Finn cracked up at his side.

My mouth dropped open. I'd been played by my sister and her two teenage sons. I grinned huge and burst out, "I love you guys."

"We love you too," they shouted from behind the counter.

"I love you, Violet," I whispered to her.

"I love you too, little sister. Be happy," she whispered back.

We both turned as the door opened behind us, and Luke and the kids burst in.

"Oh, cupcakes!" Dylan shouted when he spied a cupcake tower on the coffee table by the couch.

"No way, donut boy. Take your booty to the veggie tray over there by Uncle Asher and the kids," I answered.

He smiled and looked sheepish, but he didn't argue as he headed to their table.

"Gimme that baby," Violet demanded of Luke. He handed Calla over, and Violet took off with her to sit by Gram on the couch, where they proceeded to coo and rain attention on her. Calla loved it. Her smile was huge, and her baby squeals and giggles danced across the shop.

I took a bite of the cupcake Finn brought me, then offered a bite to Luke. He leaned over, took a bite, then licked frosting from my finger. That action inspired a lot of catcalls from our audience. "Oh my gosh." I groaned and buried my face in Luke's chest.

He laughed and hugged me close.

Rose cleared her throat. "I see that Violet and I will be fighting for maid of honor duties now." Everyone laughed. Rose held up her coffee. "But first—let's toast to Diana. We all miss her. And let's not forget that it was her and Mom who started this whole thing. Aren't you glad you didn't end up with me, Luke?" He laughed and squeezed my waist. "To Diana, to Luke and Lily, and to you too, Mom. Cheers!" We all cheered, then Luke and I were passed around the room to receive hugs and well wishes and lots of "Finally! When's the wedding?" My ring was examined and Diana was remembered fondly, which choked Luke up. Finally, it was just Luke and me at a table in the corner sipping coffee and eating cupcakes while the room disappeared around us. I was so happy that everything else faded away. I looked into Luke's eyes and knew down to my bones that no matter what happened, we would get through it. Together this time.

The party carried on for a couple of hours before people started filtering out, back to their own lives. The happy bubble was coming to an end, but I was still riding the high.

Violet had yet to give up my baby, so Calla was content. I had relented and let Dylan have a cupcake, so he was content as well. Luke and I were still attached at the hip, so we were both super content. This day was the best I'd had in a long time.

"Mommy, I have to go to the bathroom," Dylan came up and announced. The bathroom was down a wide hall that also held a small storage room. It led to the back door of Violet's shop. I had previously told Dylan that he wasn't allowed to go back there by himself. Call me overprotective, but I didn't want him back there alone. I got up to walk him back and wait in the hall.

"Come on, bud," I said, and he raced ahead of me to the hallway. I saw light from the back door shining into the hall, which was odd; Violet always kept it shut and locked. She didn't want anyone sneaking in through the back.

"Dylan, wait!" I rushed into the mouth of the hall and saw the good-looking, ponytailed, Hawaiian-shirt bad guy named Derrick come out of the storage room. He lunged for Dylan and grabbed his arm, pulling him toward the open back door.

I ran forward to jump on his back. Reaching around his neck, I pulled at his nose, I kicked and I scratched. I hit him over and over until Dylan was able to break free. "Run, Dylan! Get Luke, get help," I grunted.

Dylan stared at me for a second as tears filled his eyes, then he shot off down the hall.

I was glad he didn't see me get thrown off. I was glad he didn't see me get shoved into the wall and punched in the side of the head.

After that, I couldn't see either. Everything had gone black.

Chapter 31
Luke

"Dad!" Dylan's terrified scream echoed through Violet's shop, sending us all into a shocked silence as he came barreling through the swinging doors that led out of the back room.

Liam clapped my shoulder as he ran around me to follow Dylan's path through the doors. I darted toward Dylan.

"What happened? Where's your mom?" I barked, kneeling to gather him into my arms. "Someone call for help!"

Violet handed Calla to her grandmother and fumbled in her apron pocket, removing her cell. "I'll get dad on the phone. He's with Cade."

Liam reentered the room, stopping at my side. "The back door was wide open. No sign of Lily or anyone else."

Rose joined me on the floor. "Dylan, honey, tell us exactly what happened."

"That mean man Derrick was back there. He hit her and took her away. He tried to take me first, but Mommy wouldn't let him." Tears rolled down his face, wetting my shirt. His shoulders shook with sobs.

When I found them, it would take everything in me not to end that man. Rage, cold and prickly, wound through my body, coiling me tight, forcing my mind back to the time when most of my existence was fight or flight and required my entire focus to stay alive.

"Think really hard, Dylan. Did you see anyone else? Could you see out the back door?" Liam asked as he knelt next to us. "Did you see a car running out there? Or anything that could help?"

Dylan looked at Liam and his eyes lit up. "Yeah, I did. I saw a car. It was red but not shiny and it looked like Darrell Cartrip from *Cars*."

"Oh, that's a Monte Carlo," Nick said. "Good job, Dylan."

"Did you see the license plate?" Rose questioned. "Could you see any letters or numbers?"

"No. But it had one blue door with a big dent in it. And that other guy in the pictures at Grandma's house was in the car," he added.

The coil in my gut tightened as I waited for Violet to relay information from her father. I needed a starting point.

"You are such a good helper, Dylan," Rose told him as she pushed his hair back from his face and dried his cheeks with a napkin.

"Really?"

"You sure are," Liam answered. "This will help find your mom."

"Take him, Rose." She reached for Dylan. I stood. "We have to find her."

"We will." Liam's tone launched me back into our past. "Nothing else is acceptable. Focus."

"Focus," I repeated. "Ready."

"Ready," he chanted back to me. "We'll get her."

"I'm closing the shop," Violet informed us. "We're all going to the house. Trevor is headed there to wait with us. Dad and Cade are on the way to Portland." She scribbled down an address then handed it to me. "Meet him there. Between the car description and the partial plate numbers they have an address to start with."

"Dylan, I'm so proud of you," I cupped his cheek, wiping away a tear with my thumb."

Rose picked him up. He buried his face against her shoulder, crying too hard to answer me. "I've got him. You go get my sister," she said through her own tears.

"I will." It was a promise.

Liam and I headed to my truck while everyone else loaded up to head to Ben and Dahlia's place.

"Should we stop at my house first? Do you think they'll let us borrow any of their weapons?" Liam asked. "Because I do not intend to stand around and wait."

"Probably not. But we don't have to stop. I have what we need locked in the back of the truck along with my other tools."

He laughed. "Of course you do."

I drove us out of town, gathering speed once we merged on the highway toward Portland. My mind raced through endless horrific possibilities, but I shut each of them down while keeping one thought at the forefront: *I will find her*.

We made it to the address Violet gave us, which was an old diner across the street from a warehouse. I pulled to a stop next to Ben's SUV to see it surrounded by what were clearly unmarked police cars.

I got out and unlocked the toolbox in the bed of my truck and removed the metal case I kept inside. I passed Liam a Kevlar vest and took one for myself. I put it on, gesturing for Liam to choose what he wanted from the case as I headed over to Ben.

Chapter 32
Lily

I woke up in a trunk. Before I could even try to remember how to get out, it popped open. I blinked rapidly as my eyes adjusted to the dim light. I looked up and saw a huge, hairy bad guy glowering down at me. He reached out and touched the side of my face. Even though he looked concerned I flinched away from him. I didn't care about his concern. I was in a freaking trunk, for flip's sake.

"I don't care what's going on. You don't punch a girl. You okay?" he barked.

I nodded. "Are you going to let me go? Please?"

"No. I can't." The trunk slammed shut, sinking me into darkness once more. I listened to his footsteps fade. I was pretty sure he'd walked away.

I knew, *I just knew*, if I got happy, something or someone would come along and mess it up. Something like being in a motherflipping, effing, fucking trunk. I squinted in the dark, trying to see the safety lever. I had spent time in the trunk of a car on several occasions during my youth. Cops and Robbers could get kind of dicey with my brothers and sisters.

My eyes finally adjusted enough to see it. This was an older model car and I was lucky it even had one. My hands were cuffed behind my back, so I flipped over to reach it. For once, I was glad to be short; it allowed me room to maneuver. I just wish I didn't have heels on. Being a slob could pay off sometimes, and I would kill to be wearing my jeans and sneakers right about now. However, the pins in my hair would probably come in handy.

I pulled the lever and sat up when the trunk lid popped open. It appeared that I was in a warehouse type of building. The roof was very high, but the space was not open. It had been divided up with walls that gave it a maze-like quality. The ambient sounds bouncing off the metal walls echoed in my ears. I tried to focus my eyes in the dim light. Luckily, I could see the sun peeking through the high windows, and I hoped I would find my way out before it grew completely dark. My head pounded, and the side of my face felt tight from the hit at Violet's.

I pushed up onto my knees and half-stepped, half-rolled over the side of the trunk and landed on my ass on the cement floor. I tucked my legs to my chest, tight as they could go, so I could slip my feet through my arms. I didn't even need to take my shoes off.

God bless my brothers and sisters and our deranged childhood games.

God bless Will and his excessive self-defense lessons.

I reached into my hair and located a bobby pin. I used my teeth to take off the little plastic thingy on the end, then bent it at an angle. The trick was to stick the pin only halfway into the lock mechanism. I did it! My hands were now free.

I kept the handcuffs in my hand as I looked around for something else to use as a weapon while simultaneously looking for a way out. There had to be a garage door somewhere around here—someone had driven a car inside, after all. I walked around one of the makeshift walls and saw more walls. Some had doors that probably led to small rooms, and some just snaked around and led to who knew where. I decided to follow pathways that were wide enough to drive a car through. I needed to get to an outside wall. Then I could follow it around until I reached a doorway.

Instead of a way out, I found Hawaiian-shirt Derrick with his stupid effing ponytail and handsome but hostile grin. I held the cuffs in my fist and immediately took a swing at him, clocking him hard in the throat. He immediately started gagging and gasping. He also immediately got pissed off and moved to hit me back. Ducking his swing, I kicked him in the balls. He doubled over and I swear he started to cry, but I wasn't going to stick around to find out. I turned on my heel and ran the opposite direction, forgetting Will's and Cade's and my father's previous instructions to completely incapacitate an attacker. I should have kicked him in the head a few times.

Too late now. I was already running around the corner, turning around weird, nonsensically placed walls and stacks of boxes and crates. I was hopelessly lost in this ridiculous, cavernous warehouse. I froze when I saw Derrick's partner in front of me holding a gun.

I dropped the handcuffs and held my hands out to my sides. He gestured for me to go to him, so I did it. At this point, I was out of options and a little bit out of my mind. I stopped in front of him, and he grabbed my arm and zip tied my hands behind my back without saying a word.

He pulled me through a narrow pathway forged between stacked-up boxes and crates. Dust kicked up with every step and filled my nostrils until I couldn't breathe. I gasped as I struggled not to fall. I stumbled once, and he hauled me up by my arm, shaking me forcefully. So much for his earlier concern.

It was getting darker, and the sound of our footfalls stomping and scraping across the dirty floor echoed throughout the warehouse. We reached a door, and he shoved me into a pitch-black room. Careening through the doorway, I tripped on my heels. But instead of hitting the floor, I hit a body.

I assumed it was a man, given his size and the fact there were no boobs when I hit the chest area. I balanced precariously against his chest as he curved his shoulders forward to prevent my fall. He was solid, and he tried to keep his footing as he helped steady me. I managed to lower myself to the floor and sit down, then he sat near me.

As my eyes started to adjust to the dark, I could make out his features a bit. It almost looked like my stalker, but I couldn't be sure. But if he was tied up too, he couldn't be the jerk who had been messing with me.

"Are you the one messing with me?" I asked, just to be sure.

He sighed. "Yes."

"And?" I asked, and he sighed again with annoyance. "What the hell is going on?"

"You know Tara?" he asked.

"Tara? Trevor's wife, Tara?"

"Yes. She's my sister. Did you know about the divorce? Why they were getting it, all of that?" he asked.

"Yeah, she cheated on him. He only took her back because she had cancer, so she could stay on his insurance and keep the same doctors," I answered. Trevor was a saint and a great dad. I loved him like another brother.

"Right. I'm not proud of what she became. But she was my sister, and I had to protect her and the kids. Mostly Madison."

"Explain. All of it, right now," I demanded. What did Trevor and Tara have to do with any of this? Had Will known?

"Madison might not be Trevor's. At first, Tara just didn't want him to know. She was just concerned she would lose some of the child support—you know how she was." He shook his head. "Then she found out she was terminal, and she didn't want Madison to be taken from Trevor if he wasn't her father. The prick she cheated with had been blackmailing her."

"What does Trevor's marriage have to do with me and Will?"

"I'm a police officer. My father is a detective. In Brighton."

I shrugged. I didn't know where Brighton was.

"It's a tiny town about halfway between here and Tacoma?" He gave me another look.

"Yeah. So?"

He shook his head at me. "So we needed money to help Tara. We went to a local guy for a loan." He cast his eyes downward.

"You mean like a loan shark?" I asked, and he nodded. "You idiot," I said. "You're a police officer. You should know better. Mortgage your house, sell your car, or, I don't know—arrest the blackmailer."

"We did all of that. He kept wanting more and more, and Tara was desperate—and dying. And Madison, she's a little angel. She can't be taken from Trevor."

"I understand. But why am I here? Why did that guy try to grab my son? I have nothing to do with Trevor and Tara's marriage, or you." All his explaining hadn't enlightened me at all. I was still confused.

"The guys who have us are the loan sharks. They figured out who Dad and I were, and then they didn't want us to pay them back. They wanted to use us instead. They got ambitious, wanted to branch out, and who better to help them than two cops they could get dirty? We were in way over our heads. We couldn't ask Trevor for help. First, because we aren't close with him for obvious reasons. And second, we didn't want him to find out about Madison. We asked Will for help instead. We figured he wouldn't want her to be taken from Trevor either, so he might help us on the down low."

I narrowed my eyes at him. "Will died over a year ago. Why is this happening now?"

"Will was working with us to bring these guys down. I'm pretty sure they killed him."

I gasped. "No . . ." My heart dropped to my stomach. Not my sweet Will. Tears filled my eyes, but I resisted letting them fall. I could think about this later; I couldn't afford to fall apart now. Instead of sadness, I let myself feel rage. Will had been a good man, the best, and I would always love him. "What made you think they killed Will?"

"At first, we thought what everyone did—that it was a random hit-and-run. But now, I'm pretty sure they did it. A few months ago, they figured out that it was us who tipped Will off, and that we were working with him. They wanted us to gather any evidence he had managed to collect. I knew Will had the flash drive because I gave it to him. I tried to tell them it would be useless without knowing what it was. I mean, it's just lists of places and routes. Will never found anything that would stick, and our word against theirs would have been useless without proof. We needed to find tangible evidence. I tried to explain that we had nothing on them, but they became so paranoid and reckless—"

"You broke into my house?"

He nodded.

"You know, you are a really crappy stalker. I knew you were watching me. I knew you were following me," I accused.

"I wanted you to know. I wanted to scare you so you wouldn't be alone in that house with your kids. I'm not a bad person. I made a stupid decision, but I never wanted anyone to get hurt. I thought if I scared you enough, you'd get protection. You would go hide out with your father, or your cop brother, or even Trevor. I didn't want to hurt you, or your kids. I sure as fuck didn't want Will to die. I never wanted any of this to happen." He was so earnest I felt compelled to believe him.

"Why didn't you just explain all of this to me? Why didn't you just turn yourself in?" I asked. "This is out of control."

"Because they have my dad," he bit out. "They made him take vacation from work so no one would realize he was missing, and they locked him up. They had me out trying to get the flash drive from you. They put me in here about two days ago when they figured out I was trying to warn you. Dad and I were tapping Morse code on the walls to communicate with each other. He hasn't responded since yesterday. I don't know what happened to him, and I'm worried. His heart isn't too good. And Madison—that can't come out." He sank back against the wall and shut his eyes.

I felt kind of sorry for him. He was trying to help Madison. I loved that little girl like my own, and there wasn't much I wouldn't do for her either. But Trevor was going to find out. It was inevitable now.

"We have to get out of here." Once more, I tucked my legs through my arms. I stood up, raised my hands above my head, then quickly brought them down, breaking the zip ties. I'd seen this trick on the internet, and it actually worked. I plucked another bobby pin from my hair, removed the plastic part, then went over to— "Hey, what's your name?"

"Jeff," he answered dejectedly.

"Well, turn around, Jeff. I'll get the cuffs off you, and then we are getting out of here." He looked at me doubtfully and stayed where he was.

"I'll leave you here if I have to. But I was hoping to use you as a human shield. It's the least you could do," I grumbled.

He finally turned around. He looked surprised when I freed him from the handcuffs. Jerk. I didn't have time for naysayers or sexists. I could pick a lock, I could throw a punch, and I was getting the hell out of here and back to my family, damnit.

I made myself keep feeling the rage. It made me focus instead of panic.

"Thanks," he mumbled. Jeff reached out and jiggled the door handle. It was locked, of course.

I pulled another pin from my hair—I needed two pins for the door—and set about picking the lock. Luckily, it was just a regular inside knob lock, not a deadbolt or something that required a pick set, or a hammer, or a battering ram, or a motherfreaking cannon.

I turned to Jeff with a smug smile after opening the door. "Lead the way," I offered.

We crept out into the narrow hallway. It was quiet and getting darker by the minute. I hoped that Jeff could find his way out of here without light because we were losing it fast.

"I want to find my dad," Jeff whispered.

"How about we get out of here and get help?" I countered. And what if his dad was hurt, or dead? I needed to get out of here. Dylan was probably beside himself. Remembering the look on his face before he ran for help broke my heart all over again. I cut that line of thought off, then decided to give it another direction instead—back to rage. They'd tried to take my son.

Focus. Anger gave me focus. I took a deep breath. Jeff took my hand and guided me forward.

"You're probably right," he whispered. "I need to get you out of here. I have no idea why they brought you."

We crept down the dusty makeshift hallway. "Where are we?" I whispered.

"This is a warehouse in Portland. They were small-time, but they've been branching out all over the place, running drugs. Mostly meth. They had me and my dad delivering it. I mean, who's going to pull a cop over?" He laughed bitterly.

"Okay, well, that sucks," I said. I couldn't find anything appropriately sympathetic to say to him. I was all out of caring thoughts for the moment. Right now I was running on adrenaline and rage with a small sprinkle of fear over the top to keep me alert.

We continued walking for a bit before he held his arm out to stop me. I froze at his back. I stood on my tiptoes to see over his shoulder. Jeff bumped into me as he took a step back.

"They're right there, blocking the way out. Turn around. *Hurry*," he hissed. I blinked at the dark when I turned around.

I felt Jeff close to my back. He took my hand again and tugged me back the way we'd come.

"Is there another way out?" I whispered. There had to be. In my quick peek around the corner before turning around, I had seen a regular door, not a garage door or a sliding door or anything big enough for a car to drive through.

"Yes, there are dock doors. Let's hurry." He tugged on my hand and I hurried after him.

Chapter 33
Luke

Six hours.

She had been missing for six hours.

Someone had taken Lily, and I was terrified. My heart was with her. My chest felt empty. Dread coursed through my veins like ice water. I had let myself slip back into my old thought patterns. Years and years of training had taken over until I had only one objective. But the fear wouldn't stop creeping into my thoughts and throwing me off. I was glad Liam was here to help me retain my focus.

"Any more intel?" I barked at Cade. He shook his head.

"No, only what we already know." I watched Ben get out of his SUV just as a few more cruisers arrived.

"I'm going in there," I said, and with a nod, Liam immediately moved to follow me.

"Wait a minute," Cade said. "We're not going to just storm the gates—"

"She's in there. I'm not storming anything. We go in quietly." I checked my weapon, then tucked it away. I was wearing a Kevlar vest—we all were. Plus, I had stashed all my usual weapons of choice in their normal spots. I glanced at Liam. He had done the same. It felt like the old days, except that this time, I had way more to lose than just my life. The fear had gone straight to my soul, and I couldn't shake it, I couldn't bury it, but I couldn't let it consume me.

Liam clapped me on the shoulder. "Luke. Steady," he said, and I nodded.

We all froze as a commotion started up from the side of the building. A bearded man came barreling around the corner, dragging Lily behind him. My whole body sighed with relief for a split second, then I snapped into action, following behind Liam, who had already started running in their direction.

"Shit!" Liam yelled as the two men we'd identified earlier as the probable kidnappers burst out from a door on the side of the building. The bearded guy with Lily let her go, turned, and rushed the bigger of the two kidnappers, tackling him to the ground.

"Go, Lily, go, go!" he yelled at her.

She looked back at him for a brief second, then turned in my direction. When she spotted me, she ran faster. She screamed as the ponytailed kidnapper caught up to her and grabbed her from behind, lifting her off her feet. Liam and I had almost caught up to the fray, with Ben and Cade close behind.

Lily swung her head forward before slamming the back of it into ponytail's face. She did it hard enough I heard the impact. She shoved herself forward out of his grasp, then turned and punched him right where she had headbutted him. He stumbled back a foot or so and almost lost his balance. He fell after she kneed him between his legs and shoved him.

But Lily didn't stop. She tackled him as he fell, landing with both of her knees in his stomach. He let out a sickening *oof* as her weight hit him and his breath wheezed out in a rush. Using her closed fist like a hammer, she hit him in the face again and again, all the while screaming and cursing at him about how he killed Will and how he wouldn't scare her son or hurt anybody else ever again.

"Lily, stop." I had finally reached her, along with Liam, Cade, and Ben. She pushed herself to her feet and collapsed in my arms, sobbing.

"He killed Will. He tried to take Dylan," she cried.

I held her tighter, then picked her up.

Ben put cuffs on Derrick, who was surprisingly still conscious. And Cade had the big one. Officers pulled their cruisers up to where we were and one of them cuffed the bearded guy who had run out with Lily.

She shuddered against me. "I'm okay. You can put me down, Luke."

I couldn't do it though. I wanted to keep her close and never let her out of my sight again. I could have lost her, lost everything. Instead of setting her down, I released her legs, then held her up with my arms around her hips. Her arms wound around my neck. With her breath on my cheek and her heartbeat next to mine, I calmed down.

"I knew you would come," she whispered. The only thing I could think to do was kiss her. My mind had blanked of every-thing but the relief I felt from having her in my arms again. I put her down. She held my hand and stood at my side.

"That's Jeff," she said and pointed to the bearded guy. "His dad is in there somewhere. He's the one who was following me around and watching from the backyard. He's also the one who broke into Gram's house. In his own stupid way, he was trying to help me. He was locked up in there too." She addressed the officer handcuffing Jeff, "Don't let him go. You should arrest him. I'm sorry, Jeff, but you know it's true."

He just looked at her and nodded.

"If his dad is okay and doesn't need an ambulance or some-thing, he should be arrested too" she said to Ben, who had just finished putting Derrick into the back of a cruiser.

"Dad!" Jeff yelled as two officers led an older man down the warehouse stairs.

"I'm okay, son!" the man yelled back.

Ben pulled Lily into his arms and squeezed her tight. "You scared me, baby girl," he said into the top of her head. That started her tears up again.

Cade finished securing the second kidnapper, rushed to Ben and Lily, and took over the hug. "You really kicked his ass, Lily. Dad had to scoop him into the handcuffs."

"I did? I don't really remember," she said sheepishly.

"Blind rage," Liam said. "Now you know what you're capable of. Bet your head hurts. That was one hell of a head-butt. Not to mention your hand." He held out his fist, and Lily bumped it softly with hers, then threw herself into his arms. He looked surprised but leaned over and hugged her back.

"I knew she'd have it," Cade said. "Lily is one of those quiet people you have to watch out for. Plus, she is a redhead." He nudged her arm with his, then hugged her again. I heard him whisper, "I don't know what I'd do without you, Lily. I was so scared." She wrapped her arms around his waist, and they held on to each other.

I glanced over at Liam, who was watching them like I was, both of us wishing we had grown up with that kind of closeness, that kind of love. With people who would drop everything and do anything they could, no matter what. Liam and I had acted like a couple of blind fools, keeping ourselves distant from the friendship we'd fallen into with each other over the years.

"I love you, man. You were there for me today. You're always there," I said to him.

He blinked, then a small smile crossed his face, and he clapped his hand onto my shoulder. "Love you too."

Lily was crying again when she said, "We're all going to be okay."

Chapter 34
Lily

Never had I been happier to pull into the driveway of my parents' house than I was today. I saw my family running out of the house as I hopped out of Luke's truck and ran straight into my mother's arms. I hugged her, but over her shoulder I searched for Dylan. He stood on the front porch, next to Violet, who cradled a sleeping Calla in her arms. Tears streamed down his little face, and I ran to him. I scooped him up and held him, absorbing his sobs into my body while wishing I could take this whole day away and erase it from his memory.

"Luke told me you're my little hero," I whispered into his ear. He squeezed my neck and continued crying. "You saved my life, Dylan. I am so, so proud of you."

"I love you, Mommy," he said through his tears.

"I love you too, little bug." He wiggled for me to put him down, so I did.

He ran down the drive to Luke who picked him up and hugged him.

Tears filled my eyes once more as Rose wrapped her arms around me from behind. Violet leaned in, and I kissed Calla's sweet little cheek. "Thank you for taking care of her," I murmured. Violet nodded at me with a smile.

"Lily." Rose's voice broke on my name as tears streamed down her face. I turned and hugged Rose tighter while Violet and Gram moved over to one of the porch swings and sat down near Finn and Nick.

Trevor and his kids came out the front door. Mikey and Maddie crashed into my legs. I leaned down and kissed their cheeks. Trevor kissed the top of my head and told me goodbye, and he would see me tomorrow. I did not want to tell Trevor the things Jeff had told me about Tara, but I would, because he had to know. He needed to protect Madison. That girl was his, even if she wasn't. Now was not the time though. He led the kids to his car, and they took off.

Luke, with Dylan in his arms and Rocky jumping around his feet, made his way up the walkway to the porch steps followed by Liam and my mother.

Dad and Cade had gone back to the station to bust the bad guys or do whatever they did after they arrested people.

Asher came out of the front door bearing an ice pack, which he handed to me after hugging me. I pressed it to my sore face with my sore hand and held it there. Mark and Mara were with their other grandparents. I would see them this weekend. I was sure my mother would be doing something extra for Sunday dinner.

Levi and Jude were up next, followed by Finn and Nick. I hugged them all and suddenly missed Holly. It had been almost a year since I'd seen my baby sister.

But then she appeared, walking out the front door like the blond goddess she was. She ran into my arms. She had to lean over because like almost everyone else in my family, she was way taller than me. We hugged, then she cradled my face, gentle with the bruises and swelling that had arisen along the side where Derrick had hit me, and studied my eyes. "I just got home a few hours ago. Walked through the front door to find the house was full and everyone going nuts. I have been so worried, Lily."

"I'm sorry you had to go through that, Holly," I said, and she laughed.

"Typical Lily. You get kidnapped, yet you are apologizing because I worried about you. I love you."

"I love you too."

Luke and Dylan had come up behind me. Dylan ran around me to one of the padded couches on the porch and sat down. Rocky hopped up beside him and cuddled into his side.

"Hey, Luke. It's good you're finally back. I missed you," Holly said.

He smiled and wrapped her up in a hug.

Luke let go, and Liam greeted her. "Hi."

I saw Liam see Holly, and I saw Holly see Liam, and *whoa*. This would be interesting. Mom noticed it too, because she gave me big eyes from Liam's side.

"Liam, this is my sister Holly. Holly, Liam is Luke's B-F-F." His eyes never left her face.

"It's nice to meet you, Liam. I'm going inside to crash. I'll catch up with you later, Lily." Holly jogged off.

Mom stood up and announced, "Everyone is staying here tonight. My nerves won't be able to take it if anyone goes home." For once, I agreed with her. A night with everyone under the same roof sounded perfect to me.

"Liam, your room is ready. Come on, honey, and I'll show you where everything is." Liam followed my mother into the house. He was staying here tonight as well, instead of going back to Luke's house.

"Good night, kids. I'm going home, but it's just right over the garage, so I think your mama can handle that." Gram winked and took off. Violet handed Calla off to Luke, then headed inside. One by one, everyone trickled in after her until it was just Luke, me, Dylan and Calla, and, of course, Rocky, left on the porch.

My little family. Surrounded by my big family. Safe and sound.

Epilogue - Lily

"You've already started planning my wedding?" I was incredulous. We were having a girls' lunch on the patio by the pool at my parents' house. Mom, my sisters, and I were eating, toasting my engagement, and poking over the events that had happened this summer. Well, we were talking about Violet's marriage and my relationship with Luke, and Rose was dodging questions about Trevor. She'd spill it eventually. Or, more likely, one of us would overhear or witness something.

"Of course. Rose, Violet, and I started planning it when you and Luke went out on your second first date," Mom said, looking at me like I was stupid or something. Like I had some nerve wanting to participate in the planning of my own wedding. I glared accusingly at my sisters.

"Don't look at me. I wasn't here for all that nonsense," Holly said. I raised my glass, and she clinked it with hers. At least I had one of them on my side.

"You don't even like planning parties," Violet said. This was true, but so not the point.

"Um, this is my wedding. This is different."

"We decided to let you pick the dress," Rose said. "We have a folder full of options." What the what?

"Come on, darling. Just look at what we've got so far," Mom said, pushing the wedding binder closer to me on the table. "Please? You won't be mad once you see what we've planned."

I sniffed and looked away. I took a sip of my iced tea and gave them all a good bitch face. Except for Holly, I smiled at her. She shook her head at me and grinned.

"We haven't chosen the cake yet, or the food. That's what you really care about anyway. Am I right?" Rose said knowingly, and Holly laughed—the traitor.

Okay, *yes,* she was right. I wanted to pick the cake and go cake taste testing. That was the most fun part of planning a wedding. I'd never done that before, and I had always wanted to. Will and I had eloped—no planning, no cake, no big dinner. I wanted to eat a bunch of tiny cakes, damn it. Some girls dream of the dress. I dreamed of the dessert.

"We made an appointment at the bakery tomorrow," Violet said as a peace offering.

I perked up. "Fine. Tell me what you've got so far." I decided to stop being mad. Cake went a long way when it came to earning forgiveness from me.

"Yay!" Rose yelled. "It will be very *Midsummer Night's Dream*—very enchanted forest. You'll love it."

Oooh, pretty, pretty. I had to admit it—they knew what I liked.

Mom chimed in. "I've ordered a ton of lily of the valley and baby's breath. All the flowers will be white. We're going to practice making flower crowns later." She looked quite pleased with herself. "I bought white twinkle lights and flameless candles and cute little jars—"

Violet interrupted, "It will be over there." She pointed to the edge of the property, near the forest before the trees started to get thick. "We'll wrap the trees in white organza and lights and hang jars full of flowers. Oh, and evergreen wreaths wrapped with twinkle lights will be strung up too."

"But I get to pick the food and the cake, right?"

Mom nodded. "Do you want to pick your dress and shoes too?" she asked.

"No, you guys can do that."

They all looked at each other smugly.

Whatever.

I sat back and relaxed. I was going to have a beautiful wedding.

And it would be delicious.

* * *

I stood in front of the full-length mirror in my mother's bedroom. I couldn't look away from my own reflection. I looked like a fairy princess! This was not bragging, because I'd had nothing to do with it. I didn't even look like myself.

Mom had hired a hairstylist to fix my hair. It was pulled back and twisted around the sides of my head to coil in thick spiral curls down my back with lily of the valley, little crystals, and tiny evergreen spikes woven throughout.

My makeup was like something out of a movie—or Instagram. I'd tried to memorize what the makeup artist was doing so I could do it myself, but it was impossible. I would never have enough skills to do what she did. Is this what having "on-fleek" eyebrows was like? I didn't even have to suck in my cheeks to see my cheekbones. I pursed my lips at myself in the mirror and was even tempted to take a selfie. *Gah!* Amazing.

And my dress? The only word for it was *ethereal*. I was glad I hadn't chosen my own dress, because if I had, it wouldn't have looked this good. I turned side to side in the mirror. This fabric was shimmery and floated around my body, and even had a little train in the back. I remembered Violet's voice on the phone with Rose when I was trying it on for the first time. *"It's satin under tulle. It has a sweetheart neckline and spaghetti straps, floral embroidery, and tiny crystal beads. It's beautiful on her. It's white, it's sexy, it's sweet, it's perfect. This is the one. We're getting it."* Then she'd snapped my picture and texted it to Rose. She'd been right, it was perfect for me. But it was more than what I looked like that kept me staring. I was happy. It shone through all the makeup. It shone through the satin and flowers, the hairdo, the dress, and the party to come.

And I had a surprise for Luke. They say pregnant women glowed. Well, I was glowing like a mother. I hoped I could make it through the ceremony without puking. I hoped my morning sickness—what bullcrap, because it was constant sickness—would go away, so I could eat cake. I really wanted that cake.

Rose popped her head in the room to inform me, "Lily, it's time." She wore a pink dress similar in style to mine, except hers was knee length and didn't have all the fancy extras added to it. Holly's was pink too. Violet's was lavender, of course.

It had been a long battle between Rose and Violet as to who would be the maid of honor. I'd almost been tempted to pick Holly, but she said she didn't want to get in the middle. Violet said she deserved it for her subtle matchmaking machinations. Rose insisted she deserved it because we were twins. Eventually, Rose decided that being my identical twin outranked everything else, and she didn't need to be the maid of honor for everyone to know I loved her most—*insert eye roll here*. They'd been fighting simply for the sake of fighting but Violet and Rose were good at that. At least it was entertaining.

Rose opened the door all the way and came inside. Holly and Violet were behind her, full of smiles, but Violet dabbed her eyes with a hankie.

"No crying, Vi. If you cry, I'll cry. Look at my face. There is no way I can fix this if I mess it up."

Violet took a shaky breath, and her eyes cleared. "I'm just

so happy for you, Lily. And only five percent jealous." She leaned in and hugged me.

Rose joined the hug, saying, "I'm one hundred percent jealous.".

"I'm not jealous at all," Holly added right before she too joined in.

We had a fancy-dress sister group hug for a minute longer. Then we headed out to do this thing.

Epilogue - Luke

I waited for her. Under an arch made of flowers and lights, I waited as my heart overflowed with love.

I could finally breathe. I felt my chest expand to let more than just air inside.

Liam stood at my side, and Cade beside him. They were standing up for me on this day, just like they always had. Only now, I could finally see it. Now I knew I was worth it and could turn around and give it back. My eyes had been opened.

I was finally, truly home.

Liam slapped my shoulder as we heard the music start and whispered, "I'm happy for you, man." I smiled at him and knew he would be okay. There was no way I would have it any other way.

We watched as Lily's nephew Mark led Dahlia to her seat in the front. She winked at me, and I smiled back. Holly was next, followed by Rose, then Violet. They each took their places on the other side of the arch.

Everyone oohed and ahhed as Dylan, clad in his little tuxedo, walked down the aisle with the rings on a pillow. He hugged me, then stood between me and Liam.

But everyone collectively lost their minds when Madison

and Mara began pulling Calla down the aisle in a little white wagon. They were all dressed in the fluffiest pink dresses I'd ever seen and wore crowns made of flowers. They threw white rose petals along the aisle. Mara had to keep pulling the petals away from Calla, who was more interested in putting them in her mouth. After they reached us, Violet went to the wagon and carried Calla up to stand in her place, then Mara and Maddie stood in front of Rose and Holly.

It seemed like I had been waiting for her forever, and now I was finally finished marking time. She would be mine again. Forever this time.

The music changed, and I lost my breath as I saw her and Ben step forward. My breath returned with each step she took toward me until my lungs were so full I thought I'd burst.

The vows we took went by in a blur even though I meant every word.

Then, finally, we were dancing. I could hold her in my arms, and I never had to let her go.

She lifted her head from my chest and pulled my head to hers. "I have a wedding present for you." She leaned in to whisper in my ear, "We're having a baby."

My eyes filled with tears, and they fell straight down my cheeks. I couldn't stop it even if I wanted to. I lifted her straight up with my hands under her arms and kissed her belly, where our child grew. She giggled. I lowered her a bit and shifted my arms around her hips, but still held her aloft.

The train of her dress billowed out as I twirled us around in a circle. I was so happy right now, twirling her around was all I could think to do.

"Oh, God. Don't spin again, Luke." Lily gulped.

I set her down gently and cradled her face. "What do you need?" I whispered.

"Just you. And something slow and steady. Don't bust any more moves," she teased.

I took her hand in one of mine and grabbed her waist with the other.

"Hop up," I said.

She laughed and stood on my feet. I began to execute a perfect—meaning very slow—side to side step. Her head rested on my chest as she sighed against me.

Violet came up to us with Calla and handed her to me. "Does all of what I just now saw mean what I think it does?" she asked.

I nodded, and her eyes filled with tears. "I'm so happy for you guys right now. This is as it should be. Finally." She cried and hugged us both.

Dylan came running over. "You're going to be a big brother again," Lily told him, and he beamed.

She held his hand, and he held mine. Lily wrapped her other arm around my waist and leaned in to kiss Calla's sweet little cheek.

Then we all held each other and danced as the news circled around the room and the cheering started.

Want more happily ever after?
Scan the QR code below for *Two Tiny Hearts* - A Luke and Lily bonus scene!

About the Author

Nora Everly is a lifelong bookworm. She started reading the good stuff once she grew tall enough to sneak the romance novels off the top of her mother's bookshelf and it has been non-stop ever since.
Once upon a time she was a substitute teacher and an educational assistant. Now she's a writer and stay at home mom to two small humans and one fat cat.
Nora lives in the Pacific Northwest with her family and her overactive imagination.

Find her at noraeverly.com

Also by Nora Everly

The Sweetbriar Mountain Series:

In My Heart

Heart Words

From the Heart

Heart to Heart

Change of Heart

Honeybrook Hollow:

Next to You

Make You Mine

By Your Side

Sweetbriar Short Stories:

Holiday Hearts

Conversation Hearts

Let It Snow

The Cozy Creek Collection:

Fall at Once

From Smartypants Romance:

Oh Brother!

Crime and Periodicals

Carpentry and Cocktails